'I regard myself

Rhys continued, 'Tho[...] times are still troubled. The King's men are everywhere and soldiers, off duty, can pose problems for vulnerable women. I am sure that I do not have to explain that to you?'

'Are you our protector or our jailor?' she said stonily, and his eyes opened wide and darkened.

Hastily she added, somewhat lamely, 'I meant that—I do not understand why you should appoint yourself our guardian.'

He shrugged. 'Perhaps because Fate cast you both before me as being in need. Is that not a good enough reason, my lady?'

Haughtily she shook her glorious hair, which lay unbound in heavy red-gold waves upon her shoulders. He felt a strong desire to pull her towards him and run his fingers through it. He took himself firmly in hand. She was young, vulnerable and under his protection. He must hold himself in check.

Joanna Makepeace taught as head of English in a comprehensive school before leaving full-time work to write. She lives in Leicester, with a Jack Russell terrier called Jeffrey, and has written over thirty books under different pseudonyms. She loves the old romantic historical films, which she finds more exciting and relaxing than the newer ones.

THE TRAITOR'S DAUGHTER

Joanna Makepeace

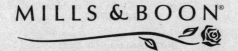

MILLS & BOON®

First published in Great Britain 2001
Harlequin Mills & Boon Limited,
Eton House, 18-24 Paradise Road, Richmond, Surrey TW9 1SR

© Joanna Makepeace 2001

ISBN 0 263 82742 9

Set in Times Roman 10½ on 12 pt.
04-0801-87742

Printed and bound in Spain
by Litografia Rosés S.A., Barcelona

PLANTAGENETS
Houses of York and Lancaster

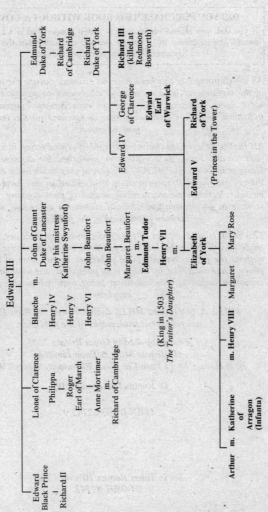

Chapter One

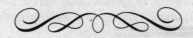

Summer 1503

Philippa Telford stole a hasty glance at her mother as they stood together with their squire, Peter Fairley, on the quay at Milford Haven. Her mother had been very sea sick during their crossing from the port of Damme, in Burgundy, and Philippa had been very concerned for her. The crossing had been rough and the two women had been almost thrown from their bunks several times; Philippa's mother had not slept for one moment of the time. Philippa had tended her, since they had been unable to bring a maid with them from their lodging in Malines where Philippa's father, Martyn, Earl of Wroxeter, served the dowager Duchess Margaret of Burgundy—the sister of England's late King, Richard III. Now, on dry land at last, Philippa was anxious to get her mother quickly to an inn where she could rest and recover from the hardships of the journey.

She was glad that they had followed Peter's advice and donned their warmest cloaks, since a mist had enveloped the harbour and coastline as they had disembarked and the air was chilly and damp, despite the fact that it was early

summer. Philippa sighed as if this inclement weather was
a presentiment of misfortunes yet to come.

Peter had already settled their dues with the captain of
their carrack, *Le Grande Dame*, and had assembled their
saddle bags of extra clothing and necessities upon the
greasy cobblestones of the quay. The bad weather had,
apparently, caused the town's inhabitants to seek drier
quarters and the quay looked bleak and almost deserted,
which was fortunate, since it was imperative that their arrival should not be unduly noted.

Philippa could see a huddle of uninviting buildings, behind which were the faintest of blue outlines, veiled by the
sea mist; she presumed them to be hills. The prevailing
sea mist hid from the travellers the sight of other vessels
docked in the harbour, though glimpses of tall masts and
the creak of timbers came to them eerily from the dank
half-darkness of the early evening. This, then, was Philippa's first sight of the land which had been her mother's
home. Again a shiver ran through her. This place seemed
exceptionally inhospitable. She prayed that matters might
improve with better weather prospects in the morning
when they began their journey to her grandfather's manor
near the town of Ludlow. Had not this land of Wales been
described to her by many fellow exiles as a most beautiful
one?

Peter led them to an inn situated at the far end of the
quay, having discounted a tavern in the centre of the harbour, from which they could hear the sounds of noisy banter, as being unsuitable for his charges, and also considering the necessity of not encountering anyone from near
the town of Ludlow who might be staying here in Milford
on business in the harbour. It had been many years since
the Countess of Wroxeter had been back in her home land,
but it was essential that she should not be recognised by

anyone who might have known her in childhood, before she had left her father's manor to journey to Westminster where she had married the Earl and whom she had followed into exile almost twenty years ago. All three of them were acutely aware of the danger which threatened them constantly on arrival; only the dire need to be with Philippa's grandparents during the serious illness of her grandfather Sir Daniel Gretton had brought them to this dank unwelcoming shore.

Philippa was wryly amused to see the inn's crudely painted sign of the White Dragon creaking and swaying from the corner of the eaves.

'At least it is not a red dragon,' she murmured in her mother's ear, recalling that her father had often referred to the court of King Henry VII at Westminster as the lair of the red dragon, contemptuously speaking of the Tudor King's personal device of the red dragon. To Philippa's father, the present English King would always be a usurper who had unlawfully taken up arms against his true King, Richard III, and, aided by traitors, had defeated him at the battle of Redmoor near Bosworth, where Wroxeter's friend and liege lord, King Richard, had been slain. Now Philippa's father was a proscribed traitor within his own home land, living in exile, unable to accompany his wife and daughter on this journey on threat of a hideous death should he be discovered and arrested.

Cressida made no answer, but Philippa could tell that her mother also was not impressed by the coincidence of the somewhat ominous inn sign.

The tap room appeared as crowded as the other tavern had been, but slightly less noisy. Talk stopped as the eyes of the men gathered round the scratched and stained tables were turned upon the newcomers in open curiosity. Philippa considered that they all looked vaguely alike to her, medium-sized, sturdily built men, dressed in homespun, dark avised; their language, which had come to her in snatches when they had entered the room, was totally incomprehensible to her.

Peter engaged in talk with a slightly taller shambling fellow who announced himself as mine host. He, at least, appeared to speak English, though his accent was very marked and singsong in rhythm.

'I require a private room for my sister, Mistress Weston, and her daughter, my niece. I am escorting them to visit a sick relative who lives near to Ludlow. Can you oblige, master innkeeper?'

The man shook his head emphatically. 'I have but one private chamber which is already spoken for. The ladies must make do with the common sleeping room. There are but two women sleeping there tonight. You must sleep down here in the tap room, or the stable if you would prefer that.'

Peter turned to confer, but Cressida said hastily, 'Peter, I would much prefer to sleep within the stable with Philippa and you nearby. Can that be arranged?'

The innkeeper scowled and the men seated nearby within earshot whispered to their neighbours. It seemed that only certain members of the company understood English and needed a translation of what had transpired. Curiosity increased. Strangers, most likely, some merchant's wife and daughter, were usually content enough to share the women's common sleeping chamber. An atmosphere of resentment seemed to grow within the tap room, making the ale-stinking place chillier than it had been at the outset when they had entered.

'Aye,' the innkeeper growled, 'if the lady insists, but if it's food ye want you'll have to be fetching it yourself. I can't be waiting on folks across the courtyard. I've customers in plenty in here. You can eat here if ye've a mind to, all of ye.'

Cressida smiled politely and once more shook her head. 'Innkeeper, I mean no offence. It is just that we are wearied and would eat and sleep in quiet. We shall be glad to see to our own needs, they will be simple enough, some ale, perhaps, and bread and meats or cheeses.'

'Oh, aye.' The man turned away, then taking a lanthorn from a hook behind him, came from his place nearest to the ale barrel in present use and moved towards the inn door.

'Come this way then, folks and I'll show you the way to the stable. I take it ye've no horses of your own?'

'I intend to buy mounts for the land journey tomorrow,' Peter informed him. 'We have only lately disembarked from the carrack, *La Grande Dame*, just in from the port of Bruges. My sister's husband had been living there for some years as he has business interests there.'

The innkeeper sniffed and moved in his clumsy, shambling walk to the door, opened it and held up the lanthorn so they could see only dimly across the unlit courtyard. 'Directly opposite is the stable door. There are only three stalls occupied at the moment. The lord who has taken my private bedchamber has a horse stabled there with that of his squire and my own cob is there as well. There'll be plenty of room for the three of ye, and there's clean straw in plenty for your beds.'

Peter thanked the man civilly and took the proffered lanthorn, murmuring that he would take particular care with it within the stable, then the three of them stepped outside into the mist—shrouded air again.

The cobbles of the courtyard were slick with rain and mist and they were forced to watch their steps, the ladies holding their skirts high to avoid any ordure or refuse from the inn or stable as they crossed.

'My pardon, my lady,' Peter murmured, 'I had thought to provide you with better accommodation than this poor place this night. God's blood, it appears that what they say about this benighted land of Wales is true, the inhabitants are barbarians. Did you hear those outlandish peasants chattering in their singsong tongue?'

'Peter,' laughed the Countess, 'remember that I lived in the Welsh Marches throughout my childhood. We had many Welsh servants at the manor and, though I could not speak their tongue, I grew to respect and like them very much. We would have been regarded with just as much outright curiosity wherever we had fetched up. We shall do well enough if the stable is dry and we shall have privacy which is most important.'

'Yes, mistress, but you have had a rough time of it on board ship and I hoped for better conditions for you both than these.'

'I prefer to have you within call, Peter,' Cressida said quietly, 'and I am sure you and my lord have slept in many worse places than this over the years.'

He glanced at her sharply and Philippa glimpsed a wry twist to his lips as he pushed wide the stable door and held up the lanthorn for them to enter before him. The missions the Earl had undertaken for the Duchess Margaret in her relentless intrigues against the Tudor king had often meant danger for them both and, indeed, they had many times been forced to live for quite long periods of time in disguise and in vastly uncomfortable circumstances.

The warmth and familiar scent of horseflesh met them and they heard the restless movement of wickering within the stalls as the horses were both disturbed by their unexpected arrival and alarmed by the sudden lanthorn light.

Peter held the lanthorn high, glimpsed a hook suspended from the thatched roof to hold it and hung it securely. Surprisingly the place looked well kept. Obviously it had been cleaned that very morning, possibly in expectation of the arrival of the lord the innkeeper had spoken of. Philippa moved to inspect the mounts. Two were sturdy Welsh cobs, she surmised, one belonging to the innkeeper and the other to the lord's squire. The third horse was a black courser, a large, heavy-boned, finely muscled animal, extremely valuable, she guessed. Of the three, this one was the most restive and she moved closer to the stall and spoke gently, reassuringly.

'Steady there, my beauty, we mean you no harm nor any to your master.'

Cressida uttered a sharp warning as her daughter reached out a hand to pat the creature's velvet nose, aware of how dangerous destriers could be, bred for warfare as they were, but Philippa turned, shaking her head gently. She was patient and the sound of her soft voice did eventually reassure the animal and it stood docilely while she ran her hand gently down its silky well-brushed nose.

'There, there, I have no apple for you. Perhaps I will have tomorrow. I will try to find some and reward you all.'

Philippa adored horses and had very little opportunity to ride, let alone own a mount while at her parents' lodging at Malines. Her father had been forced by limited means to hire mounts only when he had need, but he had managed to have his daughter taught to ride and she was glad now that she would have no problem during their journey to Gretton.

Peter had busied himself, piling up clean straw in one of the stalls furthest from the horses and the door for Philippa and her mother. He intended to make his own bed well away from them and near to the door so that he might be aware of anyone entering unexpectedly during the coming night. Possibly the lord's squire would come before retiring for the night to ensure that all was well with his master's horses and might intend to sleep within the stable. Peter frowned as he considered that might pose a problem and hoped the fellow would either sleep across his master's doorway as he himself had been used to do for Lord Martyn or content himself in the warmer and more comfortable tap room. He would meet that problem if and when it presented itself.

Philippa sank down thankfully upon the sweet-smelling straw and watched as her mother took off her cloak and laid it down upon the bed Peter had formed for her.

'There, Peter,' she said, 'it is as I thought, we shall manage very well here and be spared any awkward questioning we might have to face within the common sleeping chamber. If you could go across and fetch us something to eat and drink, we can settle down soon and get some sleep. We have a long journey in front of us.'

Peter nodded, looked round to assure himself that he had made his charges as comfortable as he could, then moved to the stable door.

'I should keep this barred, my lady. Make anyone wishing to enter declare himself and, even then, I would advise you to wait for my return before admitting anyone.'

Philippa smiled in answer. 'Be assured we shall do that, Peter.'

He left and she snuggled close to her mother, still huddling within her own frieze cloak. 'Aren't you chilly? I am still. Why don't you put your cloak back on for a while?'

'No, don't fuss. I am quite comfortable out of the damp air.' Cressida looked round the gloomy stable and gave a little petulant shrug. 'I shall be glad when we are well on our way tomorrow.'

'Grandmère will be glad to see us.'

'Yes, indeed. I only hope and pray that we are in time to see your grandfather.'

Philippa made no answer. She was aware that her mother entertained little hope that Sir Daniel would continue to survive the collapse which he had suffered some two weeks ago, which had left him partially paralysed. The message which Lady Gretton had managed to send to her daughter in Burgundy had informed Cressida that her father had lost the power of his speech. Philippa knew, as her mother did, that attacks such as these were often followed by others, which, eventually, led to the death of the sufferer. Cressida had pleaded with her husband to be allowed to journey to Gretton to see her father and take with her their only daughter, his grandchild, whom he had never seen. Reluctantly, the Earl had given his permission and allowed Peter Fairley, his trusted squire and friend, to be their sole protector.

Philippa watched as her mother stretched wearily out on her straw bed.

'You do believe that we shall be safe,' she queried softly, 'that at Gretton the servants can be trusted and...?' Her voice trailed off uncertainly.

Cressida lifted her head and gazed doubtfully at her daughter in the flickering light of the lanthorn.

'Nothing can be certain, child. The servants have been with your grandparents for years and will, I believe, be discreet. They loved me as a child and they are all aware of the dangers. Travelling under assumed names, we should be safe enough, but if you are afraid I could instruct Peter to see you safe on a ship bound for home—'

'No, no, I insist on going with you. I am most anxious

to see my grandparents,' Philippa declared passionately. 'I am most concerned for your safety. Papa was saying that the King's spies will be extra-vigilant since the Yorkist gentlemen will be in a state of great anger and agitation due to the summary execution of Sir James Tyrell and the lying confession about the murder of the Princes, which was published after his death.'

Cressida sighed heavily. 'When will this realm be fully peaceful? I doubt if I shall see it in my lifetime, yet the Tudor King holds the state firmly. He should be able to do so,' she added bitterly, 'he has managed to destroy all the rightful heirs who might have challenged him for power and then he married the Yorkist Princess, Elizabeth, in order to secure the loyalty of some of the disaffected nobles.'

Philippa bit her lip as her mother once more lay down. The journey had tired her so. She needed rest badly. Philippa had rarely seen her beautiful mother so downhearted and distressed, not even when the Earl, her father, had risked himself on hazardous adventures for his patroness, the Duchess Margaret, who had struggled over the last twenty years to bring down the Tudor monarchy.

Philippa's father had made her aware of the situation which had made him a hunted traitor in his own land, even though she herself, now seventeen, had been born after the tragic events which had caused it.

She knew that for over fifty years, since 1450, there had been struggles for supremacy amongst the Lancastrian and Yorkist heirs of King Edward III. In 1461 the weak Lancastrian King Henry VI had proved so incompetent that his cousin, Duke Richard of York, had challenged him for power. He had been killed in the fighting which had broken out, but his son, King Edward IV, had finally won a bloodthirsty battle at Towton in Yorkshire and had then assumed the throne and ruled ruthlessly and competently for over twenty years, despite sporadic outbursts of violence which had threatened the peace. Unfortunately he had died unexpectedly in 1483, leaving the protectorship of the realm and care of his two young sons and older five daughters to the care of their uncle, his younger brother, Duke Richard of Gloucester.

Almost immediately the peace was threatened again due to the minority of the young King, Edward V, who was just thirteen years old when Richard brought him to London to be crowned. On the journey the Queen's relatives made a bid for power which was defeated and two of them were executed. The Princes were placed for safety within the palace of the Tower of London, traditionally used to house the new monarchs before their coronations.

Philippa was aware that her father, Martyn, Earl of Wroxeter, had been a trusted friend of Duke Richard and eventually left his own estates on the Welsh Border to become his confidante and spy master.

The Bishop of Bath and Wells had made a surprise announcement at a meeting at the Tower, revealing that the late King's marriage had not been lawful and therefore his children were illegitimate. He, himself, he had declared, had betrothed the king formally to Lady Eleanor Butler and that lady had still been living when the King had married the widow of a Lancastrian nobleman, Lord Grey of Groby, and betrothals were binding, so much so that a dispensation from the Pope was required to break one. This revelation had thrown the realm into disarray once more and Duke Richard had finally been persuaded to accede to the throne as King Richard III. Philippa's father had served him faithfully and fought for him at the tragic battle of Redmoor two years later when Henry Tudor, descended from the Lancastrian, Prince John of Gaunt, and his mistress, Katherine Swynford, had arrived in England in a bid to seize the throne. The King had been treacherously betrayed by Lord William Stanley, who was married to Henry's mother, and his brother, Sir William, on the very battlefield and had died in a last courageous charge.

Since that time the Earl's fortunes had been totally destroyed as he lived in almost penniless exile in Burgundy. Philippa knew, only too well, that her chances of finding a husband, since she had no dowry, were hopeless.

This business of Tyrell's execution had heightened their danger, she knew. Sir James, like her father, had been a member of the late King's household, but had been on a mission for King Richard to France at the time of Redmoor so had taken no part in that battle. He had made his peace with the new King, Henry, and had served the Tudor house, though his estates had been confiscated and he had been deprived of his official posts in Wales. He had been later appointed Governor of Guisnes and, for the following sixteen years, had remained in France, then, suddenly, he had been accused of treasonable correspondence with the Earl of Suffolk, the late King's nephew. He had refused to surrender himself, but had allowed himself to be lured from the safety of his castle and on to one of King Henry's ships in Calais harbour by the promise of safe conduct. He was then captured and taken to the Tower of London and, later, unceremoniously executed. After his death it had been announced that he had confessed to the murder of the Princes, King Edward's young sons, who had disappeared from the Tower, on the order of their uncle. This slur upon the honour of the dead King Richard had naturally angered many of the late King's former supporters. A little shiver ran through Philippa's body, for she suspected that her father knew more about the fate of those young princes than he would ever divulge, not even to his closest family. Was this the reason why King Henry hated him so much and wished to have him in England directly in his power? She knew, only too well, that in the dungeons of the Tower men could be forced to divulge their closest-held secrets. If the King could hold the Earl's wife and child as hostages, would not her father come to their help and surrender himself, as Tyrell had done? The secret of their journey to Gretton must be kept at all costs.

Her thoughts ranged to her friends, Richard and Anne Allard, who had been her companions four years ago when she had gone to Westminster to serve King Henry's queen, Elizabeth of York. They had all been forced to flee together from England when Richard had involved himself in trying to help the young Earl of Warwick, who had been a prisoner in the Tower. Philippa sighed deeply as she remembered how that unfortunate young man had been executed with another pretender to the throne, Perkin Warbeck. Richard and Anne had been pardoned and returned to England. Philippa would have dearly liked to see them while she was here but knew that would be dangerous for all of them.

Peter appeared to be taking his time, she thought, and rose to go to the door and unbar it. After moments her eyes became accustomed to the darkness and she could see that the courtyard appeared to be deserted and she could see in the distance the dim glow of candlelight in the windows of the inn. Surely it would not have taken the innkeeper so long to provide Peter with a flagon of ale and bread and cheese? He would not linger, she knew, being always concerned for the safety of his charges. Philippa turned and looked anxiously towards her mother, who had sat up the moment she had heard her daughter stirring.

'What is it? Can you hear someone coming?'

'No, it is just that it is taking Peter rather a long time.'

'Has it? I must have dozed.' Cressida frowned. 'It is unlike Peter to delay.'

'I think I should go and look for him.'

'Philippa, no. He warned us—'

'I know all that, but I don't think we have a choice. I fear something might have happened to him.'

Cressida rose and joined Philippa at the stable door. Together they peered anxiously into the dark courtyard.

'It is indeed very strange that he hasn't returned before now. Had it been anyone else but Peter…' Cressida shook her head worriedly. 'He is not the man to allow himself to be drawn into some gambling ploy.'

'He would never leave us unprotected for so long. Something must have happened to him.'

The Countess shook her head again and bit her lip doubtfully.

'Mother, I must go back to the inn and ask after him.'

'I do not like that idea at all.'

'I don't myself, but if anything has happened to Peter we have to know about it, even—' Philippa broke off abruptly, averting her face so that her mother should not see how very alarmed she was '—even if we cannot do much about it.'

She dared not put into words the fear that harm could have come to their squire and, if it had done, what they could possibly do without him as escort.

'You stay here by the door and keep watch.' Philippa put up her cloak hood and drew its comforting warmth about her. 'I shall not be gone for more than a moment or two. The landlord is bound to know what has occurred. It may be that Peter heard of some suitable mounts for hire or purchase and thought it imperative to go immediately to find out about them.'

'At this late hour?'

'I know that it seems unlikely, but it is the only reason why he might have left us for so long.' Gently Philippa shook off her mother's detaining hand upon her wrist. 'Do not be anxious. I shall come back immediately and will not allow myself to be drawn into talk with any of the men in the tap room. At all events, most of them do not appear to be able to talk English.' She made a little wry twist of the lips in her attempt to humour her distraught mother.

Reluctantly Cressida released her and stood back as Philippa pushed the heavy stable door further open and, with but one reassuring glance behind her, stepped out into the yard. It seemed very black, but she could not take the lanthorn and leave her mother in darkness and she could just make out her way ahead by the flickering light of the candles within the inn building.

She was about halfway across when she heard some slight movement. She stopped dead still and listened, but her frightened heartbeats sounded so loud within her breast that she knew any other sounds would be drowned out by them. Reproving herself for cowardice, she crept forward cautiously. She was not wont to be so foolish. The sound could easily have been made by a night-prowling cat. She could hear the noise of talk now from the inn and she stopped again, calling upon her courage to enter the tap room alone. The outright impudence of the customers' curiosity when they had first arrived made her hesitate. As Peter had said, the travellers had certainly not been welcomed. So intent on her determination to proceed was she that she went sprawling suddenly across something directly in her path. The breath was shaken out of her and she stifled a sudden cry, recovered herself and turned to stare down at the body of the man who was lying senseless, his head in a puddle. Her eyes had become more used to the darkness now, though it was a moonless night, and, as she crouched to examine the injured man, she knew instantly that it was Peter Fairley.

He made no sound as she carefully explored his clothing, wet with the damp mist, and she gave a little gasp of fear and pity as her fingers, when lifting his head, discovered some fluid more sticky. The wound was bleeding copiously. No wonder he was unconscious and made no answer to her softly uttered urging to answer her. Had he stumbled and fallen in the darkness? Like her he carried no lanthorn and it was just possible, but Peter was a cautious man and he would have waited before proceeding to cross, allowing his night vision to develop. Unless he too had stumbled across some obstacle in his path, it was unlikely. Terror struck her forcibly as she thought he must have been deliberately struck down, but by whom—and why? Surely it had been obvious to everyone in the tap room that they were not wealthy travellers—yet Peter had made it known that he was carrying a considerable amount of coin in order to hire or buy horses for their journey. To men living in poverty that would have been invitation enough to attack and rob him. She half stood up after her efforts to rouse him had failed and looked round apprehensively. Peter was a big man. She could not lift or drag him to the stable, but dare she call for assistance from the men in the inn?

As she stood for moments, irresolute, she was taken totally by surprise as brutal hands suddenly pulled her backwards and caught her wrists in a cruel grasp, thus freeing one of her attacker's hands to clasp over her mouth before she could draw breath to call out.

'Softly there, my little beauty,' a voice, speaking in English, though with a singsong lilt she had come to identify as that of a Welshman, whispered in her ear. 'There's no

call for you to be making a scene and, like as not, you'll
not end up as your servant there if you're wise.'

She was trembling with anger as well as fear and tried
desperately to free herself from the man's grasp, but he
continued to drag her backwards, her heels trailing helplessly on the cobbles. The fellow appeared to be alone and
yet he was so strong that she feared he would be able to
drag her where he wished and that she would be helpless
to prevent him. Even in her desperation she feared for
Peter. If she were unable to help him, he could die there
in this dank straw-spattered courtyard, an ignominious end
for a man who had faced often far greater dangers. And
she—she could not doubt her own fate and knew with
blinding clarity that her attacker would be unlikely to leave
her alive after he had finished with her. Would he make
for the stable? If so, her mother, also, was in deadly danger, but no, he was aware that the stable was inhabited and
he would not risk her mother screaming for help and the
possibility that in the ensuing chaos his prey would perhaps manage to free herself. She tried to keep calm. He
obviously knew of some other shelter where he intended
to drag her. If she waited for the opportunity, surely she
would then manage to free herself momentarily, at least to
shout out a warning to her mother. Yet, even so, she coolly
debated the wisdom of that. Her mother would have a better chance of escaping this fellow's attentions if she, Philippa, remained quiet and allowed him to do what he
wished. As these thoughts raced through her mind there
was no time for hysteria or panic. Her fear was absolute,
but for the present, she was helpless to affect her own fate.
The time it took to drag her to some secluded spot seemed
elongated. In actual fact it could only have taken moments,
yet she appeared to have opportunity to think out rationally
what she could and could not do and what would be best

for her mother's safety. It would be only minutes now before she was pulled into shelter and she did not doubt that her molester would free her mouth only to render her senseless with a blow to the face.

She prayed to the Virgin and to St Catherine, the patron saint of maidens, to give her the courage to face what must be. Then, suddenly, miraculously, another voice spoke menacingly behind her. She could not understand the words for they were uttered, presumably, in Welsh, but the import was unmistakable. Abruptly she was released to fall forward onto her face.

Sobbing with terror, she scrambled up and half-turned to find her attacker had been seized from behind, as she herself had been, and, even in the dim light of the darkened courtyard, she could see the dullish gleam of a dagger held against the fellow's throat. She staggered back, unsure if she were being rescued or had fallen into the hands of another merciless attacker. The man who had first seized her was crouching awkwardly, making inarticulate sounds of rage and fear. Unceremoniously he was dragged to his feet, still with the dagger menacing his throat, and pulled some distance clear away from her.

She could not see the man she hoped was her rescuer clearly, but by his bulky shape, wrapped in a dark frieze cloak, she realised that he was a big man, towering over his prisoner, who was now continuing to babble incoherently in Welsh, his terror only too apparent.

The newcomer spoke again commandingly and the blubbering ceased. Another sharp command, in English, this time, alerted a third man to the scene who, apparently, had been waiting his opportunity to come to the newcomer's assistance.

'David, come, take possession of this fellow and cart him off to the nearest constable. I've felt him for weapons and found only a single dagger, but take care.' He tossed the weapon down at their feet where it clanged on the cobbles. 'You can never tell with these ruffians where they manage to conceal others. Hold him for a moment while I secure his hands.'

Still trembling, Philippa felt unable to move, let alone run. She could not see clearly what her rescuer was about, but guessed that he had used some belt about his person to make her attacker secure. The fellow was still murmuring promises and pleas, which were abruptly cut short, so she thought he had been unceremoniously gagged.

The man addressed as David, also a well-muscled fighting man, judging by his lumbering bulk, jerked at his prisoner's bound arms and dragged him away. Since he had made no answer to her rescuer's orders but instantly obeyed them, Philippa gathered that he was used to doing so and was, probably, his servant.

She managed to let out a little, breathless gasp at last and the man who had come to her rescue came instantly forward and put out a hand to steady her.

'Are you hurt? You are, I take it, one of the English travellers just arrived at the inn and taken up residence with my horses in the stable, or so the landlord informs me?'

'Yes,' she whispered throatily, 'I thank you, sir. My mother is in the stable and my…' she hesitated, then recollected herself suddenly and the need to guard her identity '…my uncle lies injured some paces off. No, I am not hurt, that fellow had only just grabbed me as—as I was trying to help my uncle. He—he took me by surprise but—but he had no time to—hurt me.'

'Thank the Virgin,' he said curtly. 'Show me where your relative lies and I'll summon assistance from the tap room, then you must go to your mother.'

She was feeling even more trembly now and she staggered and would have fallen had he not once more put out a sturdy arm to catch her. She felt an unaccountable tremor pass through her at the touch of his fingers and struggled a little to pull free, but he continued to hold her firmly.

'What is it? You are not afraid of me, are you?' The voice was clear, slightly lilting—as all voices, she thought, must be here in Wales or even on the Border, her mother had told her—but it was also hard, uncompromising, authoritative, and she wondered just who he was and if she could trust him. He had come to her rescue seemingly, but her attacker had known him or recognised his authority and she feared that he might question her, demand proof of her identity. He could well be a magistrate and answerable to the Crown for the good behaviour of those within his district.

'No, no.' She was afraid that reaction had set in and that she was liable to break into tears. That she must not do before this commanding stranger. 'I am sorry, sir, that I have not yet recovered my balance, it seems. Please…'

She led him to where Peter lay and was thankful to see, as they approached, that Peter was slowly coming to himself now and giving sharp little cries of pain.

Philippa's rescuer gestured her imperatively to stand slightly aside and dropped to one knee beside the sufferer and examined the head wound gently, as she had done. She marvelled at the gentle, sensitive touch of those strong large hands.

'It appears that he was struck from behind, possibly with the hilt of a dagger, mistress. Fortunately the wound does not seem to be too serious as already he is coming to himself. Head wounds can be dangerous and unconsciousness can sometimes last for hours—or even weeks.'

He stood up and removed his cloak so that now she

could see that he was, indeed, a tall, muscular man with massive shoulders, though she thought by the hardness of his body, as he had held her momentarily against his chest, that there was not an ounce of surplus fat upon him. Obviously he kept himself in superb fighting form. Was he a soldier, a mercenary?—but his commanding manner gave her the impression that he had some standing in the district and was more than likely a knight. Could he possibly be the lord the landlord had spoken of?

As if in answer to her unspoken question he addressed her as he rose to his feet once more. 'Allow me to introduce myself. I am Sir Rhys Griffith and, like you, I am accommodated at the inn.'

So her surmise had been correct. He was indeed lordly. No wonder the innkeeper had not offered to request that he vacate, for her mother's use, the private room he had bespoken.

He was continuing. 'You can leave this man's care in my hands, mistress, and go to your mother. She will be frantic for news of you both, I am sure. I will see to it that your uncle is conveyed to the inn and then I will come and inform you what is best to be done.'

Philippa still felt that her limbs would let her down if she did not find some support soon and she had the strange feeling that she must not allow this stranger to touch her again, let alone hold her as closely as he had done formerly. She was close to tears again and inwardly she castigated herself, since her immediate danger appeared to be over and she had no outward reason to distrust this man— nor yet her own feelings regarding him. It was just that he had taken over so completely, overwhelmed her by his compelling personality. Yet he had said little to her to bring out this strange, dubious excitement. Certainly he had offered her no discourtesy. She struggled to find words to thank him adequately.

'I am—most grateful, sir. I do not know what would have happened had you not come...' She swallowed and averted her face from his hawklike gaze.

'I think you must certainly have realised what would have happened, mistress,' he said a trifle harshly. 'I can understand your concern for your uncle but, really, you should not have ventured out of the stable alone.'

She was a trifle angered by that suggestion. He was reproving her for what had happened, as if it had been all her own fault. What would he have had her do, leave Peter to die out there while she remained in cowardly security within the stable?

'I had to go, sir,' she said haughtily, 'there was no one else. As for the attack, it all happened so suddenly. My uncle left us to fetch food from the inn and he was such a long time gone that I was forced to believe something had happened to him—which, indeed, it had. I stumbled over his body and, while I was kneeling by him, I suppose I was so frightened and intent on my uncle's fate that— that I did not hear anyone approach. This fellow grabbed me from behind before I could so much as pull away or cry out and—and...'

She sensed that he had relaxed his grim demeanour now, as he said more gently, 'Best not to think about it any further as no real harm has been done.'

He put out a hand to offer to lead her towards the stable. She attempted to draw away from him so that he might not touch her again, but he would brook no denial and took her hand firmly and turned her towards the stable door.

'It was fortunate that I happened to come along when I did,' he said. 'I have been visiting a friend in the town and came into the courtyard by the back way. Providentially we—that is, my squire David and I—heard noises, which indicated all was not well. I heard the man threaten you and instructed my squire to stand back while I came to your assistance. On rounding the gate post I saw at once that you needed it fast.'

She still could not see his features clearly and was glad that he must not be able to see her. She must be in a fine state after that terrible struggle. She could feel her hair straggling about her face and she wondered if she had transferred blood from Peter's wound and filth from the cobbles on to her cheeks. Certainly her hand felt sticky and dirty and he must be aware of it. How stupid, she told herself, to concern herself about such paltry matters at such a time, yet her desire to remain aloof from all strangers on this journey and the strength and determination of this man made her acutely uncomfortable in his presence. She was also anxious that he should not get too close a glimpse of her mother or guess at the real reason for their need to sleep apart in the stable.

She had felt the fine wool of his sleeve and had smelled the tang of a good-quality leathern jerkin when she had been close to him and judged that he was, as he claimed, a knight. With luck they might never meet again, but she had a strange desire to see his face clearly before their final parting. Surely that was natural, she thought, simply a wish to see the features of the man who had saved her honour and her very life.

They were approaching the stable door and he released her hand. 'I should go and give assistance to your uncle. Everything will be done for his comfort and I will ensure the future safety of you and your mother.' These last words were spoken in so stern a voice that she wondered if she suspected her attacker had been given information about the latest guest from someone inside the inn and was determined to investigate the matter further. She gave a little shudder and did not envy the men whom he would face in that tap room. He was one man, alone, yet he would deal with any rabble, she was sure of that.

A voice called anxiously from the opened door of the stable, 'Philippa, is that you? Whatever is wrong? Peter has not returned and I am—frightened.' It was so unlike her courageous mother to sound so querulous and pitiful that Philippa's heart bled for her, alone in that stable, fearful, dreading the worst for her daughter and her squire.

Sir Rhys gave a slight bow to the shadowy woman in the doorway. 'Your daughter and—your brother have encountered some difficulties, lady. Your brother is injured and I intend to see that he is cared for. Please remain together in the stable until either I or my squire can come and inform you that all is well.'

Falteringly the Countess said, 'But who are you, sir, and how—?'

'Your daughter will explain. Do not be alarmed.' He bowed also to Philippa. 'Sit down upon the straw and recover yourself. I can see that you are still trembling. I will send you both some strengthening wine. Do not concern yourself about your attacker. He will not trouble you again. My squire will see to that.'

Before either woman could reply he had strode off in the direction of the inn doorway. After the stress of all that had occurred, Philippa fell sobbing into her mother's arms.

Cressida forbore to question her daughter until the anguished sobbing had stopped, then she drew away from her, gently holding her at arm's length, and stared into Philippa's eyes searchingly.

'Tell me truly exactly what happened. Do not be afraid to do so. Whatever it is, I shall understand.'

Philippa drew a hard breath. 'I was attacked but he—the attacker—could not finish—what—what he hoped. That gentleman came to my rescue in time. His servant carted the man off to the constable so—so I expect the knight must be well known here. He—he handled the whole episode with such authority—' She broke off and dabbed at her streaming eyes with the knuckles of one hand. 'Mother, it was all so dreadful and now—now I do not know what to make of the rescuer. If he is important here, he might well demand to know more about us and—'

'Child, calm yourself. I could not see him well, but he appeared civil enough. I thank all the saints that he was able to help you in time. Who knows what—what would have occurred had he not come so promptly.'

'He—he frightens me and—and I do not know why. He was kind and courteous, yet…'

'Philippa, you are naturally upset by everything that occurred and you are alarmed for Peter.'

'I know.' Philippa took a hard grip upon herself and tried to stop the trembling and deadly chill, which had seeped into her body and sapped her strength. 'I am not usually so foolish. I am safe and unharmed but—but I cannot help thinking that this man could be dangerous to us.'

'But why? He came to our assistance and, once given, he will most probably forget our very existence.'

Philippa whispered, 'I am not so sure of that. He said he would call on those people in the inn to help Peter. He was attacked as I was. I found him lying unconscious and his head was bleeding. I could not rouse him and then—and then—' Her teeth began chattering again as the full sense of shock assailed her. 'I heard nothing. He must have been very practised in his trade for Peter to have been overcome like that.' She buried her face in her hands. 'All the time I knew—knew what he—and afterwards that he would kill me and I did not even try to bite at the hand he held over my mouth and call out because—because—'

'You were afraid he would render you unconscious and then find me,' Cressida said quietly. 'I know, child, I know.' She, too, drew a shuddering breath as she realised fully how close both of them had come to disaster and now—they must wait to discover if Peter would recover.

As if in answer to that unspoken fear, a voice called softly from the stable doorway, 'May I come in, ladies?'

'Yes, yes, of course.' Despite her recognition of the rescuer's voice and the readiness of the invitation, Cressida stood protectively in front of her daughter as he entered and stood limned against the door post.

Stepping slightly clear of her mother, Philippa could see her rescuer more clearly now as the lanthorn light played on his tall, massive form, broad shoulders and slim hips. He was equipped with heavy broadsword and dagger and, though his clothing was of good quality, as she had felt when he had touched her, he was not richly clad, being in serviceable travelling garb of leather brigandine over homespun dark doublet and hose. He had a broad, open face with a dominating beak of a nose and firm chin, dark brown eyes set well apart, beneath a mop of dark hair curling to his shoulders. He had, apparently, scorned the present fashion of curled fringe, nor did he wear the new sleeveless long gown, lately worn at court. His tanned complexion spoke to her of a life spent mostly out of doors. There was an imperious air about him, but his manner towards them could not be judged arrogant. It was difficult for her to guess at his age, but she imagined that he must be in his middle or late twenties, for his massive form had not yet run to fat; she thought he had spent his life in soldierly pursuits and continued to keep fit by hard exercise.

He was unsmiling as he bowed to them courteously. 'I do not think your escort has come to any real harm, my lady. He took a bad bang on the back of his head, which has bled profusely, but he had fully regained consciousness when we carried him into the inn and his wound has been dressed. He is resting in the tap room, concerned now about you both, naturally. I have made arrangements for you to be accommodated within the chamber allocated to me. You will be much more comfortable there and I shall do very well in the tap room where I can keep an eye on your—uncle.' There was a slight, sardonic curve of the lips as he uttered the last word and Philippa frowned, in doubt. Did he believe that her mother was travelling with her lover and wished to conceal the fact? She blushed darkly and averted her gaze from those piercing dark eyes of his. She was truly grateful to this man for his assistance, but he had no right to judge them contemptuously; however, he was putting himself out for their welfare and she felt constrained to utter words of heartfelt gratitude.

Though her immediate thought was to refuse his offer of the use of his private bedchamber, she knew it would be better for her mother if she accepted graciously.

'I have to thank you again, Sir Rhys, for all your kindness to three strangers and we accept most gratefully your kind offer.' She gave a little shiver of horrified remembrance. 'Indeed, I think we could not remain alone here in the stable without feeling apprehensive after—after what happened.'

He nodded. 'Naturally. Please, will you follow me and I will see you settled.'

He unhooked the lanthorn from its place and stood by the stable door to light their way. His free hand he prof-

fered to the Countess as she stepped into the darkened
courtyard. 'Allow me, my lady. It is dark out here and the
cobbles slippery. If you take your mother's other hand,
mistress, you will be less likely to slip.'

The landlord was obsequious as they entered the inn and
Cressida went hastily to Peter, who was sitting up in a
hard-backed chair by the fire looking pale and anxious,
but, otherwise, his true self. Philippa was thankful that the
blow did not appear to have affected his memory for he
was lucid enough.

'Do not fret, sister. I am feeling better already after im-
bibing some of the landlord's best wine. I'm only angered
at myself for being less cautious and rendering you both
without protection and leaving you open to danger.'

'This good knight has proved to be our saviour,' Cressida said reassuringly. 'Now, rest, Peter and get well. We
must see how you fare in the morning before we decide
to travel.'

He was about to argue, but she prevented him with a
gentle squeeze upon his hand.

Sir Rhys led them above stairs, after ordering the landlord to serve them with the best supper he could provide.

The room was surprisingly large and comfortably appointed. Philippa looked round appreciatively. 'I am sorry,
sir, that you must be put out....'

He laughed as he picked up a saddle bag which, presumably, contained a change of clothes and necessities for
travelling. 'I assure you that David and I have slept in far
worse places than the tap room of this inn and, as I said,
it will be wiser, considering that it appears to harbour
thieves, a matter which I shall take up with our host. Please
make yourselves at home and try to rest and, at last, sleep
after your trying adventures. I will send David up with
your belongings.'

He brushed by Philippa in order to reach the door and she felt herself trembling again at his touch. He bowed to her mother. 'Please, Lady Wroxeter, accept my apologies for these unfortunate events, happening so soon after your arrival back in your native land after such a long absence.'

Philippa saw her mother give a great gasp of surprise and shock and she herself put a hand to her mouth in dismayed astonishment.

'Sir—'

He stemmed Cressida's attempts at denial with a lordly wave of his hand.

'Sir Daniel Gretton's beautiful daughter could not be mistaken for any other, my lady. Her fame spread through the Marches and I had the advantage of seeing you once with your father in the market in Ludlow. That was considerably before you married my lord Earl.' He smiled broadly. 'I was merely eight years old then but, like all the other males in the district, I fell completely under the spell of Gretton's faery princess.' His gaze passed to Philippa and dwelt on her slight form, trembling now with another fear that he was aware of their true identities. 'Your daughter, my lady, has been blessed in inheriting your golden loveliness. I am honoured to be of service. I will pay my respects in the morning. Please excuse me now.'

He withdrew and closed the door before either of the astounded women could say a word in answer.

Chapter Two

Philippa woke to find sunlight coming through the un-shuttered casement and almost blinding her. She slipped from the bed, careful not to waken her mother who was still sleeping beside her. She went to the window and found, to her delight, that the mist and dampness of the previous day had disappeared and the sun was already well up. She gave a sigh of relief. Provided that Peter was well enough to travel after yesterday's misadventure, they would be able to make an early start and be well on their way before midday.

She had slept well considering how frightened and disturbed she had been last night. Exhaustion had taken its toll of them both. Her thoughts went to the stranger lord who had come to their help. It had been extremely kind of him to put his private chamber at their disposal, but she recalled her mother's alarmed expression when he had announced that he had recognised her. It would be well if they could avoid seeing him again, though Philippa doubted that that would be possible.

A sound from the bed alerted her to the knowledge that, despite her care not to disturb her mother, Cressida had woken and was already sitting up.

'Is there something wrong?' she enquired doubtfully. 'Have you heard someone at the door?'

'No, no one. The inn servants are already about their business. It is a fine day. We should be able to leave soon after breakfast as long as Peter is well enough.'

Cressida thrust back the bed covers and stepped from the bed. 'I'll dress at once. We must call a physician to Peter if there is need.'

Philippa went to her mother's side to help her dress. Since they had decided it would be best, for this journey, to travel without a maid in attendance, it had been necessary for them to help each other with back lacings.

Once her mother was dressed she hastened to dress herself and was relieved that she had done so when she heard a knock on the door.

Peter Fairley's voice called softly, 'It is I, my lady, Peter. I have brought you some breakfast.'

Philippa hastened to let him in, relieved to see he was up and about.

'Peter, how are you this morning?'

He set down a tray on which was laid fresh manchet bread, a small pot of honey and a plate of ham and cold meats and a stoup of ale.

'I'm very well except for a bump on the back of my head as big as a pigeon's egg.' He rubbed it ruefully. 'I blame myself for total lack of caution. I could have put us all in danger.'

'You mustn't blame yourself,' Cressida reassured him. 'Who would expect to be attacked in the inn yard?'

'To speak truth, anyone should, my lady. My only excuse is that we were all tired and chilled and I was in haste to see to your needs.'

'Well, all is well.' Cressida smiled. 'We will breakfast quickly and try to make an early start.' She frowned in thought. 'I have some coin left which, fortunately, I kept in a money belt beneath my gown, but the loss of some of our funds in the robbery is dire. We shall have to be careful on the journey and settle for accommodation not of the best.' She had already put out a small pile of coin upon the bed. 'Take that and make the best bargain you can over mounts, Peter, but first, have you eaten?'

'Yes, my lady. I shall get off at once. Sir Rhys's man, David, speaks of a reasonably honest horse coper, who has a stable in the street behind the harbour.'

'Good.' Lady Wroxeter nodded her approval.

Then Philippa said thoughtfully, 'Did you discover anything about our rescuer of last night, Peter? Unfortunately he appeared to recognise Mother and we are anxious to avoid his company now.' She coloured. 'That seems to be very ungrateful, but you understand the need better than any of us.'

With his hand on the door latch, Peter turned, clearly hesitant to speak. 'Sir Rhys Griffith, my lady, is master of the greater part of my lord Earl's estates. His father was granted them following the battle of Redmoor, for his services to the new King. Sir David was killed in a hunting accident a year ago.' He grinned somewhat wolfishly. 'He was somewhat appropriately gored by a boar and did not recover from the wound which festered, and his son, Rhys, who had been knighted the year before, inherited.'

There was a deadly silence as the three exchanged alarmed glances.

Philippa exclaimed hotly, 'So the man has robbed my father of his lands and—'

'He cannot be held responsible for what his father did at Redmoor,' Cressida reproved her gently, 'but I confess this news is catastrophic. The man could prove a very real danger to us, indeed.'

'He has enquired after you both,' Peter said grimly. 'I'm afraid that it will prove very difficult for us to leave the inn without encountering him.'

'And his manor is far too close to Gretton for our peace of mind,' Lady Wroxeter said regretfully.

Philippa paled. 'Do you think our going there could put Grandmère and Grandpère in danger?'

Lady Wroxeter shook her head. 'I do not think so, though it will not enhance their reputation as Yorkist sympathisers. They are not proscribed and are in no danger of arrest.' The fingers of one hand tightened on the bedpost. 'I am so very anxious to see them. It has been so long since—' She broke off, her voice choked with emotion, 'Neither of them has ever seen you. I think we should take the risk.'

'But this man does know we are going there?'

'I imagine so. Since he lives so close I would think he is aware of how ill my father is. It is to be hoped that he will have enough humanity to leave us in peace and not inform the court authorities of our presence there.' She sighed. 'Our visit will only be a short one. We dare not remain long.'

'You miss your home at Gretton, don't you?'

'I always loved it dearly and when I heard of the proposed betrothal to your father I was most reluctant to leave it. Of course, then there was every possibility of being able to come home on frequent visits but since Redmoor…' She shrugged helplessly.

'You gave up everything to be with my father in exile, a safe secure home, money sufficient to fill all your needs, everything.'

Cressida smiled fondly. 'When you fall in love, Philippa, you will understand that nothing is important save being with the one you love.'

Philippa bit her lip uncertainly. The way matters stood that possibility seemed very far off, if at all.

Her mother suddenly remembered that she had given Peter Fairley no instructions about settling their score. 'I should have asked him to settle with the landlord on his way out to the horse coper,' she said. 'The sooner we can leave the better.'

A decisive voice from the doorway settled the matter for her. 'You need have no doubts on that score, Lady Wroxeter, I have already paid the landlord and the moment your man returns with your mounts we can leave immediately. It will be well to do so since the day promises to be a fine one.'

Sir Rhys Griffith stood poised in the doorway which Peter must have left slightly ajar in his agitation on leaving them.

'I beg pardon for the intrusion, but the door was open sufficiently for me to overhear what you said, my lady. May I come in?' He bowed courteously and Cressida, somewhat startled and flustered, nodded hastily.

'Please do so, Sir Rhys. This chamber is yours, after all, but I cannot allow you to stand our score. We have slept in this chamber, and most comfortably, I thank you, and have eaten two meals. I...'

He had advanced slightly and was regarding Philippa smilingly though he must have seen at once that her manner was somewhat hostile.

'You have no choice, my lady. I have already settled the matter. Under the distressing circumstances of last night it was the least I could do as a gentleman knight and for a neighbour.' He undid the purse suspended from the military-styled leather belt he wore round his waist and proffered a small leather bag to Philippa.

'There, mistress, is the coin that rascally thief stole from your man. I rose early, called on the constable with instructions as to charging the fellow and retrieved your money. You will need it when you arrive at Gretton or later on your journey home. You need not concern yourself about expenses occurred on the way to Gretton Manor since it will be my most pleasurable duty to escort you there.'

Philippa gave a great gasp of shocked surprise and anger. 'That will not be necessary, sir. Peter Fairley, my father's trusty squire, is perfectly capable of seeing us safe to Gretton.'

Her tone was now unmistakably hostile and his dark brows rose in assumed or real astonishment.

'Forgive me, Lady...?' He paused and looked enquiringly at Lady Wroxeter.

'My daughter is Lady Philippa Telford, Sir Rhys, and she owes her safety from molestation and her life to you,' Cressida put in hurriedly. Though she herself was anxious to be free of this man's presence, she had no wish for Philippa to antagonise him deliberately.

He bowed again, smiling. 'Forgive me again, Lady Philippa, but I must point out to you that neither you nor your squire appeared last night to be perfectly capable of protecting yourselves. It is my desire and my bounden duty to provide a suitable escort. Both my cousin David and I are soldier-trained and with your squire, who is too, we should prove a sufficient force to keep off any opportunity-seeking robbers on the road.' He shook his head, gently reproving, 'I fear the roads of Wales are no more safe from thieves and outlaws than any other rural community, though preferable in many ways to the hazards of London town or even Ludlow after dark.'

Philippa looked to her mother for support in her rejection of the idea, but Cressida shook her head gently. 'We shall be grateful for your continued care of us, Sir Rhys,' she said quietly.

Sir Rhys glanced round the chamber to see if their saddle bags were packed and nodded his satisfaction.

'I will inform your man Peter when he returns with the horses and send him up to you. I should not advise you to come down to the tap room until there is need. The clientele of this place is hardly salubrious, as yesterday's misadventures bore out.' He bowed again and withdrew.

Philippa said angrily, 'Why did you agree to his escort? We do not need or want his company.'

Lady Wroxeter sighed. 'I do not see how we could refuse. To do so would only appear ungrateful and incur his displeasure, if not his downright anger. We cannot afford to antagonise the man, not only for our sakes but for those of your grandparents as well. Since he is well aware of our destination he could inform on us after our arrival, so it makes little difference.'

'I would have preferred not to have his company,' Philippa said sulkily and her mother turned on her in sudden irritation.

'You were glad enough of Sir Rhys's services last night, young lady. Be good enough to acknowledge our debt to him.'

'I doubt if he acknowledges any debt to my father,' Philippa snapped in answer and turned away to see to the final packing.

Philippa was forced to acknowledge Sir Rhys Griffith's need for caution, however, when they were eventually called downstairs by his squire, who informed them that Peter Fairley had arrived with their horses and his master had declared himself ready to leave. The atmosphere in the tap room was decidedly frosty; the small number of men seated at the ale-spattered tables stared at the women in open hostility and the landlord was surly. Obviously news concerning their imprisoned companion had reached them and the blame for his likely fate placed at the women's door. Sir Rhys received them cheerily and conducted them to the door with a show of deliberate courtesy. Philippa shivered in spite of herself and was glad of his presence.

Peter had managed to procure an elderly palfrey for Lady Wroxeter and two sturdy Welsh cobs for himself and Philippa. To her irritation, Sir Rhys insisted upon inspecting them before allowing his charges to mount. As if Peter was incapable of judging good horse flesh when he saw it, Philippa fumed inwardly. She watched, frowning, as Sir Rhys ran his hand down the legs of each of the mounts and inspected their chests and mouths. Apparently satisfied, he came back to the waiting group and nodded his approval.

'You have made as good purchases as possible under the circumstances,' he informed Peter.

'If you were not sure of his abilities, you should have accompanied him to the horse coper,' Philippa murmured under her breath and he turned and grinned at her. She was not sure if he had actually heard, but he made no comment.

'It is necessary to have good mounts for our journey,' he explained. 'We have almost a hundred miles over undulating country, some of it mountainous.'

Cressida nodded. 'I travelled it only once when—when I left England in 1486 and we were somewhat hurried,' she said quickly.

'I imagine you have not ridden a great deal over the last years?' he enquired.

'No, there has been little opportunity or need,' she agreed.

Peter stepped forward to help his mistress into the saddle

and Philippa was chagrined to find Sir Rhys at her side to do a like service for her. She found herself swung up lightly, the touch of his hand gentle yet firm upon her body. Confused by such close contact, she turned and fumbled awkwardly with the reins, only to find them deliberately placed into her hands.

'You are used to riding, Lady Philippa?' he enquired. 'If not, you can ride with me.'

'That will certainly not be necessary, sir,' she said coldly. 'Though I do not ride often in Malines, my father has been at pains to see that I learned well and had adequate practice.'

'Good. As I said to your mother, we have a hard ride in front of us.'

He stood back to confer with the two men, then gave a signal for all to mount up and swung himself lightly into the saddle of the courser an inn groom held ready for him. He moved his horse beside that of her mother's as they rode beneath the courtyard arch and Philippa rode behind with the two squires flanking her.

The day was pleasantly warm and she flung back her cloak and slipped back her hood, allowing the sun's gentle warmth to touch her body. Her new mount seemed amiable enough and soon became accustomed to her touch upon the reins and she leaned forward to pat the cob's shaggy neck. Peter smiled at her encouragingly and she grinned back, thankful, at last, to be away from the inn.

Soon they were out of the mired streets of the harbour and free of the unaccustomed smells of sea air and tar and the green undulating countryside stretched before them. Yesterday's misty dampness had refreshed the air and Philippa began to find the ride pleasurable.

She could hear Sir Rhys in talk with her mother and

rode slightly forward so that she could catch everything which was said.

'I would suggest that we make three stops upon the way at inns known to me,' he said.

'But, Sir Rhys, I had thought Philippa and I might be accommodated at two nunneries I know of.' Lady Wroxeter hesitated, her colour rising, as she went on, 'You must understand that expense is a feature of my decision...'

'I think not, my lady,' he brushed aside her objection. 'Nuns are notoriously curious. They lead such sheltered lives that they are fascinated by the backgrounds and news brought from the outside world of everyone who comes to stay. I imagine you are anxious to avoid as much gossip as possible. Do not concern yourself about expense. I have already made provision for David and I upon the journey so it will be no extra drain upon our resources.'

'But surely—'

Philippa saw him lean towards her mother and place a restraining hand upon hers. 'Please, Lady Wroxeter, place yourself in my hands and, I assure you, you will reach Gretton without either incident or undue notice.'

Philippa considered what he had said and raised an enquiring eyebrow in Peter's direction. He merely shrugged his shoulders in answer. They were in this man's power and she realised they were helpless to change the situation.

She regarded his unyielding back as he rode ahead and mentally reviewed the encounter of the previous night. Her mother was right. Had this man not come to her rescue, they would not be travelling this road today. A great shudder ran through her at the thought. Had she not discovered that he was a loyal Tudor supporter and, worse than that, had inherited her father's confiscated estates, she would have been more than ready to acknowledge her debt to him. What was his motive in offering them protection?

Would he lead them into some manor upon the way where they could be arrested and held during the King's pleasure in hopes that her father would come to England to plead their cause and try to obtain their release, so placing his head on the block? It was a likely prospect—yet how could they manage to evade this fate? Peter had clearly accepted defeat—for the moment. She must wait patiently until he was able to suggest some way of escaping Sir Rhys's vigilance, but even should they accomplish this—and it would be difficult and hazardous—their plans to visit her dying grandfather would have to be abandoned and she knew her mother had set her heart upon this visit. She sighed a little too loudly and Sir Rhys turned in his saddle to regard her, eyebrows raised.

'Are you tired already, Lady Philippa? Do you wish to stop? I know that unaccustomed riding can cause saddle soreness.'

She blushed hotly at the thought and shook her head. 'No, no, sir, I was just—considering the length of the journey facing us.'

'I shall try to make it as easy for you all as possible,' he returned mildly.

Their first stop for refreshment was in the Tudor stronghold of Pembroke. Philippa looked up at the looming castle apprehensively. Here, surely, Sir Rhys might well achieve his aim and put them in the hands of the King's officers. More than likely he would obtain the King's favour by so doing though, knowing the Tudor monarch from her days in attendance at Queen Elizabeth's court, she doubted that he would be paid in coin or lands. King Henry kept a very tight hand on the treasury purse strings. Nevertheless all his supporters were well aware that to be in the King's debt would be advantageous.

Sir Rhys drew his small company off the main street which was crowded with carts and market stalls, their proprietors calling hoarsely the worth of their wares to passers-by, into a street behind where he drew his mount up before an inn displaying the sign of the Red Lion. Despite her assurance to Sir Rhys that she was not weary, Philippa was glad to have Peter lift her down and to join her mother in the inn's one eating room where a sweating landlord came obsequiously forward to enquire what service Sir Rhys required.

Curtly the knight ordered a dinner of meat and vegetable broth, pease pudding and what tarts the fellow had to offer which would please the ladies. Philippa and her mother were escorted up the rickety stair to a small dark chamber where a slatternly maid brought them water and towels, plus chamber pots, so that they might refresh themselves. Thankfully they returned to the eating room to find the food already upon the table. Philippa, who had been dry-mouthed with alarm at what might transpire in the next hour or so, discovered that, despite that, she was hungry and was glad of the hot tasty food and the rye bread which accompanied it. This inn was not apparently able to provide the fine white manchet bread to which Sir Rhys was more usually accustomed.

Her mother was rather quiet over the meal and Sir Rhys accepted her need for silence in courtesy. Above stairs, away from his presence, Philippa had thought it best not to alarm her mother with her fears. Catching her eye across the table, she understood that her mother had already considered the danger.

Nothing happened, however. They completed the meal, then David, Sir Rhys's squire, rose to pay the score. Peter had already gone to assure himself that their mounts had been fed and watered. Sir Rhys offered his hand to Lady Wroxeter to lead her outside to the courtyard.

'I considered it wiser to chose a less frequented inn, this being market day,' he explained. 'The fare was nourishing but hardly acceptable to finer palates used to food prepared in the Duchess Margaret's establishment at Malines.'

Cressida shook her head. 'The food was excellent and the place unexpectedly clean,' she replied.

Since Peter was engaged in mounting his lady upon her palfrey and David was still about his business in the inn, Sir Rhys lifted Philippa once more into the saddle.

'These merchant's clothes form an excellent disguise, and were well chosen,' he remarked as he fingered the wool of her russet gown.

Angrily she flashed back at him, 'These garments are no disguise, sir. We live in virtual penuary at Malines while you live in luxury on my father's estates.'

He looked from the tip of her proudly held young head to her little booted foot resting in the stirrup. How very lovely she was, even dressed, as she was, in these dull, outmoded clothes. Her golden curls peeped provocatively from beneath her simple linen coif, for she had thrown back the hood of her travelling cloak.

He had said earlier that she possessed the same golden loveliness of her mother, but in Philippa now that beauty was enhanced by vibrant youth. Her skin glowed with health and her green-blue eyes, almost turquoise in the sunlight, sparked with angry vitality. There was a seeming childlike fragility about her in her exquisite petiteness, which he had noted when he had come to her rescue in that darkened courtyard. It had brought out a protective tenderness in him, yet now his pulses raced as he thought how much of a true woman she was. He sensed the inten- sity of her bitterness towards him, read it in the set of her little pointed chin, in that hauntingly elfish, heart-shaped face, in the hard-held line of her lips, despite their sensuous fullness, which now he longed to lean forward and kiss.

He had met and known many women at court, and other, more earthy voluptuous beauties who had lived on his estates and granted him favours, daughters of his tenants and servants, but none had stirred him as this woman did.

When Philippa had risen, trembling, from her attacker and he had felt her quivering fearful young body pressed against his heart, he had recognised the inner strength of her, the courageous determination to recover quickly so that she could rush to her mother to warn and protect her, her genuine concern for their squire, even under the stress of her own ordeal.

She was in fighting form now, and amused admiration for her warred within him with the sudden surge of desire which ran through him.

He chuckled inwardly. She would need to be managed—for her own safety and that of those she might imperil if she gave way to rashness brought on by her own contempt for him.

'Ah,' he murmured, his dark eyes flashing in understanding, 'so that is the rub, Lady Philippa, and the direct cause of your suddenly adopted hatred for me. Your man has informed you about my estates and how my father obtained them.

'I hate no one, sir,' she said coldly. 'That would be against the teaching of Holy Church. Contempt would be nearer the mark to explain my feelings towards you.'

'You think I should have refused to accept my inheritance?' He gave a little dry laugh. 'I would have thought you would have gained a better knowledge of the ways of the world than that, Lady Philippa. I am quite sure your father's many services to the late King won him the pre-ferment he both desired and earned.'

She went white to the lips and, seeing her unwillingness to reply to that shot, he bowed and moved towards his own mount.

Lady Wroxeter had not been able to hear their conver-sation, but, feeling instinctively that Philippa had insulted their escort, she turned in the saddle and gave her daughter a warning look.

They travelled for the rest of the day without incident and arrived at dusk at an inn on the outskirts of Carmar-then. Sir Rhys had chosen one less fashionable but appar-ently clean and respectable. He arranged for a private chamber for the ladies, informing the landlord's wife that Lady Wroxeter was a cousin of his, who was travelling with her daughter and brother to visit a sick relative who lived in the Marches. He, himself, he said cheerily, would make do with the common chamber and, as Peter Fairley announced his intention of sleeping with their horses in the stable, he ordered David, his squire, to join him there.

After a hearty meal the ladies retired and assisted each other to undress.

'Philippa,' Lady Wroxeter said, wrinkling her brow in concern, 'you have not quarrelled with Sir Rhys, have you? I asked you to have a care. I thought there seemed something of an atmosphere between you after our stop for dinner. We are in enough danger as it is. Do not an-tagonise the man.'

Philippa shrugged irritably. 'I merely made it clear to him when he passed an opinion on our state of dress that our straitened circumstances are due in part to his enrich-ment at our expense.'

'But that is hardly true. King Henry would have granted

your father's lands to, if not Sir Rhys's father, then another one of his supporters after your father became a proscribed traitor.'

'But Sir Rhys's father turned traitor to his rightful king at Redmoor,' Philippa snapped.

'I doubt if Sir Rhys was quite old enough to fight for the Tudor either at Redmoor or Stoke and can hardly be blamed for what his father did,' Cressida reminded her. 'In all events, those battles were over long ago and we have your future to consider now.'

'You wish that my father was not so concerned with the Duchess Margaret's machinations?' Philippa posed, somewhat shocked by such a suggestion.

'Like most women, I wish your father would sometimes consider the cost of his outdated allegiance and think a little more of us,' Cressida rejoined tartly. 'I love your father with my whole heart and will remain loyal to him whatever he chooses to do, but I do have you to think about.'

Wearily she climbed into bed and Philippa thought it best to say nothing further.

She lay wakeful. Her fears had been thoroughly aroused in Pembroke and would not be put to rest. Her mother had not been present during that dreadful journey to the coast, four years ago, when she had been forced to flee from England with her friends, the Allards. The King's body squire, John Hilyard, had followed them and attempted to take Philippa prisoner, to hold her hostage for her father's compliance to King Henry's will. It had been a hard fight when he had overtaken them and Philippa had been little more than a child then, but she had known real heartstopping fear that they would be killed. John Hilyard had paid the price and lost his life as a consequence of that encounter and his body had been thrown over a hedge. In retrospect she recalled how they had all set their teeth and struggled on, their friend, Sir Adam Westlake, severely wounded in the fight and Richard Allard still suffering from the effects of the torture he had endured as King Henry's prisoner in the Tower of London. Report of Hilyard's death must have reached the King. Philippa doubted if she would ever be forgiven. If she could be captured now, on this visit, how great a prize she and her mother would be if Rhys Griffith decided to hand them over. Somehow she must convince her mother of their danger and try to escape from Rhys's clutches.

Cressida had fallen into an exhausted slumber at her side. Cautiously Philippa climbed from the bed and pulled her gown over her head, but was forced to leave it unlaced at the back. She thought it most likely that, despite his avowed intention of staying with the horses, Peter had more than probably stolen back to sleep nearer to his charges. She must seek him out and confer with him about their next move.

She looked back to see if her mother had wakened but Cressida stirred, then turned over and went back to sleep again. Philippa gave a little sigh of relief, stole to the door and carefully undid the latch. She had not dared to light a candle and found herself in total darkness on the landing when the door opened. The crack in the shutter had lightened her chamber sufficiently well for to see there, but now the blackness appeared absolute and she hesitated for moments to allow her eyes to adjust. After a second or two she could begin to see dimly in greyness and was about to step forward when she stumbled against something soft and yielding right before her feet.

'Peter,' she called softly but, before she could bend to examine the sleeping form further, her ankles were caught in a tight hold and she fell backwards into the arms of the man who had risen, cat-like, into a crouch at her advance. A hand fastened cruelly over her mouth and almost cut off her breath.

A harsh whisper came from the darkness. 'God's Wounds, mistress, what are you about? Not again! Did your previous hazardous encounter teach you nothing?'

She struggled ineffectively in her captor's arms, realising, in fury, that she had been caught by the very man she had wished to avoid.

'If I remove my hand, will you cry out and waken everyone in the inn?' he demanded softly. 'If not, shake your head and I will oblige.'

She shook her head vigorously and he released the gagging hand so that she could draw in ragged gasps of breath again. Her knees felt weak—she feared they would let her down and leaned against the door for support. He had risen to his feet fully now and was still holding her by one shoulder, then he urged her silently but imperiously down the stairs where he pushed open the door of the tap room in front of her and thrust her inside.

'We can talk more privately in here.'

She made to argue hotly but he lifted a hand impatiently to prevent her, and stood facing her, hands on his hips.

'Now, mistress, I demand to know what business brings you from your chamber half undressed.' His eyes passed insolently over her body on which her gown hung loosely and one shoulder was bared to his hard gaze. 'I take it that your mother is unaware of this escapade? What are you doing, Lady Philippa? Are you in search of Master Fairley?'

She was about to agree that she was until she understood by the hard gleam in his eyes that he thought her reason for doing so was quite unacceptable. Her cheeks flamed and she went hot with embarrassment and anger that he might have so little regard for her sense of propriety.

'How dare you question me!' she snapped impatiently and turned to hasten towards the door again in order to make her escape, but he caught her by the arm again and pulled her towards him roughly.

'I have every reason to do so since I have made myself responsible for your safety.'

'No one asked you to,' she flared back.

The room was, of course, deserted and she was aware that her voice had risen and that she might well have awakened someone upstairs who might come to discover what was causing a disturbance in the night. The room seemed chilly and she turned towards the fire where the embers had been banked down but a residual warmth was still being given out. Despite the day's summer warmth, it had been kindled to allow mulled ale and spiced wine to be produced for travellers and customers who requested it. She realised suddenly that she was quite alone with this man she regarded as an enemy and knew that her shivers were caused by something other than the chilliness of the summer night.

Tiredly she said, 'Allow me, sir, to return to my chamber now. I am wearied.'

'Not too wearied to be wandering about. I will allow you to go, mistress, when you provide me with a suitable explanation for this wanton behaviour.'

'It does not concern you. I do not have to answer to you, sir.'

He did not favour that remark with an answer, but released her arm and stood dominatingly before her, feet apart, arms folded.

His very attitude and the fact that he had dispensed with the courtesy of affording her her proper title but had addressed her as 'mistress', rather than 'my lady', fired her to anger once more.

'If you must have an explanation, yes, I was, indeed, looking for Peter.'

'Why?'

The single word was uttered without any courteous preamble.

'As I have said, it is of no concern of yours. I—I—' She flailed about in her mind for an acceptable reason. She dared not give him the true one. 'I—I simply wanted to talk with him—about the problems of the journey and—and did not wish to alarm my mother.'

'You are sure you have no other reason for not alarming your mother?' The question was disconcertingly blunt, so much so that she gasped aloud.

'Are you suggesting—?'

'I am suggesting nothing. The facts seem plain enough. You get up in the middle of the night, half undressed, in order to see your father's squire. It requires little more speculation on my part.'

In sudden fury she lashed out at his cheek, but he caught her hand before it could do damage and held it in a punishing grip, so that she cried out in pain. 'Little hell·cat,' he murmured softly and deliberately.

She struggled to free herself. His grasp was delivering real pain and she knew there would be bruises to show for it in the morning. He released her at last and she stumbled backwards.

'How dare you!' she stuttered, very close to tears. 'How dare you imply that Peter and I would—' Her breath ended in a splutter of unutterable rage. 'Why, Peter, unlike you, is the soul of honour. He is totally devoted to our interests and discreet and my father trusts him with all our lives...'

'I do not doubt that, mistress,' he said grimly, 'but can

he trust him with his daughter's honour? Last evening, as I recall, you were supposedly out looking for him then because you said he was late returning to you and you were worried about him.'

'That was the truth,' she retorted, sparks flying from her lovely blue-green eyes. 'Perhaps you would like to question my concern for his welfare and put that down to a dishonourable reason. I imagine you are less concerned about the welfare of your own retainers.'

He was silent for a while, not rising to her taunt, watching the angry rise and fall of her breasts, the looseness of her unfastened gown more than normally revealing. Once more he marvelled at her loveliness, so exquisitely formed, like a faery sprite, more beautiful than he had remembered her mother to have been when she had captivated his boy's heart so long ago. He felt an ungovernable anger. Philippa Telford might look like a child, but she most certainly was not. He had the evidence of that before his eyes. She was radiantly lovely, enough to seduce the whole of the male population within the Duchess Margaret's court, he thought, yet she was here in search of her father's squire, a man surely too old and unworthy to be her lover. Was he judging her too harshly? Was she really innocent at heart, simply anxious to talk with the man, as she had said, about the difficulties of the journey ahead? Unaccountably he found himself wanting to believe her. She was so young—sixteen, seventeen perhaps—and he believed her parents had kept her well chaperoned. Yet, the thought came to him that, beautiful as she was and well born, she had not concealed how poverty-stricken they were in exile in Burgundy. She must be fully aware of how difficult it was going to be for her father to provide her with a suitable husband. How galling that must be to her...

He sighed heavily. In her present mood he was going

to find it hard to convince her that this rash behaviour was indiscreet, if not downright dangerous.

'Lady Philippa, you know, I am sure, that this is a difficult and dangerous time for your mother and you. It behoves you to be circumspect.' He lifted a hand imperiously as she made to interrupt him. 'No, hear me out. I cannot imagine why you should wish to seek out your father's squire at this hour of the night, but there must be no more of these escapades. Do you hear me?'

'I hear you,' she grated through clenched teeth. 'I would like to know just why you were sleeping outside our door rather than in the common chamber where you said you would be.'

'I have already explained. I regard myself as your protector,' he returned mildly. 'Though the wars are over, the times are still troubled. King's men are everywhere and soldiers, off duty, can pose problems for vulnerable women. I am sure that I do not have to explain that to you.'

'Are you our protector or our jailer?' she said stonily and his eyes opened wide and darkened to obsidian.

Hastily she added, somewhat lamely, 'I meant that—I do not understand why you should appoint yourself our guardian.'

He shrugged. 'Perhaps because Fate or the Virgin cast you both before me as being in need. Is that not a good enough reason, mistress?'

Haughtily she shook her glorious hair, which lay unbound in heavy red-gold waves upon her shoulders. He felt an irresistible desire to pull her towards him and run his fingers through it. What was she doing, he thought savagely, appearing before a man in the night like that? Had she no sense of decorum? Didn't she realise what temptations she could arouse in men? He took himself firmly in hand. She was young, vulnerable, and under his protection. He must hold himself in check.

'I am not sure,' she said icily, 'whether either my mother or I are gladdened that fate decided to take such a hand in our affairs. Now, sir, will you please stand aside and allow me to return to my mother?'

He nodded slowly and stepped aside from the door so that she might move towards it unhindered. He could not allow himself to touch her, not again.

He said a trifle hoarsely, 'Certainly, Lady Philippa, but be assured that I shall resume my post outside your door the moment you are settled inside.'

She did not deign to reply, but sulkily moved past him and mounted the stairs back to their chamber.

He followed and settled himself, seated with his back to their door. He was bewitched as if she had thrown faery dust before his eyes and taken possession of his very soul. How could this have happened to him and so suddenly? Not only was she so beautiful that just to look at her caused an ache within his loins, but she had spirit and courage. He could only pray that those very virtues he admired in her did not bring her into further dangers.

He pondered upon her reaction to his unvoiced accusation that she was wandering out to meet her lover. She had rejected it out of hand and with considerable indignation. Could he believe her? Would she not, if caught out like that, react in exactly that way? And had he any right to be angered by her behaviour?

He allowed himself a little secret smile. Certainly she had made no bones about admitting the fact that she despised him. Why? Simply because he was in possession of her father's former lands? Had she expected to arrive in England and find those estates and manor houses empty and neglected? Was it not usual for the victor in any combat to hand out spoils to his supporters? At Duchess Margaret's court, intrigue-ridden as it was, she could not be unaware of those situations.

He had recognised Lady Wroxeter on sight and on impulse offered her his protection on this journey. He knew of the distress of her parents at being so long parted from their daughter by circumstances they were powerless to alter and of the present serious illness of Sir Daniel. It had seemed reasonable and his duty to assume responsibility for the safety of his neighbour's kin. He had not expected such a hostile reaction from Lady Philippa. He sighed. They would be thrown together for several more days. In honour he must control his growing feelings for her. He had gravely insulted her by his suggestion that she had acted wantonly. There would be time for him to discover if he were, in fact, mistaken and, if so, to attempt to repair the damage.

The darkness upon the landing was beginning to lighten to grey. He settled himself more comfortably, yet in a position to continue his nocturnal watch.

Philippa stole back to her bed, careful not to disturb her sleeping mother. Her cheeks were still hot with embarrassed fury directed at the man who was separated from her only by the thickness of the chamber door. Her plan would have to be abandoned. Rhys Griffith would not move from his post this night. She would have to try to find some other opportunity to have talk with Peter away from the man's insufferable vigilance.

She punched the straw-filled pillow violently to relieve her feelings and wriggled down in the bed. Yet sleep evaded her. The vision of the man's dark presence continued to dominate her thoughts. She tossed and turned restlessly. She had never before encountered a man so bluntly and insultingly spoken. No one in the Duchess's retinue, nor even any nobleman at Queen Elizabeth's court at Westminster, would have dared to question her so accusingly. He was hateful and she had no way of proving to him how shamefully wrong he was in his suspicions. Peter was a dear and trusted friend whom she had known from childhood. Never could she think of him as—she blushed inwardly at the thought—as a lover. Even if they had had more intimate feelings towards each other, neither would have behaved so indecorously. Peter would have regarded such desires as a blot upon the knightly honour to which he had once aspired. Knowing how vulnerable her position was at court, she had been particularly careful that she was never alone in any man's company, since her dowerless state would have made it impossible for any man to offer her honourable marriage.

Rhys Griffith had immediately jumped to the wrong conclusion. Indignantly she asked herself what business it was of his? He had no hold over her. It was as if he were— jealous! The idea was laughable.

Once more she pounded her pillow in impotent fury. Somehow she must convince him that he had accused her falsely, but without alerting him to the true reason for her determination to meet with Peter privately for that could put them all in danger. Strangely she was most anxious that Rhys Griffith should not think ill of her, though, for the life of her, she could not understand her own reason for caring.

Chapter Three

They travelled by easy stages through the lovely Welsh countryside, through Carmarthen, Landovery and Buith Wells, and stayed at last at an inn in Leominster. The weather stayed fine. The rain, which had fallen before their arrival in Wales, had laid the dust and the roads were reasonably comfortable as a result, neither too miry or too dusty and hard ridged.

As on the stops they had made previously, the inn Sir Rhys had chosen was comfortable and clean without being luxurious or fashionable. Philippa had had no opportunity to speak with Peter Fairley privately during the journey. Though they had ridden side by side, she was conscious that Sir Rhys, riding with her mother only some yards ahead of her, could hear anything they had to say and, therefore, she had had to talk of everyday things, the comforts or disadvantages of the inns they stayed at, the beauty of the scenery, or the weather. At all times, whether he was looking at them or not, Philippa was aware that she and Peter were under close scrutiny and it irked her.

At Leominster she had an excuse at last to follow Peter down to the stables, hoping to find him alone. Her little Welsh cob, of whom she had grown very fond, was limp-

ing just a little by the time they arrived and she expressed
a desire to go and ask Peter to discover, if he could, the
reason and pronounce his opinion on whether she were
well enough to proceed next day. Sir Rhys was absent from
the eating room for the moment and Philippa's mother
nodded her agreement.

Philippa was fortunate to find Peter alone and he was,
as she entered the stable, examining the cob's right fore
hoof.

He looked up, smiling, as he saw Philippa. 'She has
gathered a small stone. It isn't serious. I'm removing it
now.'

'Will she be able to carry me tomorrow? I don't want
to further lame her.'

'Yes, my lady, she will be fine when she's rested.'

Philippa approached him and looked back to see that no
one was near the opened doorway.

'I've been anxious to speak with you alone since we left
Milford Haven.'

He nodded. 'It has proved difficult. I would have preferred to have closer access to your mother, also, but it
seemed unwise.'

'Peter, do you think we are in danger from this man?'

'Sir Rhys? I doubt it, though he is the King's man. Had
he any intention of betraying us he would have done so
before now.'

'Yet he could involve my grandparents in the crime of
harbouring us if we are discovered there after we have
actually settled in at Gretton. Should we not try to part
from his surveillance after we leave Ludlow and, perhaps,
postpone our arrival at Gretton?'

Peter scratched his chin thoughtfully. 'Neither you nor
your mother are proscribed traitors. There can be no real
reason why you should not visit. I, on the other hand, could

find myself arrested both for having fought at Redmoor and at Stoke and for being in your father's service and close confidence. However,' he said, smiling. 'I do not believe that Sir Rhys Griffith thinks I am important enough for him to concern himself about my doings.'

'I am not so sure of that,' Philippa replied coolly.

He glanced at her quickly. 'Oh?'

'He thinks you are my lover or that you aspire to be.'

Peter's expression of alarm was so comical that Philippa burst out laughing and she quickly explained to him what had occurred when she had attempted to slip out on that first night in Pembroke to see him.

'I hope you disabused him of that idea. Your mother would be scandalised and as for your father's reaction to such news—' He broke off, horrified.

Teasingly she said, 'Don't you find me attractive, Peter?'

His brown eyes surveyed her somewhat myopically. 'You are the most beautiful girl I have ever seen, Lady Philippa, barring your mother when she was the age you are now, but I would never betray your father's trust, you know that. I love you as a...' he sought blindly for words '...as a beloved sister perhaps. I would gladly die for you if there were need, but—'

'You do not love me in the way the troubadors sing of. I understand,' she said blithely, 'and that is just as well for I, too, regard you as a dear, elder brother.' She frowned, considering. 'Then you do not think we should try to escape Sir Rhys?'

He sighed. 'It would prove impossible. If he should decide to call out a search for us, all roads to any coast would be blocked.'

She bit her lip uncertainly. 'Then we can do nothing?'

A cool voice from the doorway answered her with another question. 'What is it you wish to do, Lady Philippa?'

She turned guiltily to face Sir Rhys as he entered, his
cold gaze passing from her to Peter.

'We were conferring about my mount, sir,' she retorted,
staring back at him defiantly. 'You may have noticed she
was limping when we arrived and Peter tells me she has
picked up a loose stone which he has removed. I thought
we might require the services of a smith.'

'Ah.' He did not take his gaze from her for moments
and then turned to Peter. 'Will she be fit to carry your
mistress tomorrow, think you?'

'Oh, yes, Sir Rhys, there should be no difficulty about
completing our journey.'

'Good. We do not wish for any delay as I am sure your
grandmother will be anxious to see you, Lady Philippa.
Now, if you will come at once, supper will soon be served
and your mother will wish you to join her.'

He held out his hand commandingly and she was forced
to take it and allow him to lead her from the stable after
a murmured 'thank you' to Peter.

Outside she snatched her hand from his grasp and
rasped. 'I wish you would not insist on spying on me when
I am with Peter. I have told you before, he is my father's
trusted squire and companion and nothing more to me than
a friend.'

He regarded her quizzically. 'Since you give me your
word on that, Lady Philippa, I must believe you, but I do
regard it as my duty to keep you safe from…' he paused,
thoughtfully eyeing her speculatively '…all harm.'

She flounced ahead of him into the inn and hastily went
to join her mother at the table. Lady Wroxeter was puzzled
by the strange gleam she saw reflected in her daughter's
eye. She had known throughout the journey that Philippa

had strongly resented their need to accede to Sir Rhys Griffith's desire to escort them to Gretton, but tonight she thought something further had passed between them. She sighed inwardly but said nothing. This problem would soon resolve itself. Tomorrow they would arrive at Gretton and she doubted if they would see more of their protector. Her father had written on several occasions that his neighbours were inclined to shun him, since he was found to be under the displeasure of the King and her parents had become virtually isolated on their own manor.

Philippa was particularly interested in the small market town of Ludlow next day as they rode in. This was their nearest town and her mother knew it well. Unlike Milford Haven, it seemed relatively clean and peaceful in the afternoon sun since today there was no market and no vociferous traders. Most of the shops were closed apparently over the dinner hour and there was a sleepy air about the place, dominated as it was by the former Yorkist stronghold of Ludlow Castle. She glanced at the grim walls curiously as they passed through. Here it was that Edward, the elder of the two Yorkist princes, had finally ridden out to meet his uncle, Richard, on his momentous journey to London to be crowned. It had never happened. He and his brothers and sisters had been declared illegitimate, the two boys placed in the royal apartments of the Tower of London from which they had mysteriously disappeared. She thought how furiously angry her father had been to learn only days ago that a proclamation had been made that Sir James Tyrell, recently executed, had confessed to their murder on the instructions of their uncle. She bit her lip uncertainly and cast a glance at her mother, who had turned in the saddle, finding her also tight-lipped. Did her mother believe the slanderous tale, despite her father's

avowals that the confession was a lie which had either
been forced from Sir James while in Tudor hands or fabricated after his death, a lie which could not be denied?
Sir Rhys had reined in his mount in order to allow the two
ladies to view the castle. Philippa cast him a venomous
glance. Undoubtedly Sir Rhys believed it.

As they left the town Philippa was impatient to reach
their home manor, but her anticipated pleasure was shad-
owed by the fear that they might not find her grandfather
alive.

Sir Rhys gestured her forward as they entered her grandfather's lands so that the two women could be together.
Philippa saw that her mother's eyes were bright with un-
shed tears and she reined in close and, reaching out, took
her gloved hand in her own encouragingly.

'We have come as soon as we could, *ma mère*, I am
sure we shall be in time to—' She broke off, too emotion-
ally choked to continue.

Sir Rhys said quietly, 'I saw your grandfather just before
I left for Milford Haven. I was able to conduct some business for him there. He was incapacitated but able to talk
and was as well as could be expected. Your grandmother
informed me that the physicians had told her they had no
reason to fear the worst.'

Lady Wroxeter nodded, grateful for his reassurance. So
he *did* visit her parents, apparently, undeterred by his
neighbours' unpopularity. Her mother must have had cause
to be grateful to him during those recent difficult and anx-
iety-ridden weeks.

Philippa was filled with surprised delight when she
caught her first sight of Gretton Manor. The evening sunlight caught the mellow building with its strong rays. The
undercroft was stone built, with an upper storey of timber

and plaster lath painted yellow which showed to advantage against the dark-stained oak beams. The manor house itself was approached through a gatehouse arch which at one time had housed a guard room but, probably due to the settled times and King Henry's proscriptions against the keeping of retainers, was now disused. From the front it was not possible to see the outbuildings and stables but, as the small party approached, grooms ran quickly forward to take the lead reins of their horses. One gabbled to Sir Rhys in Welsh, which he answered fluently. Any hopes Philippa might have had that he would leave them now, having delivered them safely home, were dispelled as both Sir Rhys's horse and his squire's were led off with their own. Peter Fairley lifted her down and she turned, a little flustered, to see a woman standing upon the top step leading to the hall to greet them. She came down immediately the moment she recognised the new arrivals. Cressida, who had been assisted to dismount by Sir Rhys, ran to her with a little choking cry of mingled delight and anxiety. Philippa could see little of her grandmother's features as her head was bent over the shoulders of her weeping daughter. She could just distinguish that Lady Gretton was of no great height, like her daughter and grandchild, and was plumply rounded in build.

Philippa came hesitantly towards the two and just caught the whispered questions each gave to the other.

'Father, is he…?'

'Well enough, child, and very anxious to greet you, but not sufficiently recovered to come from the hall yet.'

Lady Gretton had posed her question even more softly.

'Martyn, is he safe?'

Philippa's mother's answer was even softer, barely whispered. 'He was safe in Malines and well when we left him a sennight ago.'

Lady Gretton gave a little satisfied sigh. 'Good. It was unsafe for him to venture with you. Times are troubled here, even yet.'

She looked up and held her arms wide for Philippa to run into them. 'Come, child. You will never know how long we have waited to have a sight of you.'

Philippa was enveloped in a motherly embrace, scenting the fresh, country fragrances of rosemary and lavender. She was hugged so tightly she could hardly breathe and withdrew finally a little breathless, half-laughing and half-crying in the sudden emotion of greeting.

Now she could see that Mildred Gretton was indeed short and plumply attractive still in late middle age, but with nothing about her of her daughter and granddaughter's famed ethereal beauty. Her pleasant features were relatively unlined except for the little crinkles around her round, dark eyes, which betokened good humour. She was dressed in a dark green silk gown, somewhat outdated but of excellent quality, and she wore a small tight-fitting linen cap, but had not yet adopted the new French fashion of attached velvet veil Philippa had seen worn at the English court.

Still holding her grandchild by one arm, she turned smilingly to Sir Rhys Griffith.

'Rhys, how good to see you here, and in the company of my loved ones. As always you are very welcome to Gretton. Daniel will be so pleased to see you.'

He bowed courteously. 'Thank you, Mildred, but I will not stay. I have business to conclude at home and you both will wish to have this time with your loved ones alone. I found them on the harbour at Milford Haven and made it my business to see them safe to Gretton. How is Sir Daniel?'

'As you saw him a week ago, Rhys. He frets that he

cannot yet walk well or sit a horse. He sleeps below stairs as getting him above to our bedchamber has proven irksome, but the physician has hopes that he will soon be able to proceed further afield with the aid of a stick.'

Philippa gazed from her grandmother to Sir Rhys. So, they were obviously on good terms, which she found puzzling. She could but hope that Sir Rhys would honour his acceptance of their need for privacy and stay away from Gretton for some time. He was bidding farewell to her mother and she came to herself with a sudden start as he came to her side and held out his hand.

'I must make my excuses, Lady Philippa. I am delighted to hear that you will find your grandfather in good health considering his infirmities. I shall call on you all soon to assure myself that you want for nothing.'

She surrendered her hand a trifle unwillingly and murmured a polite word of gratitude for his care of them during the journey and he bent and kissed her palm. She found herself doubtfully regarding his retreating back as he left with his squire to move to the stable to retrieve his mount after it had been fed and watered. Her feelings were strangely mixed and bewildering, as if she was unsure when or if their paths would cross again and whether that would please or alarm her.

She followed her mother and grandmother up the entrance steps, through the screen doors and into the manor's hall. A man sat near a fire, which was burning on the side hearth despite it being mid-summer, and rose with difficulty at their entrance, leaning hard on a sturdy oaken stick. An elderly woman standing behind the chair clucked at him warningly as Cressida ran to him and he rocked on his feet with the suddenness of her fierce embrace.

'Now, master, be careful. Mistress Cressida, mind your father's condition.' Her admonition was unheeded as the two, locked together in the first joy of their meeting, were unconscious of the presence of any other within the hall. Philippa stood back a little shyly as, finally, tears streaming down her cheeks, her mother, helped by the elderly attendant, assisted her father back into his chair. Lady Gretton stood some little distance away, holding her granddaughter tightly by her hand. At last Cressida turned and stood aside a little from the seated figure, who was now leaning forward eagerly to view the newcomer.

'And here, Father, is Philippa. Come, child, and kiss your *grandpère*.'

Philippa, released by her grandmother, came forward and dropped to her knees before the old man. She saw that despite his illness his large, big-boned form had not withered. He had a shock of white hair reaching in curls to his shoulders and his broad, open countenance was still weatherbeaten as if, previous to the stroke which had laid him low, he had enjoyed an active, outdoor life. Like her mother, there were tears upon his cheeks and he bent and took Philippa's face between his two large hands, scrutinising her carefully, then he looked up at his daughter and wife who had come closer to the chair, and smiled.

'I had the most beautiful daughter in England and this, her child, and Wroxeter's, looks like being as lovely, and I can see spirit here in her eyes and courage. You have your mother's looks, child, but I think there is something of your father's courage and intelligence in the steadiness of your gaze and the intentness of your concern, aye, and stubbornness in the tilt of your chin, too.' He looked upwards to the elderly attendant who was standing behind his chair. 'Don't you agree, Alice? She's the child of both of them right enough.'

The woman gave a little snort and stared down at Philippa, who returned her scrutiny curiously.

Her grandfather chuckled. 'This is Alice, your mother's nurse and your grandmother's maid now, aye, and, over these last weeks, my nurse too, though I could wish her in purgatory some days when she bothers me with her strictures.'

'For your own good and you know it,' the woman scolded. 'The doctor says you'll do well enough if you take your time, but you will rush to do things.' Her expression was kindly, though her voice somewhat harsh, and she went scarlet with pleasure as Cressida seized her by the shoulders and planted a hearty kiss upon her lined cheek. She hugged her former charge, grinning at Philippa over Lady Wroxeter's shoulder.

'It's fair good to have your mother back again, sweeting, if only for a little while.' Her expression grew sad. 'The Virgin knows I wanted to go with her after—well, after—but there, it wasn't possible. It's true, lassie, you be right like your mother in appearance and like to be as much trouble in handling as she was, I'll be bound.'

'She is, Alice, she is,' laughed Cressida, 'but hardships have given her more common sense than I ever had at her age, so that's as well.'

'Aye, well, we'll see about that.' Alice turned to her mistress. 'I'll be about seeing to a meal for you all and away to the kitchen. Did I not hear Sir Rhys Griffith? Will he not take supper here with us?'

'No, Alice, he excused himself. He's just come from Milford. There are bound to be matters needing attention on his own manor. He'll be here again soon,' Lady Gretton announced.

Alice cast a quick suspicious glance at Philippa. 'Aye, I warrant he will,' she muttered as she stalked off towards the screen doors.

Cressida drew up chairs for her mother and herself as

Lady Gretton informed her, 'We have no pages or squires, now, of course. I gave the servants warning to leave us alone together for the first hour or so. I knew there would be much to discuss.'

Philippa remained seated at her grandfather's feet while her eyes roved the hall. She understood his need for a fire. Enforced inactivity, she knew, often caused a chill of the limbs and the blazing logs added an air of cheeriness to the large hall. Despite her grandmother's hint that they were short of the customary number of servants, due, she thought, to the fines they had been forced to pay shortly after the King's accession, the furniture was well kept, though sparse. There were court cupboards, on which a few remaining pieces of silverware gleamed, several finely carved chests, three armchairs, several backless stools and, in the upper part of the hall, a single trestle was covered with linen ready for the promised supper. The fine hangings which adorned the limewashed walls were brightly coloured, totally unfaded, and Philippa guessed that they had been only recently executed, and that embroidery was most probably her grandmother's chosen pastime during the formerly long days when her man had been out hunting or away from the manor on business in Ludlow. Philippa gave a little shocked gasp as something cold touched her hand and a shaggy head was thrust towards her, almost knocking her off balance.

Her father gave a little throaty chuckle. 'Is Bors bothering you? He's getting to be an old deer hound now, but he's strong still. Down, old fellow. This is your newest mistress come to visit.'

Philppa stretched out a hand to pat the shaggy head and a rough tongue caressed her cheek. 'Nay, Grandpère, he does not bother me, I love all God's good creatures and must go soon and see to it that my little cob isn't missing me or needing attention.'

'Aye, it's well you're a country mouse at heart despite all this life in palaces,' he said gruffly but fondly.

Her mother had been telling them both about their encounter with Sir Rhys Griffith at the inn at Milford Haven and their subsequent journey together. 'I was somewhat concerned that—' She broke off awkwardly. 'Since it is difficult for Pippa and I to be here, I feared he might pose a danger, but he appears to be a welcome visitor to Gretton.'

'Since he inherited he has proved himself a friend.' Philippa's grandmother paused and looked anxiously towards her husband. 'Though we are cautious as to what we say to him. His father was loyal to the Tudor and often at court, but Rhys is in London less often.' She frowned a little. 'People arrive at this house sometimes whom—well, whom we would rather young Rhys does not see.' She shook her head as the door behind the trestle table opened and two serving women entered with trays ready to serve supper. She changed the subject quickly. 'I have arranged for one of our young serving girls to be Philippa's maid Gwenny. She's a good girl but inexperienced yet. Alice will want to attend you, Cressida, as she used to do, as she serves me now.' She called to one of the women who was busied setting out wooden platters and knives upon the trestle table. 'Nan, will you show Lady Wroxeter and Lady Philippa to their chamber and call young Gwenny?'

The two ladies followed the serving woman up the newel stair, along the landing, and into a chamber behind Lady Gretton's solar. The woman smilingly indicated a further chamber beyond. 'That is much smaller, my lady, but the mistress thought Lady Philippa would like to have a room of her own. Gwenny can share it with her for there is a truckle bed which can be pulled out.' She made a little bobbed curtsy. 'I will call Gwenny and we'll come back soon with an ewer of warmed water and fresh towels, my lady.'

Cressida smiled her dismissal and turned to survey the chamber with bright tears in her eyes which she hastily brushed aside. 'Forgive me, child, you must think me a ninny to be so close to crying all the time but these are tears of joy, believe me. This was my chamber in the old days and I so very reluctant to leave it to go to court and meet your father.' Cressida took in all the familiar things she had loved—the testered bed of solid cherry wood with its holland sheets and embroidered woollen covering, the carved oak chest for her treasured belongings which were not accommodated within the press in the garde robe, the prieu-dieu with its embroidered seat cushion lovingly done by her mother—and then she ran to the casement window with its well-used seat cushions upon the wide low sill. Unlatching the glazed casement, she leaned down to gaze at the lawn below with its rose bushes and, beyond, her mother's herb garden and pleasance.

'Oh, Philippa, it is just as it always was. I hope you will come to love it as I did and that—' her throat worked oddly '—that, one day, you will be able to spend more time here.'

Philippa joined her and breathed in the heady scents of roses, sweet marjoram and rosemary, which came wafting up from the sun-soaked garden. 'Oh, but I would never wish to leave our lodging at Malines with you and Father,' she said fervently.

Her mother gave her an odd little glance, her head tilted on one side. 'I thought just like you, Pippa,' she mused, her lips curving into a strangely sweet smile, 'but then—

then I met and married your father and was content to live wherever he was.'

Philippa broke away suddenly and turned back into the centre of the room. 'It is unlikely that I shall find a suitable husband,' she said stiffly, 'at least, not a man I could love as you love my father.'

'No?' Cressida's lips curved into an even wider smile. 'Do not be too sure, Pippa. We have already met another man who is taken with your beauty.'

'But we have met no one but—' Philippa broke off in horror. 'You cannot mean…?'

'Oh, but I do,' her mother said lightly.

'But you could never countenance a match so—' Philippa drew a hard breath '—so completely outrageous.'

'You could not?'

'Certainly not,' Philippa returned hotly.

'No, of course not.' Lady Wroxeter was still smiling when the serving woman came back, followed by a gangling, awkward young girl whose strands of red hair were straggling untidily from the sides of her cap. They were laden with an ewer of hot water, a basin and clean towels. The girl, who could not be much more than thirteen or fourteen years old, stood regarding Philippa with rounded eyes until water began to slop from her ewer onto the oaken boards at her feet and she was hastily reprimanded for clumsiness by her older companion.

Philippa nodded to the older woman and asked, 'Is this my new maid Gwenny?'

'Indeed it is, my lady, and I hope she will soon learn to be less clumsy.'

'I'm sure she will. Put the ewer down, Gwenny, on that chest over there and then you can come into my chamber with me and see that all is ready for tonight when I retire.'

The girl bobbed a clumsy curtsy that nearly had her

falling over, but Philippa waited patiently until she recovered herself and led the way through into her own private chamber.

It was very small, containing only a bed, a chest and scarcely room enough for the truckle bed underneath hers to be pulled out for Gwenny, but Philippa was delighted with it. She bit her lip thoughtfully as she glanced round. Why was she suddenly so anxious to be private within the night hours, separated from the mother she dearly loved? Was it because, already, she sensed in her mother's manner towards her a different approach, a determination to get her ineligible daughter married? But to whom?

Philippa shivered as she considered her mother's last words. Not Sir Rhys Griffith, surely. He was an enemy, a Tudor supporter who could prove a danger to them all. She shook her head to try to dispel the vivid image she had of him, of the tall, upright, unyielding body, the flashing dark eyes, straight, dominant nose and the mop of luxuriant black curls. She had been less than gracious to him throughout the days they had spent together—and after he had saved her from rape and death. The man could not be attracted to the slip of a girl who had constantly taunted and insulted him. She wondered what he and her mother had talked of on that ride, on the occasions when she had been too far back from them to overhear. She looked up to find the girl waiting anxiously for her to decide what she was to do next.

'Everything seems well in order, Gwenny. Your bed is under mine. I will go now and wash in my mother's chamber and you can return to the kitchens and get your own supper. I'll send for you when I am ready for bed and you can help me to undress and brush my hair after first tidying away the toilet articles.'

The girl nodded timidly, curtsyed again, less ineptly this

time, and hastened out of the chamber. Philippa returned
to her mother who had completed her toilet and was drying
her hands.

'Will the girl do, do you think?'

'Oh, yes, she is a frightened little rabbit, but she will
soon get used to my ways. You will be glad to have the
services of your Alice again.'

'Indeed. I have missed her sorely since Redmoor.' Cressida laughed. 'She has always kept me firmly in hand and
will do you, too, if she has half a chance.'

'And now my father manages you.'

Cressida touched her daughter's bright hair affection-
ately as she removed her hood to brush and tidy her dishevelled locks. 'While I found that annoying at first, I
was glad to surrender—in the end.'

Cressida regarded her thoughtfully and they both knew
that Philippa was thinking of her dislike for Sir Rhys Griffith. 'Differences of opinion have a way of becoming settled in the marriage bed,' she said very softly.

Philippa gave a little cluck of dissent and completed her
toilet before she accompanied her mother down to the hall
for supper.

Next morning when Gwenny was assisting her to dress,
Philippa asked Gwenny, 'Have you been in service at Gretton for long?'

Gwenny, who was feeling very self-conscious about her
new duties, tugged clumsily at the laces of Philippa's
gown. 'Oh, yes, my lady, most of my life really. My
mother works in the manor kitchen and I have been working there for the last three years, but Lady Gretton thought
I was the right age to serve you.'

'And does that please you?'

'Oh, yes, my lady, if I can prove satisfactory.'

'I'm sure that you will, especially if I can rely on you to be—discreet. I do not wish you to gossip about me— in the kitchens or with any of the other servants.'

'My mother has told me that over and over, my lady.' Gwenny hesitated. 'We all know that you and your lady mother are here on a very private visit and it is not to be spoken of—in the district.'

'Yes. Sir Rhys Griffith is well aware of it. Does he come often to Gretton?'

'Quite often, my lady. He plays chess with Sir Daniel, especially since the master has been unable to get about.'

Philippa digested this information and added, 'How far is his own manor, Gwenny? Isn't there a castle?'

'Oh, yes, my lady, but that is near to Wroxeter. When Sir Rhy's father became master he considered it very cold and draughty, especially in winter, and he built a newer manor house about four miles away off the Ludlow road; very comfortable it is, with a smaller hall and proper bed-chambers, even for the servants, and all the windows are glazed. The furniture came from London, they say. None of the local craftsmen were engaged to make it and it was brought by road all that way. You'd think it would have got damaged, wouldn't you?'

'So Sir Rhys lives at the manor house?'

'Most of the time, my lady, but sometimes he goes to Wroxeter Castle. The hall there is used for the district court and there are dungeons for felons. I 'spect it's a much grimmer place than the manor though Jake, one of our grooms, worked there a long time ago for the Earl and he said it was a fine place.'

Philippa's heart contracted as she thought how her father had been cheated out of his birthright. Would he have deserted the ancient castle, the home of his and her ancestors?

Tartly she said, 'It seems that Sir Rhys has become a very wealthy and fine gentleman indeed since the new King's accession.'

At her reference to the King, Gwenny looked blankly at her again and Philippa realised that the child had no notion of who had ruled in England before the decisive battle of Redmoor or, in her limited, youthful life, thought very much about kings at all.

At breakfast she discovered that her mother had already eaten and was in her father's chamber with her grandmother. She finished her own meal and went in search of them. Her mother came from the small curtained space behind the hall, which had been prepared for Sir Daniel since his illness, to speak with her.

'Your grandfather has had a bad night, I'm afraid, Pippa. He has been excited by our arrival and I think it best if you wait until this evening before you see him again. I shall remain with my mother to tend him. Can you find some way to occupy yourself until later?'

Philippa could see by the worry lines between her brows and the shadows beneath her eyes that her mother was extremely worried about her grandfather's condition.

'Yes, of course,' she hastened to say. 'There is not the slightest need for you to worry yourself about me. I am sorry. I thought he looked very well last night, considering...' She broke off and bit her lip.

'I know. I allowed myself to become over-hopeful. We shall send for the physician from Ludlow and hope he gets over this set-back.' She smiled a trifle distractedly and went behind the curtain again, leaving Philippa doubtful and more alarmed than she had first thought. She moved away from the curtained-off alcove to allow the three complete quiet and sat for a while before the fire, which the manor servants had apparently kindled against need.

Abruptly she rose and made for the screen doors where she encountered Gwenny returning to the hall, apparently in search of her mistress.

'Is there anything I can do for you, my lady?'

'What? Oh, no, thank you, Gwenny. I have decided to go for a ride. Do not disturb Lady Gretton or my mother who are with Sir Daniel. He is less well this morning. Occupy yourself with completing my unpacking and see if anything requires mending or pressing. Can you tell me how to reach the stables?'

She had gone with one of the servants last night to see her little cob but it had been dark then and she had taken little heed of the way. Gwenny pointed out the archway which led to the courtyard and outbuildings, offering to accompany her, but Philippa declined.

She found Peter Fairley emerging from the stables, in talk with an elderly groom. The man touched his forelock at sight of Philippa.

'Good day, my lady.'

She nodded coolly. 'I would like to ride out as it is such a fine morning. Can you accompany me, Peter, or should I take one of the grooms?'

'Certainly I can come with you.' Peter looked enquiringly back towards the manor house. 'Is your mother aware…?'

'No, but she is occupied in tending my *grandpère*. She will not mind if you are with me.' She glanced down at her gown. 'I am suitably dressed, and you appear to be.'

As usual he was dressed in serviceable homespun jack and hose without a cloak since the day was already heating up.

The groom called back into the stable for one of his

underlings to bring out their mounts saddled and ready. When her cob was brought to the mounting block, Peter lifted Philippa to the saddle and settled her comfortably.

'You have visited Gretton before, in the old days,' she said as she took the reins. 'I would like you to show me my father's lands.'

Peter glanced at her searchingly but passed no comment. Together they passed through the archway and rode towards the long road which led to Gretton village.

The little place looked prosperous and was almost deserted, most of the labourers busy with the harvest, and they rode together companionably.

Peter said quietly, 'Lady Philippa, you know it does no good to think how things might have been.'

'I know,' she said calmly. 'I just want to see how it was for my father and—and I hear Sir Rhys's father built himself a new manor house and would see it for myself—from a distance, of course.'

He glanced at her sharply, but nodded and led the way towards the Ludlow road. Soon she could see evidence of well-tended strips and fields on both sides of the highway and labourers working in the distance. The animals, too, appeared to be in excellent condition and Peter grunted.

'It seems Griffith handles his labourers well. Your father would be relieved to know his lands are in the hands of a capable master.'

'I'm sure that my father would prefer to have his lands under his own control,' Philippa snapped and Peter looked at her again and grinned mirthlessly.

'That is indeed true, Lady Philippa, but as things are the Earl does well to keep his head on his shoulders, as you know well.'

They rode on in silence while Philippa took in the continuing evidence of the demesne's prosperity. She was so intent upon her survey that Peter was forced to give a shout of warning as a riderless horse veered suddenly across her path. The animal was limping badly and had, clearly, recently thrown its rider. Alerted to the danger, Philippa pulled sharply on her own lead reins and moved her own mount out of the frenzied creature's path. Her little cob stumbled to a halt and was startled by the suddenness of her move so that she was shivering violently. Philippa leaned down to pat her shaggy coat encouragingly, looking back to see the uncertain progress of the injured animal. Peter, coming up close, pointed with his whip to a huddled form lying in the road some yards ahead of them.

Together they eased their horses steadily forward and Peter jumped down to investigate. The fallen rider looked unconscious but, as Philippa scrambled awkwardly to dismount and joined Peter, he looked up from his crouching position to confirm, with a nod, that the man was still breathing.

'He's not conscious, must have hit his head on that boulder,' he said, gesturing towards a rough granite stone a foot or two to their left. 'His leg is lying at an awkward angle and I believe it to be broken. Don't try to move him, my lady, not until we've examined him further.'

She looked back anxiously to where the riderless horse had floundered by them. 'His mount must have been startled by a hare or bird or put its foot in a rutted hole. How badly is our man hurt, Peter, can you tell?'

'He struck his head, as I said, and it's bleeding, but not too seriously. We can only hope he will come to himself soon. It's the leg which gives concern,' he said dubiously, cautiously moving the injured limb in an attempt to straighten it. 'It is as well he is not conscious, for the moment. See if you can find me a long branch from in the hedgerow and I will try to splint this before he comes to.

Then he must be got back to the village, or, preferably, the town. I'm not sure how many miles that is but he may need the attention of a surgeon.'

Philippa did as she was bidden and hastened to search for a suitable branch strong enough to act as a splint. She was finally successful and brought it to Peter, who cut away the lesser branches with his knife and laid it gently alongside the now straightened limb. The sufferer moaned slightly and Peter grunted his approval. 'He is coming to himself so there is no serious brain damage, by the look of it. It's best for us to complete this before he feels more pain.'

Philippa had already torn several strips from her linen petticoat and was kneeling in the road beside Peter, steadying the branch, as the squire went about his task of securing it to the injured leg with the improvised bandages.

Now she could see that the injured man was young, or younger, she thought, than Peter—perhaps in his middle twenties, she considered. He was a merchant, by the look of his dress. Peter had turned him over so that she could see that he was pleasantly featured, his skin without disfiguring pock marks. His fair hair was worn fashionably in a curled bob to his neck and clustered into a long similar curl on a forehead that was dappled with bright blood, but was broad with level, fair brows. His nose was very slightly tip-tilted; his mouth, held in tightly against the pain as he began to regain his senses, was well shaped with a slightly over-full lower lip. Thick fair lashes flickered and grey eyes regarded her wonderingly as she bent close over him.

'Hush,' she warned gently, 'you are quite safe. Your horse threw you and we think you have broken your right leg. Lie very still for a while.'

The lashes flickered again and the man attempted to lift

his head, then gave another groan as blood trickled down his forehead to drift into his eye.

Philippa dabbed at the trickle with another torn piece of her petticoat, but was unable to pad the head wound for fear of moving the patient.

'It's all right,' she added soothingly, 'you hit your head when you fell, but we don't think that the wound is serious. We'll deal with it in a moment when the splint on your leg is fixed.'

He gave a little relieved sigh and sank back again, a faint smile forming about his well-shaped mouth.

Peter rose and stood, regarding his patient, frowning in thought. 'We need to get help now. A broken limb can be…' He shrugged and avoided Philippa's eye. Only too well she knew that fractures could cause the death of the patient or a necessary amputation of the limb and she compressed her lips in alarm. Peter was shading his eyes as he looked to his left to where a small thicket, about a half-mile away, was split as if a lesser road or track ran through it.

'That may lead to the manor house, where we could get assistance. See. It probably joins the road some miles back. I'd best ride and see if I can find some labourers who could provide a rough bier of some sort to get him to a house or to the outskirts of the town. Will you feel concerned about being left alone with him?'

'No, of course not. He needs help as soon as possible. You will not be long gone. There are bound to be labourers or servants within a short ride.'

She was giving her full attention to their patient and Peter had moved off and was about to mount up when a stern voice, calling for them to halt, arrested him in the action and Philippa turned hastily to face the newcomer. She gave a little gasp of annoyance and surprise as she

saw that Sir Rhys Griffith was riding up to them, attended
by two retainers. His gaze swept coldly from her dishevelled clothing, dust-stained and bloodstained, to Peter Fairley and then to the injured man.

'Lady Philippa, you are about early, considering your
very recent arrival at Gretton. What is this?'

One of his men had jumped down and was holding his
rouncey still for him to dismount. He was dressed, as she
remembered him, in riding clothes, a leather jerkin over
brown hose, and was hatless. He strode up to the three and
stared down with marked disapproval at their patient.

'Who is this fellow and what is he doing on my land?'

Philippa was so startled by his hostile manner that she
rounded on him instantly. 'He is on the highway, Sir Rhys,
and you must be able to see clearly enough that he has
been thrown from his horse and lies injured.'

He stood frowningly regarding the sufferer, tapping his
riding whip against his thigh impatiently.

'So it would appear. Actually, Lady Philippa, this is not
the highway, but a lesser road cutting through my demesne, and I cannot imagine what he was doing on it, but,
there, it seems he has fractured his leg and will need help
to be moved.' His dark eyes were still regarding the
stranger dispassionately. 'I do not encourage strangers,
poachers, particularly.'

Philippa was almost incoherent with anger. 'You can see
the man is no local poacher but, apparently, some merchant's apprentice or journeyman about his business, probably making his way towards Ludlow to seek accommodation.'

One dark brow rose in amusement. 'Here's heat. You
take me to task, Lady Philippa, for lack of Christian compassion, but I will see to it that this fellow is tended and

then conveyed in a cart to Ludlow town where there are several excellent physicians and surgeons to treat him.'

He turned now to Peter and she saw that her father's squire's presence, alone in her company, rather than one of her grandfather's grooms, had again displeased him. She compressed her lips against uttering further explosive words to dispel his suspicions.

'I take it you were about to go looking for some assistance…' his gaze went again to Philippa '…and about to leave your mistress alone once more.'

'There appeared to be no help for it,' she said tersely, 'since there is no one else in sight—at least, there wasn't until you rode up.'

Their patient had come to his full senses now and was trying to sit up. 'My apologies for invading your demesne without permission, sir,' he said in a low, pleasant voice, 'but I thought no harm and was riding towards Ludlow. I have business there. My master is a wool merchant in the Steelyard in London town. My name is Roger Maynard. I regret that I must give you trouble. My horse stumbled in a rut, I think, and threw me. Someone must try to find him and check his headlong dash. He could prove a danger to any child in his path.'

So he had heard Sir Rhys's ungracious comments, Philippa thought, and looked towards him, her own brows raised in condemnation. She was surprised to see that Sir Rhys was staring at the newcomer as if he knew him, but then he shook his head as if he had discovered he was mistaken and inclined his chin in acceptance of the man's explanation.

'So, it was like that, was it? Never mind. We will see to your comfort and find your mount.'

He turned to issue orders to his two retainers who had stood silently attentive throughout the exchanges, their faces expressionless, as if they were used to hearing their master put in his place by some slip of a girl.

'You two, get back to the manor and summon some men with a bier. He'd best be accommodated in the gatehouse lodge until he is fit to travel on into Ludlow. In the meantime, I will escort Lady Philippa to the manor house where she can take refreshment and—tidy herself.'

Peter said, respectfully, speaking for the first time, 'I think it would be best if I accompany you and Lady Philippa, Sir Rhys, and perhaps one of your men here can be detailed to stay with our injured friend until help arrives.'

Sir Rhys cast him a challenging glance. Obviously he had thought to command Peter to stay with his patient, but he thought better of that and barked, 'Yes, certainly, that would be best.'

'Once I am assured that this man is tended, Peter and I could ride home to Gretton,' Philippa put in.

'I do not think so, not in that state,' Sir Rhys replied, his eyes passing again over the state of her dirtied gown, 'you will alarm your mother and grandparents. I take it you were riding to review my demesne. Allow me to welcome you to my manor house.'

She flushed hotly and was about to refute his accusation then, catching Peter's eyes, let out a little frustrated sigh and bent once more to reassure Master Maynard before walking towards her own mount.

'I shall make enquiries about your welfare, Master Maynard. I am sure you will soon be safe and in good hands. I wish you a hasty recovery, but I think it will be some time before you will be able to leave Ludlow. I will try to discover your lodgings there and reassure myself about your condition.'

The fair young face flushed and he bowed his head. 'I shall pray and thank the Virgin for sending an angel to come to my help, mistress. May I know to whom I am indebted?'

Before she could answer Sir Rhys cut in, 'Mistress Weston will be staying a short time in the district and it is unlikely that you will see her again.'

Philippa smiled at Master Maynard and moved towards her own mount, which Peter was holding ready. She approved Sir Rhys's caution, but wondered if the man could have heard him address her as Lady Philippa earlier. He had appeared to be just recovering full consciousness when Sir Rhys had arrived on the scene. She dismissed the thought, feeling that Maynard must have been confused and dizzy with pain at the time and so, for the moment, her identity was still unknown and could not be talked of in Ludlow town.

Sir Rhys had already dispatched his man to fetch help. He gave orders briskly to the other man, who was waiting by Master Maynard, then he indicated to Peter that he was ready to leave, mounted, and took the lead in the direction of the small thicket Peter had noted earlier.

Philippa had feared he might insist upon taking her lead rein, but he allowed her to ride beside him, with Peter only slightly in the rear.

'I think it best if you do not communicate with this Maynard fellow directly,' he said crisply. 'I will ascertain where he is finally lodged and inform you of his condition.'

She glanced at him sharply and he continued, 'I know you consider I was harsh with the fellow but, as matters are in the county at present, and, particularly considering your mother's visit, not to say your grandparents' danger, it is wiser if we do not encourage strangers on our land.'

'But Master Maynard is surely no spy. He said he was a merchant's journeyman and...'

'I know what he said. Strangers cannot always be believed.'

She eyed him thoughtfully. 'But now that the wars are over, the King does not employ spies…'

He smiled grimly. 'All the time, Lady Philippa, that is why I urge you to caution. I grant you this Master Maynard appears to be what he seems and looks harmless enough, but he had no real need or right to be riding this way. As for the King's policy—Henry trusts no one, not even those whose loyalty he is most assured of. His creatures are everywhere, making sure the correct tallies are made of properties and taxes. Have you not heard how the new Court of the Star Chamber is kept busy?'

She was forced to give him a smile in answer. 'But, surely, you pay your own taxes on time and give true accounting of your revenues.'

His answering smile was broad and Philippa heard Peter give a chuckle behind them.

She fell into a reverie as they took a well-marked path through the thicket. Could she have misjudged Sir Rhys? Was he as genuine as he seemed to ensure her mother's and her own safety?

He gave a sudden shout of warning, as a riderless horse veered across their path and, this time, he reached over and snatched at her lead rein as her little cob squealed in terror and rose, forelegs high in the air, so that Philippa had all she could do to stay in the saddle.

'That was Master Maynard's horse,' she said shakily. 'Thank you, I wasn't prepared for that.'

'Aye, and limping badly, by all appearance. Master Fairley,' he barked, 'I must leave you to try to retrieve the animal before it causes an accident. Stay with your lady. Continue on this path and veer left as you emerge from the wood. In a mile you will see the manor house ahead of you.'

Before Philippa could properly catch her breath he had ridden off at a gallop and Peter came quickly alongside. He noted her paleness and gave a gasp of concern.

'Are you all right?'

'Yes, but I was nearly unseated. I hope he manages to catch the poor creature and return it to the stables of his manor.'

Peter's eyelashes flickered oddly and he shook his head, then before she could object, he took her lead rein firmly as Sir Rhys had done, and took the path the knight had indicated.

Chapter Four

The manor house was moated and approached over a static bridge then through a gatehouse, which appeared as they passed under to be guarded. They entered the court-yard and Philippa gave a little gasp of wonder as they passed by a guard sergeant who seemed to know at once who she was and that she had a right to be there. The house stood squarely before them, built entirely of Welsh blue stone with mullioned windows and a central door of solid oak. The sunlight glittered on the glazed windows and she recalled Gwenny's description of the place and acknowledged that it was, indeed, very fine.

Peter gave a slow whistle of appreciation. 'Though the place is guarded there is no drawbridge or portculis on the arch and no crenellations.' He peered upwards to the slop-ing roof, and saw no guards upon the leads. 'Griffith ex-pects no trouble from his neighbours. The moat appears to be decorative more than useful to deter unwanted visitors.'

'Sir Rhys seems to be well able to do that by his own innate power of authority,' Philippa commented drily, 'but, as you say, the manor house is very fine and must have cost his father near a fortune to build.'

Before she could comment further a steward appeared

at the opened door and descended the steps to the courtyard to greet them. Already grooms were running to take
their mounts.

The steward bowed. 'Welcome to Griffith Manor, Lady
Philippa. Sir Rhys's messenger, sent to obtain help for the
injured man, alerted us to your imminent arrival.' He appeared to be in no way put out by the fact that his master
was not with his visitors but led the way into the hall
which was lime washed and colourful with painted coats
of arms and then he took them along a corridor into a
winter parlour beyond. 'I will summon servants to fetch
toilet articles for you, Lady Philippa, a servant to deal with
your soiled garments and a page to bring wine and refresh-
ments. Please make yourselves comfortable. Sir Rhys will
present himself very shortly.'

He bowed himself out, backwards, as if he was dealing
with royalty, Philippa thought wryly. Since the man had
not mentioned a lady as chatelaine, she presumed that Sir
Rhys's mother was not present at the manor or possibly
had died. She knew so little about him, only that he was,
as yet, unmarried.

She found herself staring, round eyed, like a recently
appointed servant, at the luxurious comforts of the new
manor. The windows were wide and let in an abundance
of light, the walls were oak panelled and adorned with
what she believed to be French tapestries and embroidered
wall hangings. Here the fire had not been lit in the great
stone-manteled hearth, but a large earthernware jug held a
wealth of sweet-smelling roses. The furniture was of
highly polished oak, with several high-backed chairs up-
holstered in Spanish leather and there were embroidered
cushions upon the deep window seats. This room had been
furnished for a lady, probably Sir Rhys's mother. Philippa
stared enviously down at the bright rugs from the East

which replaced the rushes of her grandmother's own home. Everything within this room spoke of wealth and settled prosperity and she gave a little sigh. Peter eyed her comically and she burst into a little laugh. 'No wonder Sir Rhys has abandoned my father's castle as a place of residence.'

'Not abandoned it entirely, Lady Philippa,' Sir Rhys said as he entered, pulling off his riding gauntlets. 'I spend a great deal of time at the castle, which you must visit, before you leave England, but I am here for the present to give what aid and comfort I can to Lady Gretton, should she need me in any emergency.'

He approached her smiling, as again, she felt a sudden stab of guilt that she had once more misjudged his motives.

He looked round to see if his orders concerning their comfort were being obeyed.

'Your steward has gone to summon servants,' Philippa put in hurriedly, fearing his frown of displeasure for the unfortunate subordinates. 'Everything is being done to make us comfortable.' She glanced at him anxiously as he waved her to a chair and Peter to another. 'Did you find the runaway horse? Have you returned it to the stables here? I'm sure Master Maynard will be prepared to pay for the services of a smith, should they be required.'

He shook his head sadly, 'I'm afraid such services will not be necessary, Lady Philippa.'

She gasped in horror. 'You—have dispatched it?'

'The poor creature's leg was so badly fractured that nothing could have been done for it. You would not wish it to have suffered further, surely?'

Her hand was at her mouth in a distressed gesture, her eyes wide with sorrow. She could only think how badly she would have grieved if her own little newly acquired Welsh cob had been lost to her. She swallowed and turned

slightly away so that he might not see her tears. 'No, sir—
of course not. It is just that...'

'You cannot bear to see dumb creatures suffer pain or
die. That is another point in your favour, Lady Philippa. I
admire most a gentle heart in a woman.'

She flushed at the compliment, feeling, vaguely, that he
was teasing her, yet when she looked full at him, his dark
eyes were grave and his mouth sensitive and she knew he
had found his self-appointed task distasteful.

A servant knocked and, on his call to enter, a girl advanced with a ewer and bowls for washing hands, and
another older woman, who bore the keys of the household
suspended from her belt, curtsied and looked deferentially
towards Sir Rhys for further information.

'I think it would be better, Sir Rhys, if I conducted my
lady to a bedchamber to repair the ravages to her gown as
best I may.'

Like all the women in the Welsh Marches, her accent
was soft and singsong. She was dressed plainly in a gown
of dark blue wool and her linen cap was spotless.

'Certainly. Do your best, Mistress Cheswick,' Sir Rhys
replied smoothly. 'If you are wearied or distressed by this
recent incident, you could lie down and rest for a while,
Lady Philippa.'

She shook her head emphatically. 'It was not I who
suffered harm, Sir Rhys. Thank you, but I shall be ready
to depart for Gretton as soon as our horses have been
rested and summoned.'

He nodded, seating himself in a chair opposite to Peter,
throwing one long leg over the other at ease. 'After you
have sampled my hospitality, Lady Philippa,' he said
mildly. 'Do not cheat me of your charming company for
an hour at least.'

She felt that her flounced exit in the wake of the housekeeper was somewhat churlish but, try, as she might, the man brought out all the contrariness within her.

The airy light-filled bedchamber overlooked the pleasance and herb garden as one would expect. Like the winter parlour it was luxuriously furnished with a wide-testered bed, curtained in blue and silver damask and there were priceless rugs upon the polished floor, elaborately carved chests and press and an exquisitely carved prieu-dieu.

Philippa looked thoughtfully round at the limewashed walls and bright tapestries in appreciation.

'This is a beautiful room. Was it furnished for Sir Rhys's mother?' she asked.

The housekeeper had already set out a small bowl of liquid upon one of the chests and she came to Philippa with a linen towel and cloth.

'Yes, my lady. Unfortunately she died a year before the house building was completed, of a tertian fever. Sir Rhys completed the furnishings and oversaw the setting out of the pleasance in her memory. He loved her very dearly.'

'Sir Rhys has no sister? There is no other mistress of the house?'

The housekeeper shook her head. 'No, Sir Rhys's only brother was killed in a border skirmish four years ago, leaving him to inherit after the master was killed in a hunting accident.'

'I heard about that. How sad! Then Sir Rhys is alone without close kin?'

'Indeed, we shall all be glad when he provides us with a new lady.' The housekeeper's face crinkled in a little smile. 'He has been lonely of late—not that he and his father always saw eye to eye.' She avoided Philippa's eye then, realising she had gossiped too freely, and bent to rub at the blood and dirt upon Philippa's gown.

Philippa considered that she had asked too many ques-

tions of the woman and allowed her to finish her ministrations, encouraging only light chatter about the weather and
general household matters.

A page had brought wine and comfits when she was
returned to the winter parlour and Peter and their host appeared to be conversing without the hostility she had detected in Sir Rhys's previous attitude towards her father's
squire. Both rose courteously at her entrance and she came
to sit in a high-backed chair beside Peter.

'I thank you, Sir Rhys. Your housekeeper has made an
excellent job of making me once more respectable. I had
not realised how badly my garment was blood-stained. As
you remarked earlier, the sight would have alarmed my
mother.'

He poured wine for her. 'You are welcome to my hospitality at all times, Lady Philippa. If I should be absent,
my housekeeper and steward will see to your comfort.'

She inclined her head graciously, watching him covertly
over the rim of her wine goblet. He was a very handsome
man who exuded a spirit of pure confidence and authority.
Despite her antipathy to him, she recalled with a little in-
voluntary shiver the warmth of his body as he had lifted
her to the saddle during the journey and the clean, male
scent of him. So he had not been the elder son. The housekeeper had inferred that there had been a certain coolness
between Rhys Griffith and his father. She wondered why.
Had he been opposed to his father's sycophantic attitude
to the Tudor King? Surely not. She found his opaque dark
eyes looking at her questioningly and hastily lowered her
own.

'I have to thank you, sir, once again, for your timely
assistance to Master Maynard and to ourselves,' she said,
somewhat lamely.

'I shall see that he is cared for. You can safely leave

his welfare in my hands.' His lips twitched slightly, 'I know that you considered me harsh on my first meeting with him but, I assure you, my suspicions will not colour my need to care for him, if only for your gentle sake.'

'I wish you would not tease me, sir,' she murmured, confused. 'You know I only offered what help any passer-by would have done.'

One dark eyebrow swept up questioningly. 'I am by no means sure of that. I only ask you to be cautious in your dealings with all in the district, for the sake of your mother and grandparents.'

She felt a sudden rush of warmth towards him for his consideration. 'I promise that I will, sir, truly.' She looked towards Peter for guidance. 'We should go, Peter. My mother will be worried.'

'Indeed.' Sir Rhys rose. 'Allow me to conduct you to the courtyard.'

As Peter moved towards the stables, Philippa said impulsively, 'I saw from your mother's bedchamber the wonderful pleasance. What a lovely thought to have had it set out as her memorial. Mistress Chiswick told me of her—untimely death. I was sorry to hear of the deaths of both your parents and brother and so close to each other.'

Peter had disappeared inside the stable and Sir Rhys offered her his arm. 'Allow me to show you the roses. They were my mother's favourite flowers and they are especially splendid this year. There will be no impropriety. Gardeners are at work there all the time. We shall not be alone or unobserved.'

She flushed rosily. She did want to see the pleasance at close quarters. From the distance she had observed that it was much larger and finer than the one at Gretton and her mother had always sighed over the fact that they had no garden behind their lodging at Malines. They were able to walk in the Duchess's gardens, of course, but they were always crowded with courtiers and visitors to the palace.

They passed through a flowery arch into the pleasance proper and Philippa exclaimed at the beauty. As Sir Rhys had commented, gardeners were at work, cutting away at the low yew hedges, clipping away dead flowers and generally tidying. The lawns were well scythed and watered and standard trees grew from the grass. Further on a rose garden held a variety of fragrances and colours and were alive with the heady buzzing of bees. She saw lavender and gilly flowers and lilac trees, fairly new to this country, as she knew they'd only been introduced some hundred years earlier by King Henry IV who had brought trees back from his visit to the Holy land. Her father had told her of how he had obtained a cutting from one of the royal gardens at Kenilworth.

'It is truly beautiful,' she said softly, 'What a pity your mother could not have walked here. You must have loved her very deeply.'

'Aye.'

She turned as she caught a little catch in his voice on the utterance of the single word. 'Forgive me. I should not have spoken of her and given you pain.'

'You would never mean to give pain, Lady Philippa. She would have admired the beauty she would see in you. She appreciated all lovely and sensitive things—and people.'

'Your father must have grieved sorely, particularly after losing your brother.'

'Oh, he did mourn the loss of my brother. They were two of a kind.' She could not fail to notice the true note of bitterness now.

She was silent for a moment, then murmured, 'Your mother was not happy?'

'She was not happy,' he repeated. 'My father was blessed with a gentle obedient wife but—alas—he did not consider her a beauty and beautiful women were a passion with him—and a weakness. Oh, I could have forgiven his neglect of her. He married her on his father's command, as so many men do, and they take opportunities to seek consolation elsewhere—but he flaunted his mistresses before her—at Wroxeter and in Ludlow—everywhere.'

'And your brother?'

'Was of like mind. He was courageous and reckless and died because of it. Had he one moment's consideration for his own skin and, incidentally, for the lives of his men, he would be master here today. He loved wine and hunting—and women—many women. He showed little affection for our mother either and it broke her heart.'

Philippa was visibly shaken. She looked away, sensing his emotional distress. She swallowed and said very softly, 'I am very sorry for your loss.'

He moved slightly forward, away from her. 'Yes, life has been—difficult, but there has been much to be done.'

She sensed that during his father's time much had been neglected and thought how it might have been had his brother lived to inherit.

'You will soon bring a wife to Griffith Manor,' she said. 'Your mother would have wanted that—and she will bring you comfort.'

'If she is the right woman, yes.'

He was gazing at her very directly now and she flushed under his scrutiny as she very often found herself doing.

He said suddenly, a little harshly. 'Are you in love with Fairley?'

She started and said indignantly, 'I have told you, there is nothing between us. You misjudged my motive that night you found me from my chamber…'

'That is not what I asked.'

She swallowed hard, finding herself trembling. 'No. I am fond of Peter, but not in the way you imply.'

'Or in love with any man?'

'No,' she said evenly. 'My father cannot offer a dowry for me. The men like my father—exiles of Yorkist leanings at the Duchess of Burgundy's court—are as impecunious as he. They could not, in honour, request my hand—and I am no wanton, sir.'

His mouth twitched betrayingly. 'I humbly beg your pardon, Lady Philippa, if I ever gave you the opinion that I believed such a possibility.'

She inclined her head graciously.

'Then—what will you do?'

'You mean will I enter a convent as so many unmarriageable maids do?' Her lips were curving now into a slightly bitter smile.

'That would be a tragedy indeed—for all the men in the world who were deprived of the chance to look on you.'

'Then you need not concern yourself, sir. I have no intention of so doing. I have no vocation for life as a bride of Christ.' She lifted her chin a little defiantly. 'I shall make my own way in the world, do not fear.'

'But if your father should die?'

She gave a little gasp of horror as the implication of what he had said struck her forcibly. Always, everywhere, when away from the protection of the Duchess's court, her father, the Earl, was in danger. And lately it had become apparent that Margaret of Burgundy was ailing. She knew her mother feared the withdrawal of that support and protection. Her father could look after his own interests, she knew that well enough, he could become a soldier of fortune, a mercenary, if needs be, but he needed constantly to be assured that his wife and daughter were well provided for. She bit her lip and gave a little nervous shrug.

'Then Peter will support us loyally as he always has.'

'Why were you seeking him out if not for…?'

She avoided his eye, then said steadily, 'I was concerned for our safety during the journey. I wanted to discuss matters with him.'

'You feared I might betray you and your mother to the King's cronies?'

Again she gave a little helpless shrug. 'The thought crossed my mind. To do so would enhance your standing at Court.'

'I think you have mistaken my motives for those of my father,' he said curtly.

She was silent for a moment, then said, 'Yes, Sir Rhys, I believe that I did. You must understand that to hold both my mother and I would be a strategic triumph for the King. He knows well enough that my father would surrender himself in order to free us.'

He frowned slightly. 'Your father has been a thorn in the King's flesh for some time. It is well known in the district and I cannot conceive of any reason why he is so desirous of having your father within his hands, not now, after so long.'

'Perhaps because my father could divulge matters his Grace wishes to keep secret.'

His dark eyes flashed. 'About the Princes, you mean? But now Tyrell has confessed to their murder the King has little to fear on that score.'

She flashed him a withering glance. 'Tyrell's confession cannot be refuted. Do you think all men believe it? Do *you* believe it, Sir Rhys?'

There was amusement and some doubt in those dark eyes of his now. 'If your father knows the truth concerning the fate of the boys, why has he not spoken out? Even such a statement, coming from such a dubious source as the Burgundian court where all in Europe know how biased the Duchess is in the late King Richard's favour, would draw some considerable attention—especially from the Spanish court at this time when the King is so anxious to further cement the alliance between our countries and marry young Henry to the Infanta, Catherine.'

'My father may well have his own reasons which I have never sought to question.'

His lips twitched again as he moved towards her. 'Come, your escort will become impatient. I will send two of my men with you to Gretton. For one thing, I need to discover the condition of your grandfather. Fairley told me earlier he was not well this morning.'

She felt suddenly contrite that she had dallied so long away from Gretton and nodded, her lip trembling somewhat. He led her from the garden into the courtyard, where Peter stood waiting impatiently beside the horses.

Rhys Griffith stood watching wistfully as she rode away from him. God, how very beautiful and desirable she was! Had she any understanding of her own sensuality? He ached for her, had done since the moment he had laid eyes upon her.

That brief childhood vision of her mother he had had as a child had remained in his memory over the years as if he had known, even then, that he must wait for the woman of his dreams—and then he had encountered her at the inn in Milford. He bit down savagely upon his nether lip. He must have Philippa Telford for his bride, yet there was so much between them to make such a union unattainable. He held her father's lands, for which she must hold him in utter contempt. Yet, surely, he reasoned, making her his bride would be the one way of returning those properties if not to Wroxeter, to his descendants. But would she consent? He smiled a trifle grimly. If he knew her mettle, she certainly would not. Resentment of him and all he stood for he read in every line of her impressive, beautiful young face, in her poise, her very bearing. No, Philippa Telford regarded him as her enemy and he could not, as yet, see any way of convincing her otherwise.

He knew her mother was aware of his interest. How would she view an advance from him? The Countess must constantly be alarmed for her daughter's future. That was evident. Sir Daniel and Lady Gretton had made it plain that they too were well aware of the pitfalls to be negotiated before Philippa could be wed. In all events he would require her father's consent—and the sky would fall before Wroxeter would give it.

Moodily he moved to a bench within the rose arbour he had lovingly created after the manner his mother would have so delighted in. Seated there, he viewed those intertwining blooms of red and white above his head, heady with fragrance, emblems which the Tudor King had chosen to join in the new badge of the Tudor rose. Red and white roses decorating the streets of York had greeted the victorious monarch on his entrance into the city. Those two great houses of York and Lancaster and their loyal adherents, locked in mortal combat. The effects had lasted even after nearly twenty years, and continued to hold him apart from his desire. The King had managed to unite them, for political purposes, in his marriage to Elizabeth, the daughter of the Yorkist King. Could the Telfords be convinced in the same manner that he would prove a suitable husband for their headstrong daughter? For certainly Philippa would prove no docile bride—nor did he wish her to be. He admired her passionate espousal of her father's cause. He wanted, *needed* a mate who would match him in strength

of will and purpose. The saints knew he would never neglect her as his own gentle mother had been neglected.

He rose as his steward appeared in the pleasance archway, apparently in search of him, and another thought
struck him. If he could accomplish a match between Philippa Telford and himself it would not please the King.

Sir Rhys's steward bowed. 'The carrier has arrived, sir
and asks to see you.'

'Did you put him in my study?'

'Yes, sir.'

'I'll come at once. See we are not disturbed.'

He passed through the courtyard and into the house,
noting that the carrier's cart was standing, waiting, the
horse's head held by one of the grooms.

'We shall be some time. Unhitch the horse and take him
to the stable. Care for him well.'

He went into the house and passed to a small room near
the winter parlour he used as a place of business. A man
was standing near his desk, who turned and bowed obsequiously as he entered.

'Sir Rhys. I hoped you would be at home.'

The visitor was a small weasel-like individual with
sparse carroty-coloured hair, in his middle years and with
the awkward stance of a man who spent most of his time
seated upon the driving seat of a wagon. It was clear that
he was stiff from travel and Sir Rhys nodded towards a
stool which faced his desk and seated himself in the high-
backed chair behind it.

'I have ordered your horse cared for. After we have
completed our business, you can take your dinner in the
kitchen.'

The man grinned, well pleased, and leaned slightly forward.

'I thought you should have the news I have as soon as possible.'

'You have come from London?'

The man gave a bob of his head in answer.

'I saw my usual informant in a tavern in the Chepe. He tells me that the lord you asked news of had recently left the Duchess Margaret's court at Malines.'

'Where bound, had he any idea?'

The man shrugged, 'Only that he was seen to take the road for Bruges.'

'Ah, then your informant has obviously had very recent news. By carrier pigeon, do you think?'

'It would seem likely, Sir Rhys. It's known that the King's agents in Burgundy use such a method.'

Sir Rhys tapped his teeth with a quill. 'Then Wroxeter may well be heading for the port of Damme. Interesting.'

The little carrier wriggled on his stool. 'I also have news that a certain Master Allard has arrived in Milford Haven, or was there a sennight ago. You may know, Sir Rhys, that this Allard has Yorkist sympathies. His father is…'

'Yes, yes, I know well enough. His father is Sir Dominick Allard who fought for the late King at Redmoor and been an intimate with King Richard since childhood. Richard Allard was four years ago in London in service with Anne Jarvis who, with Lady Philippa Telford, was in attendance on the queen. She is the daughter of another Yorkist, Sir Guy Jarvis. She was married to young Allard some three years ago.'

'Then, sir, it is likely that he has gone to Milford Haven to meet some prominent Yorkist…'

'Aye, likely Wroxeter.' Sir Rhys leaned back irritably. 'What can the man be thinking of to risk coming to England now, when Henry's spies are watching every Yorkist in the country?'

The carrier's little rheumy eyes glistened. 'Do you wish me to head for Milford Haven, Sir Rhys? I could pick up enough good quality wool upon the way to make my journey both profitable and excusable.'

Again Sir Rhys tapped his teeth thoughtfully. 'Yes, if you can manage to make fair speed. Do you know what this fellow Allard looks like?'

'Aye, sir. I was given a description.'

'Good, then do that. You may encounter him on the road back. I am anxious to know if he intends to come to Gretton and, particularly if he is accompanied by a companion—or even a servant.'

'Aye, Sir Rhys.'

'Then get you to the kitchen. My steward will see you are suitably rewarded.'

The man rose and touched his forelock respectfully and edged his way out of the study.

Some moments later Sir Rhys's steward knocked and requested permission to enter.

'I have paid the man off, Sir Rhys. Is there any further action you wish me to take?'

Sir Rhys shook his head regretfully. 'We can do nothing but wait, Crawley. He brought disturbing news which I half feared, that the Earl of Wroxeter may be intending to visit England secretly.'

'Then he will join his lady.'

'I certainly hope not.' Again he sighed heavily. 'When you have made arrangements to have that fellow, Maynard, conveyed to Ludlow, see to it that I am informed where he is lodged and...' he hesitated slightly then continued '...and further, put someone in the household you can trust into Ludlow to keep an eye on the place and report the comings and goings of any strangers.'

The steward smiled and bowed slightly. 'I will see to it personally, Sir Rhys.'

Rhys sat on, his eyes narrowed. This Tyrrell affair was likely to fire up the realm. His confession, that on the late King's orders he had secretly suffocated the two young Princes placed in the Tower for their own safety, was dubious in the extreme. Rhys, himself, was sceptical about the truth of it. Why had King Henry waited nigh on twenty years to press Tyrrell to confess? He had certainly had the means to force the truth from all those purported to be in on the secret. When he had entered London victorious after Redmoor, surely the servants in the Tower could have been made to divulge the graves of the murdered Princes and produce their bodies. And what of the Queen? What did she know about the fate of her brothers? Rhys shook his head in doubt. The late King had had no reason to kill his nephews. He had already been crowned King and his other nephew, the young Earl of Warwick, who could have been said to have had a greater claim on the throne than the two Princes, had not been harmed by his Uncle Richard and had continued to live until four years ago when he had been executed on a trumped-up charge of treason, simply to facilitate the marriage of the Spanish Infanta to the late Prince Arthur. Her parents had refused to allow the marriage until they had been assured that all Yorkist heirs were no longer living—young Warwick had been sacrificed. And now she was a widow and the King was anxious that she should marry his younger son, Prince Henry. Was that the reason for this hastily conceived ruse of the doubtful confession?

Rhys's loyalty to King Henry had been severely tested then—and now this possibly lying confession which could not be refuted by the accused, since Tyrrell was dead.

Philippa had indignantly denied the truth of it and Rhys

was inclined to agree with her. King Henry had kept the peace for almost twenty years and this Rhys had staunchly admired, but now his stomach turned at this ruthless extermination of all harmless Yorkist heirs.

Did Wroxeter know the truth about the fate of the Princes, as Philippa had implied, and was this the reason why the King had stoutly refused to pardon him as he had other Yorkist gentlemen? If so, he, Rhys, must find some way to protect him and aid his escape if need be.

He had to find some way to convince Philippa that he acted only in her best interest, that he was not her enemy.

He believed he had detected some softening towards him in the rose pleasance. Her gentle heart had been touched by the story of his mother's suffering and she had not withdrawn from his touch when he had led her back into the courtyard.

She needed to regard him as a true friend she could trust. Later he would be able to reveal his more passionate feelings towards her.

Chapter Five

It was considerably less hot than it had been for the previous four days, and Philippa was enjoying the ride about the Gretton demesne. Her grandfather had insisted that she leave the manor house and get some cooler fresh air. Today and for the last two days he had been much improved and she had spent much of the time with him, talking of the old times when her mother had been a child at Gretton before her marriage, and reading to him from the new printed books he had ordered from Master Caxton's shop in Westminster. Her mother had left them alone together for the most part, knowing it was essential that Sir Daniel had ample opportunity to get to know the granddaughter who had been so cruelly kept from him over the years by force of circumstance. He'd enjoyed their time together; that was plain to see to all in the household. A healthier colour brightened his cheeks, his ability to talk had returned again and, though he had lost the greater part of his movement in his lower limbs, his servants had been able to carry him in his favourite armchair, now equipped with two long sturdy poles attached to the sides for easy carrying, out into the garden or where ever he wished to go on the ground floor of the manor house.

Today he had chivied Philippa into leaving his side for a while.

'Now, go, child. You have been cooped up with me for far too long during this warm weather and I want you to be able to explore the demesne. Your father's squire will go with you as usual. We know we can rely on him to keep you safe, but, in any case, no harm can come to you on my own land. I will see you again at supper and afterwards, we will talk together once more and I will tell you some more of your mother's youthful misdemeanours.'

He chuckled and waved her away after she stooped and kissed his cheek.

She had been heartily glad of the respite and went into the courtyard where Gwenny had informed her that she had last seen Peter Fairley. She found him chatting with one of the falconers and when she told the man she had no wish to take out one of his birds, she dismissed him back to his duties in the mews.

'Grandpère has commanded me to ride out for a while and I will enjoy that but I do not wish to be gone from him too long.' She sighed. 'Who knows if I will ever see him again after we have left here again for Burgundy.'

Peter's comely features expressed his own regret for the need. He knew, only too well, that it would be unwise for the Countess and her daughter to stay very much longer at Gretton.

'I will ride with you.'

'No, Peter, I have another task for you. I wish you to ride into Ludlow and enquire for me about Master Maynard. I would like to be sure that he is being adequately cared for and discover where he has been lodged.'

Peter looked thoughtful. 'We shall have to be discreet. Sir Rhys Griffith expressly warned you not to do that.'

She bridled. 'He has been most kind to us all here, at

Gretton, but he is not my master and I fail to see why I should obey him as if he were. He has been to Gretton every day to see Grandpère but I have not actually seen and spoken to him on any one of those occasions. If so I would have asked him myself about Master Maynard. No, I will take one of the grooms. It should be quite all right on Gretton land and you can be off to Ludlow and back with your report before supper. I would prefer not to send one of the household servants.' She looked at him a trifle doubtfully. 'That, as Sir Rhys said, might not be wise.'

Peter pursed his lips. 'If I find him, do you want me to visit him?'

'I see no harm in it. Do you?'

Peter shrugged. 'The young fellow seemed genuine. If I can have some time to chat with him I shall, no doubt, be able to find out more about his business, the name of his merchant master and so set our minds at rest that he can be no spy.'

'I think Sir Rhys is being over-cautious, though,' she said thoughtfully. 'This present King appears to be very determined to exact every ounce of tribute from all his subjects. I imagine they are sensitive on the issue and are determined to ensure no King's commissioner has set men to spy upon them.' She smiled. 'Henry's parsimony was often discussed at the court.'

'Which does not make him popular.'

'He does not need to be popular, Peter, only successful in handling the power and security of the realm, which makes him dangerous.'

He looked at her sideways. 'I am just wondering why you are so anxious to know about Master Maynard.'

'Is it not natural? We did find him in a distressed state and—and Sir Rhys was not particularly sympathetic to his needs.'

'And he is very personable, young Master Maynard,' Peter retorted drily.

She went a little pink. 'Really, Peter, I am hardly acquainted with the fellow. This is a courtesy I would do for anyone. You are as bad as Sir Rhys with your suspicions.'

'He has been suspicious, questioned you—about me?' He was gazing at her very intently, his eyes narrowed and her own eyes widened in response and embarrassment.

'I think that he fears—' She broke off awkwardly.

'I am sure that you set him straight.'

The remark was so coldly uttered that she turned sharply to look at him again. Surely, Peter, dear Peter, whom she had known all her life could not be harbouring... She shook off the disturbing thought hastily.

'Please go, Peter, quickly, and do what I ask. I'll go and ask for the services of a groom to ride out with me.'

'I'll arrange for that, but we must make sure the lad is utterly reliable. The head groom will advise me. I'll go and get my own horse saddled. See that your mother is informed that I shall be away for an hour or so in case she has need of me.'

'I will, but she is busied sorting linen with Grandmère so I think you will not be missed.'

She went slowly back to the house to change her gown for one suitable for riding and to seek out her mother. As he turned towards the stable she thought his reluctance to perform the task she had set him was very palpable.

When she returned to the courtyard she found that one of the younger lads, Tom, was standing waiting, holding the bridle of her Welsh cob and those of his own mount.

She smiled at him as he led her pony to the mounting block and helped her mount. 'We shall not be gone for long, Tom. I merely wish to explore Sir Daniel's lands and visit some favourite spots my mother has spoken of.'

He saw to it that she was comfortably settled and mounted up and soon they had left the courtyard and ridden across the rich sheep-rearing lands away from the manor proper. She saw the labourers at work on their own strips of the two large fields of wheat and barley and laughing, happy people haymaking. All seemed in order, despite the fact that the master was unable to oversee the work personally. Obviously the bailiff was competent and she wondered if Sir Rhys Griffith had made himself responsible for inspecting the work from time to time. She would not be in the least surprised to find that. She pursed her lips thoughtfully. At Gretton they had much to thank their neighbour for, yet—there was a nagging doubt at the back of her mind which made her uneasy about the fact that he was aware of Sir Daniel's danger in harbouring the kin of a traitor. She shook her head to try to dispel the unworthy thought. Her father's warnings and constant need to be on his guard, particularly of all strangers and known King's men, made her unduly suspicious of all men's motives. All the time they remained at Gretton they were, undoubtedly, putting her grandparents in danger of arrest. She shuddered at the thought of her sick *grandpère* and vulnerable *grandmère* being so ruthlessly questioned if that were to happen. Whatever gratitude and admiration she had for Rhys Griffith must be laid against her need to be wary of him.

Her mother had spoken longingly of the woods at Gretton where she had often ridden alone and she asked Tom to take her on the main woodland path towards Ludlow.

He obliged and soon they were riding along a broad track shaded by stately oaks and elms. It was pleasant here, a slight breeze adding to her delight, and she resolutely thrust aside all disturbing thoughts as she slowed her horse to a gentle walk.

They had been upon the track barely more than a few

minutes when the noise of a disturbance ahead, and slightly to their right, brought her up sharply. She saw that Tom was visibly alarmed and he drew up close and urged her to return the way they had come.

'Mistress, I think we should get back to the manor, now.'

'But, Tom, we are on my grandfather's land. What can be going on? If someone is in trouble we should discover the cause and report back to the steward at the manor house.'

He shook his unruly mop of fair hair vigorously. 'My lady, I was entrusted with your safety. I will take you back and see to it that someone is dispatched from the house.'

She caught a sudden sharp cry of pain, then a kind of roar as if a small crowd was giving utterance to its combined anger.

'Tom, that might be too late. Someone is hurt. I am the lady of the manor here and I should know what is happening.'

Without further arguing she spurred her pony forward in the direction of the commotion. A lesser track led off from the main one and she had to bend low in the saddle to avoid hampering branches. Her pace was urgent in spite of the uneven ground here and she had to encourage her pony forward with gentling words of reassurance and encouragement. She could hear Tom's horse blundering in her wake and the sound of his heavy breathing which told her of his mounting concern.

The noise was growing louder and she could distinguish deliberate shouts of abuse. Someone was in real peril. She turned to encourage Tom to faster progress and plunged on until, suddenly, she found herself in a manmade clearing in the wood, in which had been built a small cottage of mud daub and thatch. An angry crowd was milling round the rough-hewn fence and several brawny fellows had broken down the gate and were hammering on the door. One turned round to shout a word of frustrated fury towards his companions by the fence that he was being denied entrance.

Tom caught at Philippa's arm as she sprang to the ground without his help but she impatiently thrust him off.

'Let me go, Tom. I demand to know what is going on here. My *grandpère* would be horrified to hear of this rioting. Who lives here?'

Tom gave a hasty gulp as several members of the crowd around the fence, hearing her upraised voice, turned to view the newcomer. Their gaze did not strike her as being unduly hostile, merely curious.

She could see that they were peasant labourers, dressed in homespun, several of the men carrying pitchforks as if they had been drawn from their task of haymaking. There was also a fair sprinkling of red-faced women among their number and Philippa realised at once that they would not be easy to pacify.

Tom whispered urgently in her ear. 'My lady, we should return to the manor at once. The mood of this crowd is ugly indeed.'

Her demand had silenced them for moments, but now they ignored her and turned back to shouting and screaming and waving fists and farm implements. The owner of the cottage had undoubtedly raised their ire and was stoutly refusing to come out and face the mob. The imperative hammering upon the door continued and one of the men kicked it hard so that the sound of splintering could be heard. It would not hold for long.

Philippa advanced, head high. 'What is all this? You are disturbing the peace. Desist from this, at once.'

Again the crowd by the fence turned and viewed her

now with distinct hostility. One woman, brawny elbows revealed by her rolled-up sleeves, stood, hands on hips, her whole pose insolent.

'Hoity toity, what brings you here to interfere with our concerns? Be off with you, mistress, and leave us to our own business.'

'I will when I am assured that this unseemly commotion stops. Who lives here? What is this all about? Whatever it is I'm sure it can be settled without the breaking of heads. If you have some legitimate grudge against the cottager, one of you send for the village constable.'

'He'll do nowt,' one of the older men spoke up defiantly, hiding himself behind the buxom woman who had accosted Philippa first. 'He's afeared—like we all are.'

'It doesn't appear to me that any of you are afraid except the poor soul who lives within,' she rejoined tartly.

While she had been having words with the villagers she heard a definite crack as the flimsy cottage door yielded and, with triumphant yells, the men round it surged inside. There was a great deal of jostling and pushing and, eventually, the self-appointed leader emerged, holding an ancient crone by one arm, two of the others urging her ungently from the rear. A second triumphant roar of applause came from the motley watchers by the gate.

Philippa attempted to shoulder the leading woman aside so that she could obtain a clearer view of the victim of all this furore, but was angrily pushed back. Tom thrust a strong shoulder forward and cleared a path for her and, after a hastily muttered word of recognition that he was one of the manor servants, those in front gave way abruptly so that Philippa and Tom were standing slightly ahead of them on the path.

She was shocked to see how fragile and vulnerable the

object of their fury was and she advanced indignantly to demand that the old woman's captors unhand her at once.

Sullenly she was obeyed, as if the innate authority in her tone was recognised and noted, but Philippa had to run forward hurriedly to catch the old lady by the shoulder as she was about to collapse. She stood supporting her, angrily facing the mob.

'Now, one of you tell me who this old lady is and what she could have possibly done to make you so angry.'

''Er's Nan Freeman,' one of the women by the fence volunteered and the tone of her voice was insolent in the extreme. 'Mistress, 'taint none of your business. You leave 'er to us.'

'To do what?'

'Well, to duck 'er for a start. She'm be a witch.'

'What nonsense,' Philippa said briskly. 'Anyone with eyes to see knows she's just a sick old woman who needs help, not abuse.'

'If 'er be sick it be but justice,' one of the men who had dashed into the cottage snapped. ''Er 'as made others sick. My lass is 'bout to die 'cos of 'er—and what's more,' he bellowed, 'she'm be 'bout to pay for it. Let's take 'er to the duck pond in the village—now.'

Screamed imprecations followed his words and Philippa was forced to stand her ground before the hapless old woman as the two men surged forward and tried to snatch the frail old body from her. She placed her arms comfortingly about the victim and said softly, 'Do not be afraid. I'll not let them hurt you. I'll send Tom for the village constable. He'll restore order.'

To her surprise the woman's answer was stronger and more vibrant than she could have believed possible.

'It would be foolish for you to stay here, mistress, and dangerous. These louts be too worked up to see sense at the end of their noses. They'll not listen to you. Don't involve the constable. He'll not be able to help. I shall be well enough. They'll most likely 'ave calmed down by the time they get me to the village.'

'But I can't stand by and let them duck you. Have you harmed someone?' Philippa's tone was doubtful now. She told herself that these charges of witchcraft were nonsensical, yet she knew that many people, even those more learned and of the nobility, were inclined to listen to such talk. Why, King Edward's queen, Elizabeth Woodville, had been thought to be a witch and her mother, Jaquetta. And Jane Shore, the King's mistress, had been condemned to do penance as a witch at St Paul's Cross, yet she could not believe this ageing, frail old woman could be guilty of such heinous behaviour.

The old woman shrugged. 'Like as not the silly wench didn't listen to un properly and took too much of the potion. 'Twould be better if they'd let us see un but they wunt, not in this mood.'

She was right, for, already, the crowd round the fence was getting angrier by the moment. The fence was broken down in one place, then several at the front began to surge forward. The two men behind who had been the leaders of this affray were looking decidedly disgruntled. They recognised that this unknown woman had some gentility and were reluctant to cross her but, on the other hand, they were frustrated at the challenge to their right to deal with their victim as they thought proper. One of them moved menacingly nearer and Tom called peremptorily to him to stay back. They were not, however, likely to listen to some young whippersnapper from the manor stables and, after a hesitant move with sidelong glances towards his companion for support, the man advanced again, lifting one arm to shove Tom impatiently aside.

''Taint none of your business, this,' he growled. 'You'd best take yourself off to your betters and leave us to deal with this old witch.'

Further angry shouts echoed his demand and Philippa began to tremble. She could see she was not to be obeyed and she would either have to abandon her protégée or fall with her in any attack—and there was little time to consider the matter. In all events she was not about to play the coward. This old creature should be under Sir Daniel's protection and she, Philippa, had a duty to stand up for her, if only as far as demanding that authority should be consulted in the person of the village constable. Tom moved nearer to shield the two women with his body, but Philippa could almost smell his fear.

Nan Freeman buckled in their grasp and croaked, 'You'd best go, mistress, ye cannat do any good 'ere.'

Philippa turned despairingly towards Tom. 'We can't leave her—'

Her words were cut short as a flying stone caught the old woman full on the forehead and blood actually splashed on to Philippa's sleeve. The mood of the mob was becoming more and more ugly by the minute and she knew she was about to suffer as the object of their combined fury. How dared she interfere in the rightful punishment to be dealt out to their captive!

Soon more stones were flying, many, thank the Virgin, missing their targets, but some were finding their marks. Tom let out a sudden yelp as one caught him on the ear and Philippa felt the sharp sting of another on her own cheek.

She gave a little sob of despair, and, as if in answer to her prayer, an authoritative voice broke across the baying of the mob.

'What in God's name is this? Are you all mad? Cease

this rioting at once or I'll have the lot of you in chains before sunset.'

It was the voice she knew only too well. Rhys Griffith's voice, and the crowd, who had ignored everything but their own lust for blood, recognised it too and that it threatened retribution and could not be denied. They fell sullenly back as he nudged his horse close to the fence and impatiently moved aside with his riding crop those who were tardy about clearing his path. He sat coolly, reviewing the scene and, for a moment, he appeared not to have noticed Philippa standing there, badly frightened and, as usual in her meetings with him, dishevelled and bloodstained.

'So,' he said, as he slid from the saddle, and flicked his riding crop against his thigh, 'there appears to be some grounds for complaint. I hope that it truly warrants my attention and is an excuse for the lot of you abandoning your work for half a day. It had better be worth it.'

He walked through the now silent group to the cottage doorway and, gently but firmly, took the old woman, now in an almost collapsed state, into his hold. 'Tom, let us help Mistress Freeman into her cottage.' He looked coolly towards Philippa who was leaning weakly against the cottage doorpost. 'Are you hurt?'

She shook her head. 'Very little, just a scratch.'

He raised his voice only slightly. 'All of you, get back to your work and your womenfolk to caring for their brats. I want to see none of you here by the time I come back to the door.'

One of the men, the accredited leader, Philippa thought, found the courage to speak up. 'Josh Carter's lass is like to die from a potion yon old witch sold 'er. 'Er deserves to suffer for it.'

'I will look into the matter; meanwhile, Mistress Freeman is under my protection. Mistress Weston here is kin to Sir Daniel, so mind your manners. If she makes complaint of your behaviour, and rightly so, you could all be before me in Wroxeter Castle hall in the morning court. Now, get you gone.'

There was a mutter of disgruntled complaints as the group began to disperse reluctantly. As they did so, Sir Rhys called, 'Get the apothecary from Ludlow to Josh's daughter. Tell him I will pay for his services. Get about it quickly. She could be worsening by the moment.'

He had held the old woman in his arms, effortlessly, as if she were a doll. He then moved calmly into the cottage and set her down upon a bed of rushes covered with skins and rough homespun blankets which had been set against one wall.

Weakly Philippa followed and gazed down at her. 'There is water in the crock there on the shelf. I will find some cloth and wipe her face. I do not think she is badly hurt. They wanted to duck her.'

He watched her as she went about her task, Tom standing guard by the doorway. 'It is always so at these times. More than likely Josh's silly wench took too much of the penny royal Nan gave her and has made herself really sick. She should recover. Nan rarely mistakes the amount of herbs she deals out.'

'You know her, then?'

'Oh, indeed. She has been wise woman and herbal healer in these parts since her childhood and her mother before her. It is not witchcraft but experienced knowledge. The villagers are glad enough normally to depend on her services, but it is probable that Josh's lass got herself into trouble with some lad he disapproves of and this has made him more angry than usual. Her own blind panic has made the situation worse, but the apothecary should be able to save her.' He regarded Philippa steadily. 'I should not speak so openly on so delicate a matter, but—'

'I know well enough that penny royal is used to abort unwanted babes,' she said coolly. 'I am no delicate flower, Sir Rhys, as you know well enough.'

He laughed. 'Indeed I do, Lady Philippa. I am becoming used to finding you in some distressed state and with your clothing torn and blood-spattered. Most of the women of my acquaintance would be swooning at the sight of you, let alone get themselves into such situations. My lady, you appear to attract trouble as a flower attracts bees.'

'Would you have had me leave her to the dubious mercy of the mob?'

'Certainly not.' He took the dampened cloth from her and very gently began to wipe her own dirtied and blood-stained face. 'You have a nasty cut on your cheek which will require some healing salve. I doubt that it will leave a scar.'

She shrugged. 'I have taken worse knocks in childhood. Thank you'—this stiffly as he completed his ministrations. 'Will Mistress Freeman be safe here now?'

'Not for a while with the whole village stirred up against her. I will leave Tom here with her and take you home to the manor house. Sir Daniel will dispatch a couple of his men to take her to my manor where she can stay until she mends and the villagers calm down. I doubt if she will consent to stay there much longer than that.' He chuckled. 'Like you, Lady Philippa, Nan Freeman has a well-developed stubborn streak.'

Philippa went to the old woman and took her hand. 'Goodbye. I am assured that you will be safe now.'

'Oh, aye, Lady Philippa, Sir Rhys will take good care of me though he mightn't have come in time. My thanks and blessings are for your timely help.'

'You know me?'

'I knew your bonny mother, my lady. You could be the child of none other. Do ye take care and for those ye love most.'

Philippa wrinkled her brow. 'You mean Sir Daniel?'

'Aye, 'im. He 'as been a good master to me but I mean—others.' Her pale lips writhed in a smile and Philippa squeezed her hand comfortingly.

'Are you not too old to live here alone now? Would you not be safer and better cared for nearer to the manor?'

'The mother will care for me, my lady, and take me easy when the time comes.'

Philippa's brow wrinkled again in puzzlement for the strange words but Sir Rhys drew her gently to the door. 'They will be sending men out in search of you. We must go.' He addressed Tom. 'I'll despatch the men quickly. You won't be alone with her for long.'

Tom nodded and knuckled his forehead and Sir Rhys drew Philippa towards her pony and lifted her effortlessly into the saddle as he had carried the wise woman. He felt her trembling in his grasp and her small hand was chilled to his touch as he handed her the pony's lead reins.

'You have been truly shocked by this. I will get you home and into your mother's care. You are quite safe with me, my lady.'

She smiled gamely back at him. 'I know that, sir. It seems I must always be in your debt. You handled that mob so confidently. Were you not just the slightest bit afraid that they would defy you and turn on you too?'

He raised one black eyebrow and grinned at her. 'It did cross my mind that I had no stout men-at-arms at my back, but they know me well. I am the magistrate for these parts; if heads had been broken, there would have been fines and imprisonment to follow. Once the first fury cooled they were aware of that.'

'Yet you did offer to care for the sick girl.'

'She is one of your grandfather's tenants and warranted our care as much as Nan.'

'I think you are a strange man, Sir Rhys,' she said soberly, 'but I discover new facets to your character every time we meet.'

She urged her pony forward and they rode steadily back towards the manor. After a moment she strove to wipe the ugly scene from her mind momentarily by engaging in more general conversation.

'We talked of my family the last time we were together, Lady Philippa. Have you found it lonely at Malines? You are your father's only child. Were there other children with whom you could play at Malines?'

She shook her head, smiling. 'Very rarely. We moved about quite a lot during my childhood while my father travelled on the Duchess's business. There were servants' children sometimes but, largely, my mother and I were forced to fall back upon each other's company. I think, perhaps, I have been indulged too much as a consequence,' she said, sighing. 'My father must have found it a hard fact to face that he has no son. In the early days I think he had hopes that he might be able to return to England and regain his lands, so he must have hoped for a son to inherit. He has never uttered a word of complaint on the subject. My mother had two miscarriages and then one little son, who was stillborn. That was a terrible tragedy for them all and now—' she looked bleakly ahead along the woodland path '—my father ails often. He took a bad wound at Redmoor and another at Stoke and his life has been hard since.'

'And there has been little money?'

Her smile was a little wistful as she turned back to him. 'It has been sufficient. The Duchess has been good to us, but all the late King's friends and supporters have suffered misfortunes over the years.'

He did not answer and they continued their ride in silence.

He was still considering her words when he found himself alone in the hall with Sir Daniel later. Lady Wroxeter had clucked her concern at the sight of Philippa, once more in a distressed condition, and hastened her away to their apartments to deal with the small wounds made by the flying stones and to comfort her. Lady Gretton, after a hasty greeting to Sir Rhys, hurried after them.

Sir Daniel eyed his neighbour quizzically after he had detailed the steps he took regarding his plans to ensure the continued safety of Nan Freeman. Already two of Sir Daniel's men had been dispatched to join Tom in her defence.

'I have to thank you again, Rhys, not only for your prompt dealing with this sorry affair, but for once more coming to my granddaughter's assistance.' He sighed and then chuckled. 'She appears to have inherited an overactive conscience and needs to come to the help of every lame dog she comes across. My Cressida was just the same at her age and I was glad to hand her into Wroxeter's care when the time came, never thinking that he, too, had this deep-rooted need to remain loyal to his principles and that Cressida would find herself in distressing circumstances so soon after the marriage. I would to God I could ensure Philippa's welfare, since her doughty spirit requires a strong and reliable mentor, but I fear that might prove difficult considering her lack of dowry.'

Rhys was silent for moments as he drained a goblet of

malmsey an attentive page had placed on the trestle table at his elbow.

'Can I ask if you are in direct contact with the Earl, her father, Sir Daniel, or would that be too delicate and dangerous an enquiry?'

Sir Daniel stared back at him thoughtfully. 'I imagine you have a definite reason for posing such a question and not merely wanting to probe my own loyalty to the King.'

'If I could reach the ear of Wroxeter, I would beg him for his daughter's hand in marriage.'

It was so blunt an announcement that Sir Daniel blinked in astonishment. He hesitated and played with his own goblet, moving the base in circles upon the table top.

'I cannot have failed to notice your interest in my granddaughter,' he said at last, slowly, 'but have you considered the consequences of such an alliance, even should it prove possible?'

'You mean I would lose the favour of the King, even come under his strong displeasure, so much so that I could suffer for it? Yes, I have done.'

'And you would still wish to proceed with such a marriage, were Wroxeter to prove willing?'

'It is the greatest desire of my heart.' He leaned forward eagerly. 'I think I fell deeply in love with Lady Philippa the first time I encountered her in the courtyard of the inn at Milford. Since then I have discovered much more about her that pleases me. As you say, she is headstrong and impulsive but her heart is warm with sympathy for those she meets, especially those requiring her help. He gave a great gasp of longing. 'She is as beautiful as some faery creature. Sometimes I look at her and can hardly believe she is of this earth. I long to possess her, Sir Daniel, and to keep her safe from all possible dangers, and, as you and I have both observed, she is likely to put herself into peril as often and as naturally as a bee pollinates flowers. I know there are obstacles to the match. I have the misfortune to possess her father's lands, and for this she holds, quite naturally, a decided grudge, but surely that very fact has an advantage. Only just now, as we rode in, she expressed what she believed must be her father's regret that he had no son to inherit his title and lands, but, as my wife, she would do so and our children after her, Wroxeter's descendants.'

Sir Daniel nodded gravely. 'You and I can see the advantage of that, Rhys, my friend, but will Wroxeter? And, most important of all, will Philippa?'

Sir Rhys shook his head. 'I think he will consider what can be gained. Did you consider Lady Wroxeter's wishes when you arranged her marriage to the Earl of Wroxeter or were you constrained to make the best alliance possible for her?'

Sir Daniel gave a wry smile. 'In all honesty, I was forced to give my consent. It was the late King's express wish and I can tell you I had my doubts, for Cressida was every bit as headstrong as her daughter, but Wroxeter proved the right man for her and she fell deeply in love with him, a love which has endured through all the dangers and hardships of the last twenty years.' He looked away from his guest, across the hall, his eyes narrowing in thought. At last he said slowly, 'I will talk to Cressida on this matter and send to you when I have received her own opinion.'

'And she has means of reaching her husband?'

'That may take some time.'

Sir Rhys nodded. He understood that since the Earl of Wroxeter was in the Duchess of Burgundy's service he must be off upon his travels often so that his wife was unaware of his whereabouts. He said softly, 'And may I know your own thoughts, Sir Daniel?'

Sir Daniel turned back and regarded him steadily. 'I have a deep admiration for you, Rhys Griffith, as both a man and as a fair and right-minded magistrate and lord. I have to say that since you, too, have undoubted determination you could find my Philippa something of a handful.' His lips twisted in some private amusement. 'But I believe you could manage her and that goes far in my consideration of her future. Cressida has spoken of her fears regarding the Duchess of Burgundy's health.'

'If she were to die, Wroxeter would lose her protection and patronage and, more than ever, he would need to secure his daughter's welfare.'

Sir Daniel inclined his head.

Sir Rhys said quietly, 'Has Lady Philippa spoken of me to you?'

Again Sir Daniel gave that little wry smile. 'She has asked questions about you but, no, she has not expressed an opinion of your character.'

'Do you think she hates me?'

'No, I think she has a certain respect for you, somewhat tempered by her concern about your loyalties.'

Rhys sighed. 'That will ever come between us.'

'I fear so, yet—' he waved one hand dismissively '—I have known successful marriages based on even more difficult grounds.'

'Then I must be content to wait.'

'I fear so. Time and force of circumstances, only, can affect Philippa's attitude towards your offer.'

Rhys saw that his host was beginning to tire. He rose, bowed and made his excuses. He decided he would not attempt to speak with Philippa again today and took his leave of his host and rode from Gretton.

* * *

Philippa was relieved, later that evening, to learn from Tom that Nan Freeman had been conveyed to Griffith Manor by two of Sir Rhys's stout men-at-arms.

'She will be safer there, under Sir Rhys's protection, than here at Gretton, mistress,' Tom assured her. 'While Sir Daniel is so ill and unable to get around the demesne.'

Philippa understood that and was content with the arrangement. She wondered how the poor lass who had taken too much of the old woman's potion had fared and if, should Sir Rhys be right in his assumptions, she was so deeply unhappy, having been abandoned by her light of love. Philippa sighed inwardly. It was ever the way of the world for women to receive no consideration from their menfolk. She pushed aside the unworthy thought that Sir Rhys had shown her every consideration. Rhys Griffith could be considered a fine, upright man for the right woman—that was, the one who shared his political sympathies.

Wistfully she wondered how things might have been had he not been master of her father's lands and she a fugitive. She could not dismiss the sight of him from her mind. How wonderful it had been to see him at that cottage, just when she had been in darkest despair! She had known then, instinctively, that with him beside her she had nothing to fear. And yet—always at the back of her mind was that nagging doubt: could she really trust him?

Her heart yearned to acknowledge that she could. Resolutely she put aside that treacherous longing. Soon she would be gone from Gretton and from England and would never see Rhys Griffith again.

Despite her determination to face that fact squarely, her lip trembled and she felt ready to break into tears as she had so many times lately. During these last days when he had come to Gretton and made no attempt to see and speak with her…

It was all so bewildering. Never had she felt like this before—not even when she had been most afraid.

There could be no more thoughts such as these. If not her enemy, Rhys Griffith was certainly her father's. There would always be too much between them. She must never harbour thoughts of love towards him. To do so would spell disaster for all of them.

When Peter Fairley sought her out later she learned that the injured Roger Maynard was considerably improved, his broken leg set, and was comfortably lodged at an inn near Ludlow Castle.

'It seems,' she said thoughtfully, 'that Sir Rhys has done his best for the man in spite of his earlier suspicions.'

Peter looked dubious. 'I doubt that the fellow could learn much to Sir Rhys's discredit in Ludlow where all seem to respect Griffith for his fair dealings.'

'So,' she said lightly, 'the knight is a paragon. What a pity he is one of King Henry's cronies.'

Since her grandfather insisted that, after her perilous adventure, she keep to the manor, Philippa saw no more of her rescuer for the next few days. Once or twice she was puzzled to see her mother closeted with Sir Daniel and, afterwards, Cressida seemed somewhat abstracted and followed her daughter with her eyes as if she would read her very soul. Philippa waited patiently for her mother to impart to her the source of her disquiet but Cressida appeared secretive about whatever had been discussed with her father. A sergeant was dispatched from the household on some mission, which was not discussed, and Philippa wondered if her mother was attempting to contact Lord Wroxeter. Knowing how dangerous a move that could be, Philippa was more than ever disturbed. Only something very serious could bring her mother to seek to be in touch with the Earl, her husband, while she was under the Gretton roof. Such a move, were it to be discovered by one of the King's minions, could be hazardous for all of them.

Philippa found her own mood to be restless and distracted, also unusually crotchety. On several occasions she had been touchy and unduly imperious and critical, so that she had brought tears to the eyes of young Gwenny. She castigated herself, knowing the girl was doing her utmost to please her young mistress. What was wrong with her? Certainly she was still worried about Sir Daniel's condition, everyone in the household was, her *grandmère* most of all, but that did not entirely explain her own sense of disquiet. She was not at peace with herself and that she found alarming. Though there had been times when she had been fearful of what the future would hold for herself, her mother and father, Philippa was generally optimistic by nature. She knew these moods of near despair were connected with the knowledge that she could not share in the contentment of many young maidens of her acquaintance, since her dowry was almost non-existent and her father's position made it unlikely that he would find a husband for her. She had always put on a cheerful countenance whenever she was in the presence of either or both her parents, but she was aware that her outward calm hid a passionate nature. Inwardly she yearned for love, for a man who could raise her to the heights of ecstasy she had read of in the troubadours' tales, for a home of her own, for children, but all this was likely to be denied her. She was a burden to her father. Would it be simpler to profess a desire to enter a nunnery? She dismissed the thought, knowing her father would reject such a suggestion immediately, and she knew herself only too well. Such a life would be a constant torture.

She was busy the next afternoon helping her mother to sort linen when Gwenny came into the chamber.

'Lady Philippa, your grandfather requests that you go to him. He is sitting in his carrying chair in the pleasance.'

'Yes, of course. Perhaps he wishes me to read with him as we often do. May I leave you to finish this, Mother?'

'Certainly.' Cressida smiled fondly at her daughter. 'Gwenny will help me here.'

Philippa moved to curtsy, but her mother pulled her to her and kissed her gently upon the forehead. 'Listen well to your grandfather, child. Remember, we have not too long to be here. Savour the moments we have together.'

Philippa nodded and ran lightly down the stair towards the courtyard, pausing only to rid herself of her linen apron as she hastened through the hall.

She found her grandfather reading one of his falconing manuals and he looked up, smiling, as she approached. It was a warm day and the pleasance was comfortable in the slight breeze blowing without the need for them to seek shade. Someone had placed a joint stool near his chair and she ran to him, kissed him on the cheek and sank down upon it.

'How are you feeling this afternoon? Did you want company? I thought that perhaps Sir Rhys Griffith would visit today.'

He took her hand in his huge paw. 'No, perhaps later. He must be busy on his own manor, overseeing the final bestowing of the harvest.'

She nodded and reached for his book. 'Perhaps soon you will be able to take out your kestrel, Grandpère.'

He smiled wryly. 'I think those days are well behind

me, child, but I still enjoy contemplating the pleasures I had.' He noticed that she wrinkled her nose and bent to ruffle her bright hair, free for once of her headdress since they were sitting comfortable *en famille*. 'You do not like falconing or the hunt?'

'Not really, I think few women do. I went on several during my days at Court at Westminster and Richmond, but I do not like to see creatures hurt, though I know it is necessary to provide meat for the winter months. Does Sir Rhys accompany you when you hunt?'

'Yes, he has done.' He was holding her hand lightly but she noticed that he did not seem willing to relinquish it. 'What is your opinion of Sir Rhys Griffith, Philippa?'

Again she wrinkled her nose, this time in thought, unwilling to answer too readily. 'He has been good to you and Grandmère. On the few occasions I have watched him deal with villagers and labourers he seem fair and kindly, though firm. He has come to my rescue on one or two occasions and he does not lack courage.' She gave a little bird-like nod of her chin. 'I respect and admire him.' She was looking away from him across the pleasance at the rose bushes, remembering the time when she and Rhys had talked informally in the rose arbour at Griffith manor. 'I think…' she said slowly, 'that he is often lonely. He did not appear to have a happy time with his brother and father. Did he tell you of them?'

Her grandfather inclined his chin. 'We all knew in the county—what went on—and pitied Rhys's lady mother.'

'He must miss her. He loved her greatly, I believe.' Philippa shaded her eyes with one hand. 'I hope he will soon find a good wife, one who will respect and love him and deal well with his household as he would wish.'

'And could you be that woman, Philippa?' The question

was put very quietly and she turned and stared at him, mouth slightly open.

'Grandpère—you cannot mean—he has asked for me?'

'He requested that I sent messengers to your father begging the right to formally ask for your hand.'

She jumped up, startled. 'And you granted it—and you have sent—I saw a messenger ride out and wondered but—I did not think—Grandfather, you are mad? You must not allow Sir Rhys Griffith to know the whereabouts of my father. Even in Burgundy he is not entirely safe. You know that. How could you—?'

'Calm yourself, child.' He lifted a restraining hand. 'There can be no harm done. My messenger will simply return with an answer if and when he finds your father. Nothing will be divulged about his whereabouts—or the business he is engaged upon.'

Her eyes were wild, her hand hard against her breast. 'But you cannot contemplate that my father would consent to such a monstrous alliance. He—the man is our enemy, he holds my father's lands. He—'

'His father may well have been our enemy, child, but Redmoor was almost twenty years ago, before you were born. We must all live as we can. Your father knows that well enough and, like me, he must be anxious to ensure your future. Rhys Griffith could provide for you more than adequately. He is a wealthy landowner and what better than that your children would inherit your father's land in God's good time?'

She stared at him blankly, 'Then you—you see some wisdom in this—*alliance*.' She ground out the final word. 'Have you—have you discussed this with Grandmère or—' the enormity of it struck her forcibly '—with mother?'

'Yes, your mother is of our opinion.' Again his answer

was very quiet but direct. 'She knows the necessity of providing for you in the event of any accident happening to your father. You know the Duchess of Burgundy ails. The fortunes of you all could take a decisive downward turn if she were to die. We must think ahead, Philippa. Rhys Griffith professes his deep love for you. He asks no dowry.'

'And my father,' she murmured brokenly, 'have you had his answer? What does he say to this unspeakable proposal?'

'I have had no answer as yet, but your mother and I thought it best to put this to you. Who knows how long you will be able to stay here or if your father can be reached in a hurry?'

'You want me to accept, don't you?'

He was silent for a moment, then he said, 'We have pondered over this for a long time and, yes, we believe it could assure your future. I trust Rhys Griffith to provide well for you. I know this must be a shock to you, Philippa, but you must have noticed that he has had no eyes for anyone but you since you met at Milford Haven. While I realise you cannot, as yet, entertain any fond feelings for him, he is young, personable—'

'And wealthy,' she put in bitterly. 'Like most other maids of my acquaintance, I am to be sold for the best price at market.'

'Philippa, you know that is not so,' he said, looking up earnestly at her as she sprang to her feet and stepped away from him, blue eyes flashing dangerously.

'No,' she said, stepping yet further back and lifting her hands as if to ward him off, 'I thought you loved me, Grandpère, but you ask this terrible thing of me. All of you have conspired against me, knowing it would be against my will. Even if I were to harbour tender thoughts for Rhys Griffith I could never—never marry him. He is my father's enemy. How could I live with such a man, fearing for my father's safety, knowing that King's officers might call at our manor at any time demanding to know the whereabouts of my father, waiting for me to lead him into a trap? I would be forced to cut off all contact with those I love best. You know all that and yet you put this to me—for—for gain alone. Rather would I run away from you all and trust myself to a nunnery—'

She broke off in this wild tirade as she saw her grandfather attempt to rise from his chair to go to her. He fell back and again struggled to rise, then he clawed at his throat and made some terrible unintelligible animal noise. She stood rooted to the spot, horrified, as she saw his eyes roll upwards. The dreadful noise continued until suddenly it stopped and she saw he had fallen sideways in his chair. Terror impelled her forward then and she ran to the chair and knelt before him.

'Grandpère, I did not mean any of that. Please, please, you know that I love you, realise that you were trying to do your best for me. What is it, Grandpère? Oh, please, please—answer me...' Her voice rose to a shriek of despair when he did not move, as she shook his shoulder urgently, tears raining down her cheeks. She spoke to him, continued to shake his unresponsive shoulder, implored him over and over again, not knowing what she said or what avail her efforts could possibly do to rouse him.

Abruptly her own shoulder was taken in a firm clasp and a well-known voice spoke very gently. 'Leave him, Lady Philippa, let me see. Allow me to help you up.'

She turned an anguished face to Rhys Griffith. 'He—he will not answer. I—I caused this. He was—he was trying to persuade me to—Oh, Sweet Virgin—I would not listen and he—he—please, oh, please, tell me he is not...'

He lifted her gently but forcibly from her kneeling position and half-carried her to a wooden seat some feet away. 'Sit, Lady Philippa. Leave this to me. Do not try to move. Trust me.'

She buried her head in her hands as he strode away, back to the carrying chair with its stricken inhabitant. It seemed an age before he returned to her side and dropped to his knees before her, taking both her hands, now wet with her scalded tears, into his own.

'My dear, you must not weep. It happened so quickly that he had no time to fear even. I have sent for a priest. Everything will be done reverently. It is good he had you with him at the last.'

She stared at him blankly. 'He is dead?' she whispered at last. 'He is really dead?'

He inclined his head gravely.

'He cannot be, not—not now when he and I were—oh, no.' She burst into a storm of weeping and he drew her up into his arms, holding her close so that she could feel the roughness of his homespun jerkin against the silk of her gown. She sobbed against his shoulder in an access of grief and self-blame. He could feel her shuddering form pressed close to his heart and he murmured gentle words of comfort until the worst of the storm was past and still she clung to him blindly, finding some inner strength which he, and he alone, could impart. At last the shuddering stopped and he drew her down to the wooden seat again, his arm about her so that she was able to cry more naturally.

'It was all my fault,' she said again as the weeping eased somewhat. 'I knew he was ill and must not be angered or upset and I—and I—and I thwarted him and...'

'Hush now,' he said softly, though he made no attempt now to stem the renewed storm of weeping. 'None of this was your fault. He suffered a stroke months ago, Philippa. We all knew it could happen again any time and that it could prove fatal. Your mother brought you here so that he would have a chance to see you at last and his wish was granted. You were everything he hoped for. He died as he wished, with you at his side. Now I shall leave you for a moment and summon your maid. Your mother and grandmother will be busied for a while. As I said, I have already sent a messenger to summon a priest. All is in hand. When Gwenny comes, you must go to your chamber and pray and try to calm yourself. In time your womenfolk will need your support. I will arrange everything. You can trust me.'

He longed to stay beside her and continue to try to comfort her desperate grief and yet there was much to be done and he must not, at this time, take advantage of her need. He could not imagine what had passed between the old man and his beloved granddaughter that was so terrible in her eyes that it could not be faced. He frowned slightly as he rose to his feet.

'Pippa?'

In her agony of mind she did not notice the use of her mother's pet name for her. She tried to stem her tears with the back of her hand and looked up at him wonderingly. 'Yes?'

'I will send for the physician, naturally, but I know he can do nothing for your grandfather. Do you feel ill? Can you manage alone until Gwenny comes? You are shocked and should not try to stand up and walk without help for a while. The physician will mix you a posset if he feels there is need.'

She shook her head vehemently. 'No, no, I am being weak and foolish and in a time of crisis when I am most needed to be strong. Thank you, Sir Rhys, for your kind-

ness. My grandmother will—will—' she swallowed back
yet more hot tears '—will be very grateful, I know. It was
just that—that he and I...' She broke off in terror that she
might have let fall to him the hub of the quarrel between
her *grandpère* and her: those bitter words that had caused
him such hurt—had made him try to rise—had caused the
seizure that had killed him. Further words were frozen as
if her tongue clung to the roof of her mouth without the
will or ability to release itself.

He nodded, then bent and took her hand, squeezed it in
a final act of attempted comfort, then gently released her,
stood up and slowly backed away.

She watched him go wonderingly. Though she was not
aware of it, the tears were still raining unchecked down
her cheeks. Always, it seemed, he was here by her side
when she had most need of him. Had he come for his
answer? If so, what had he heard? Did he know how
strongly she had rejected his offer for her hand?

She stared blankly into the distance, not hearing the sudden commotion nearer the house when the members of the
household were told of the master's death and began to
react in stunned silence to the news and to prepare themselves for what needed to be done. There was stifled sobbing and running footsteps, but, for the present, Philippa
was unaware of it all. She could only think of her own
culpability, for, however she told herself inwardly that she
could have behaved in no other way, she blamed herself
for the tragedy which would now strike at them all. She
had refused outright to listen to him, castigated him for
the very suggestion and yet—and yet—the stark horror of
the situation was now facing her. If circumstances were
different—if Rhys Griffith were not what he was—she
would have welcomed his proposal. Even now she could
feel the strong heartbeat that had moved against her own

terrified fluttering one. She had been grateful for the strength of his arms, as he had carried her away from that disastrous scene of death. She had known, instinctively, that he would deal with the crisis: comfort her mother and *grandmère*, as he had striven to comfort her; deal firmly but kindly with frightened servants and competently with the household concerning the services, which must be performed; greet the priest when he arrived. Could any man do more for his neighbours and friends? For all the this time, since they had met in Milford haven, she had fought against the deepening feelings she had for this man, flailed at her own weakening emotions, when she had thrilled at his nearness, known the wild excitement, when he had held her close, or simply lifted her to the saddle, in a simple act of courtesy only.

Her grandfather had said Rhys Griffith had professed his love for her. Was it true? He had offered for her, knowing that she could bring nothing of monetary value to the marriage bed. Was that proof that he truly loved her? Could she trust him? Was his interest in her—and in the Grettons—heightened by the knowledge that their secrets could be invaluable, if revealed to his sovereign? And yet her grandfather knew him, must have considered his own danger and yet—he trusted him. Could she do the same? Could she allow her longing heart its way at last? Was it possible that she could lower her defences and give Rhys Griffith the right to penetrate to her most secret desires? Dare she admit, to herself, that she loved him?

It was what her grandfather had wished for her—his very last wish. Could she deny him? What would her father's answer be? She must, of course, wait for that.

She stood up woodenly when Gwenny, her cheeks tear-stained, and eyelids red with weeping unrestrainedly, approached.

'Oh, mistress, what can I say? We all loved Sir Daniel and—'

'I know, Gwenny,' Philippa said quietly as she put her hand within that of her maid. She was beginning to control the first wild passion of grief and she took, gratefully, the white linen kerchief which Gwenny offered, and ineffectually began to dab at her eyes. She could remove the stains and wetness, but her own swollen and reddened lids would proclaim to the household how terrible had been her ordeal.

Resolutely she thrust to the back of her mind the inner struggle, which had been the cause of her despair. 'We must go to my mother. They will wish me to help with— with the laying out,' she whispered brokenly, 'then the priest will be here and we must offer the services for the dead.'

'There will be others to do that for him,' Gwenny murmured soulfully. 'Sir Rhys said I was to take you to your chamber for a while, that you were dreadfully shocked, the first person to realise—oh.' She began to sob again piteously. 'Oh, mistress, how terrible for you that you were alone with him.'

Philippa compressed her lips. Would Rhys Griffith reveal to her mother that she had been so terribly distressed because she and her *grandpère* had quarrelled? If so, her mother would be aware of the cause of his excitement and the following seizure. Would she ever be forgiven?

She began to walk slowly and reluctantly towards the house, turning to try to catch a glimpse of the carrying chair and its silent, motionless figure but, already servants had arrived and were preparing to carry their dead master indoors. She gave a little shudder and turned back to Gwenny.

They were passing the stable when a sudden flurry of

hoofs alerted her to the fact that a visitor had arrived at this most inappropriate moment. A single groom came to take the newcomer's leading rein as he sprang down. Philippa half-turned, curious, then stood stockstill, eyes widening in yet more shock. There was no mistaking that tall figure, imperious in bearing, despite the homespun and workworn garments of a messenger. The man handed his horse into the care of the stable boy and followed him inside. Gwenny was staring at her mistress, puzzled as she gently urged her with a light touch upon her arm further towards the door of the house.

Philippa forced herself to move from the spot, to walk on as if nothing more unusual had occurred, as if the man who had arrived was of no interest to her. Her whole body screamed out its need to rush into the house and seek out her mother, blurt out her news with its stark warning.

The Earl of Wroxeter, her father, had just ridden into the courtyard—and Rhys Griffith was still in the house.

Chapter Six

Philippa found her mother and grandmother in the hall overseeing the setting up of a trestle table to receive Sir Daniel's body. Two of the older women servants had already arrived with an ewer of warm water, towels and sweet-scented salve for anointing. She hastened to stand beside her mother, looking anxiously around for sign of Sir Rhys Griffith. Then she discovered that he was at the door, beckoning in the men bringing in the carrying chair with its sad burden. It had been a more difficult task than usual lifting it up the steps before the hall door, since the men were afraid to jar it unduly. Philippa gave a little smothered sob and her mother reached out and touched her arm in comfort. The Countess and Lady Gretton appeared calm, though it was plain to see that both women had been weeping.

Philippa watched while the chair was brought close to the trestle and the body of her beloved grandfather carefully lifted and laid out reverently upon it. Lady Gretton bent to kiss the already cooling forehead. Sir Rhys nodded to the two men to retreat with the chair, acknowledging the sorrowing womenfolk with a grave little bow.

'Ladies, I will leave you now to your sad task and wait

in the courtyard for the arrival of the priest, acquaint him with the full circumstances of what has occurred and bring him to you here.'

Lady Gretton nodded her gratitude. 'I am thankful that you were here to order matters for us in such a seemly manner, Sir Rhys,' she said quietly. 'I am sure there must be much to be done on your own manor. Please do not think you must linger here.'

'I shall remain until I am satisfied that all is done which must be done and am sure you have no further need of me.'

He bowed again, his eyes passing to Philippa's forlorn little figure, longing to put his arms about her openly and comfort her, yet knowing that could not be—yet.

She acknowledged his presence with a wan little smile. 'As ever we are in your debt, sir.'

He moved to the screen door and when he had withdrawn she put a hand upon her mother's arm and shook it gently but with a real sense of urgency.

'Ma mère, I would speak to you within your chamber.'

The Countess frowned. 'Child, you can see that it is impossible for me to leave your grandmother at this time.'

Lady Gretton shook her head sadly. She put out a hand and touched Philippa's hand reassuringly. 'This is a difficult time for you, child, one to which you are not accustomed. I pray the Virgin such an occasion will not come to you again for a long time. You must be deeply shocked, having been with him when—when it happened.'

'Nevertheless, Philippa must realise how necessary it is that I stay with you now, Mother,' the Countess said firmly. 'She should go to her own chamber until she is more in control but I see Gwenny is with you, child, and you must manage alone, for a while at least. I will come to you when I can.'

Philippa looked at her piteously. 'My need is urgent, ma mère. You must know I would not ask else.'

Lady Gretton glanced hastily at Philippa and recognised that her pale face was not only revealing signs of shock and grief but real alarm. She said quietly, 'I think you should go with her, Cressida. Philippa is no foolish child to have a fit of the vapours whatever the cause. Go and speak with her.'

The Countess shrugged helplessly, then bent and kissed her dead father upon the cheek, nodded to the two silent attendants and pushed Philippa gently towards the spiral stair which led upwards to their bed chambers. Philippa turned at its foot and dismissed Gwenny, who was wringing her hands within her apron and hovering nearby, uncertainly.

'Gwenny, go and find Master Fairley and ask him to come to the Countess's chamber as soon as he can.'

Glad of something to do at such a difficult time Gwenny sped off, thankfully, upon her errand.

Once within their chamber, Cressida Telford faced her daughter almost angrily, then, yet more irritated as Philippa waited to bar the door against any possible intruder.

'Philippa, what can possibly cause you to act in this way now?' She broke off abruptly as, like her mother, she saw also how pale and frightened Philippa truly was.

Now Philippa wasted no more time, having established that they were closeted together in private. 'Father rode in as I crossed the courtyard. He is dressed as a serving man and is unlikely to be instantly recognised, but Rhys Griffith is still here and soon the priest will arrive and many other notables from the district to pay their respects. Some of our neighbours may well remember the Earl from past dealings.'

Cressida's face whitened and she sank down upon the bed, a trembling hand to her lips.

'You are sure—?'

'Of course I am sure. How could I be mistaken—even under such grievous circumstances?'

'Is he alone?'

Philippa nodded. 'He went into the stables. Does the head groom know him?'

'Yes, and will take precautions to see that your father remains well hidden for the present, be assured of that, but, as you say, this is the worst possible moment for him to arrive and we must take every care.'

There was a knock upon the door and Philippa hurried close to it to call, 'Who is it?'

'Peter, my lady.'

She fumbled to unlatch it and let him in.

He bowed to them both. Clearly he had been hurrying. 'My apologies, my lady, for being absent from the manor at this time of grief. I have just ridden in.'

'Did you go into the stable?' Philippa interrupted him.

'No.' He looked from one to the other of them, sensing something was wrong, even of more moment than the sudden death of Sir Daniel. 'Gwenny was in the courtyard and she insisted I come at once to your chamber. She it was who informed me—told me that Sir Daniel had died very suddenly. I left my horse in the care of a groom and came at a run. I could see that Lady Gretton was in the hall—' He broke off, averting his eyes from the naked grief he saw reflected in the gaze of the two who faced him.

'My father rode into the courtyard less than an hour ago, when they were—carrying my *grandpère*…' Philippa turned away then hastily back to him. 'Sir Rhys Griffith is still here and there will be other visitors arriving soon, the priest…'

Peter nodded hastily. 'Where is he now, Lady Philippa? Have you spoken with him?'

'No, I had no opportunity. Gwenny was with me. He is disguised, but—'

'But there will be many notables hereabouts who will still remember him,' Peter agreed.

'Our head groom will keep him within the stable for now, but—' the Countess said distractedly.

'I will go at once, my lady, and make arrangements to get him to safety, at least until nightfall.' He considered. 'There must be trusted servants who will shelter him. He came here once or twice after your marriage and was well loved.'

'Indeed, yes,' Cressida breathed. 'Our blacksmith, Rob Taylor, lives within the manor precincts. I am sure he would shelter my lord Martyn for the moment, but while the funeral arrangements are in prospect he should be got away soon, from the house, to Ludlow possibly.'

Peter smiled somewhat ruefully. 'My lord will not go without seeing you both, I wager, my lady, but he will see the need for added caution.' His brows drew together. 'I cannot imagine what has brought him here, now, when all in the country are talking of the recent death of Prince Arthur and how the King, desirous to make a new marriage for the Infanta, has ordered his officials to ensure that all is quiet within the realm and any malcontents arrested. My lord is well aware of that.'

Philippa was about to answer, then bit back her suggestion. She knew that her father was angered by the scurrilous report of Sir James Tyrell's alleged confession to the murder of the Princes, but her father had known of that for some time. Had he come to the manor to investigate, in person, the possibility of an arranged marriage between herself and Rhys Griffith? If so, she had placed him in danger. Her *grandpère* had said something about consulting him, yet he must have been very near to Gretton to receive such a message so soon.

Her mother turned to her, noting her increased distress. 'Philippa, you will be the best person to keep Sir Rhys Griffith occupied and well away from the stable while Peter makes arrangements for your father's safety.' She had made no attempt to wrap up the fact that the family was well aware of Sir Rhys's determination to make her his bride. Philippa bit her lip uncertainly. She had no wish, at this moment, to deliberately play to his desires, yet she knew well that at this hazardous time everything depended upon her. She bowed her head obediently as Peter ducked his head courteously to her mother and hastened from the chamber. He had had no time to offer his formal condolences. These normal courtesies must be set aside in face of a possible disaster. The Earl of Wroxeter must not be taken at Gretton—for the sake of everyone within the manor, as well as his own.

Cressida appealed to Philippa wordlessly as she took both her daughter's hands within her own. 'Be very careful. Keep Rhys Griffith from the stable as long as you possibly can. Naturally he will announce his intention to depart soon and—'

Philippa squeezed her mother's hands reassuringly. 'Do not be worried. Go back to Grandmother and act normally. When all is clear and Sir Rhys gone from Gretton, I will return to the hall to pray with you before the bier.'

She hated deception in any form but, for now, she must behave as the distressed woman he had seen in the garden, a woman who needed his comfort. Not that I do not, she reflected inwardly, but I am not so poor spirited a creature that I would break down now, when all have need of me.

A brief glimpse into the hall, as she sped towards the

screen door, told her that her grandmother and the two attendant women were still engaged in their melancholy task.

Sir Rhys was still in the courtyard, apparently waiting for the priest to arrive, and in talk with Sir Daniel's steward. Gwenny was emerging from the dairy and Philippa thought she had probably been gossiping with one of her friends. She summoned her as she approached Sir Rhys.

He turned at once and issued some instruction to their steward. He could see the marks of recent tears still upon her cheeks and came to her at once. 'You should be resting, Lady Philippa.'

She gave a deliberately hasty glance, first at the steward and then at Gwenny. 'I—I would have talk with you, sir, in private,' she faltered, 'perhaps within the garden…'

He took her arm at once sympathetically and led her through the rose arch, nodding to Gwenny to keep some distance behind them.

'Is your grandmother unwell, or your mother?'

She gave a little shuddering breath. 'They are obviously deeply upset but—are engaged in the laying out…' She half turned away. She had no need to assume deep distress. She could still not come to terms with the way her grandfather had died, believing that she was the cause, and her heart was pounding within her breast as she realised how close to arrest her father could be. She could not lose them both in one day. That would be too cruel.

She turned back to Sir Rhys. 'They are both so dreadfully shocked that I would not have them discover…'

He took her to the bench where he had conducted her first after his discovery of Sir Daniel's body. 'Sit down, Lady Philippa, you must be feeling faint. Your maid is within call.'

'I must beg of you…' she turned a piteous countenance

towards him '…not to reveal to my mother and *grandmère* just how—how you found me.'

'I will not say anything which you do not wish me to say, Lady Philippa, but I say again, you have no call to reproach yourself. Your grandfather's death was brought about by nothing you did.'

'But it was,' she insisted. 'I—we—quarrelled. I upset him by countering his wishes. He got agitated…'

He sighed. 'Unfortunately, in your grandfather's state, any small incident that occurred which might have annoyed him could have brought about severe agitation…'

'There you are, then, I did cause his death. If my grandmother were to discover that she would be further hurt…'

'I assure you, she will discover nothing of this from me.' He frowned slightly. 'Though I confess, I am at a loss to consider how anything your grandfather demanded of you could have caused such a violent revulsion to the suggestion.'

She took further refuge in tears, unwilling to provide him with an answer to that question. 'It was just that—' she gulped '—you know how anxious he was to ensure my safety and, after what happened to poor Nan Freeman, he ordered me to remain close to the manor house. Foolishly, I argued with him about it.'

'I see.' He gave a faint smile. 'I can understand your unwillingness to be confined, Lady Philippa, but this was such a small matter. I am sure that had he not—had things turned out differently, he would have relented and allowed you more freedom, provided that you were accompanied by a responsible servant or, perhaps, by your father's squire.'

She detected, as usual, a faint note of disapproval when he mentioned Peter. He looked down her at gravely and she avoided his eye. She could not let him know that she was aware of his offer for her hand—certainly not now. Her heart was pounding again and she felt a real physical ache in the knowledge that his nearness was agitating her. Earlier, in the first full, terrible access of her grief, he had held her close and she had never felt so safe with any man, save her father. At this moment she longed for him to put his arms around her again and hold her close, assure her that nothing else could possibly go wrong, that he would keep her and hers clear of all harm. She could have appealed to him, she knew that. One tiny gesture, one word of weakness on her part and he would do so, but she could not. She must keep him at arm's length, while encouraging him to believe that she relied upon him, needed him. She must do this until she was assured that her father was ensconced in a place of safety, or until Sir Rhys left the manor. Only then could they all breathe again. Grief and terror were tearing her apart.

He was standing before her, looking deeply into her eyes, and she knew he was uncertain how to behave at this moment, longing to take advantage of her distress yet unwilling to give rein to this base urge which he thought unworthy of him. She looked slightly to his right, not wishing to meet his anxious gaze and saw with relief that Peter had arrived at the rose arch and was talking to Gwenny. Her maid was gesturing towards the bench and Peter started towards the two of them. Hastily Philippa rose to her feet at his approach, her eyes appealing to him for reassurance.

'The priest has arrived, Sir Rhys,' Peter said quietly. 'I came in search of Lady Philippa, thinking she would wish to be present when he begins his prayers for the dead.'

'Indeed,' Sir Rhys replied, 'and I do not wish to intrude. Assure Lady Gretton that a messenger to my manor can bring me the moment she has need of any service I can render her.'

He bowed to Philippa and tentatively she offered him her hand, which he turned over and kissed upon the palm. 'Try to accept what happened as natural and right, Lady Philippa. Your grandfather loved you dearly, as he has told me many times. Your presence here had given him joy. He would not wish you to make yourself too unhappy in the future. He would want you to look back on this short time you had together with pleasure. I know it does not seem like that to you now but later, I am sure, your lady mother will be able to convince you that it was so.'

Her fingers trembled within his hold. He bowed stiffly to Peter and strode off towards the entrance to the stables.

Philippa let out a pent-up breath. 'I tried to keep him occupied until—until—'

Peter took her chilled fingers and began to guide her back to the manor house. 'All is well, the Earl is safely hidden. I will conduct your father to see you both when it is safe to do so. Come now back into the hall.'

At the door to the hall they could hear through the screen doors the murmur of voices together in prayers for the dead, led by the village priest. Peter bent very low to whisper in Philippa's ear as she was about to pass through, 'You should be too distressed to sleep without your mother close tonight. Remain with her in her chamber and keep Gwenny in yours.'

She glanced at him searchingly and he nodded, then he led her into the hall and, together, they approached the bier.

It was a simple matter to do as Peter suggested. Gwenny readily accepted Philippa's avowed need to sleep in her mother's bed. When the thick oaken door was closed on the maid, Philippa was convinced she would soon fall asleep and allow her mother and herself private talk with her father. Lady Gretton had gone to her own chamber, worn out with grief and worry about the future and Cressida drew her daughter into her bed and held her close. Both wept silently and Philippa was glad of her mother's nearness as, despite the summer evening, she felt chilled.

When she heard Peter's soft scratching upon the outer chamber door she slipped from the bed and let him and his hooded and cloaked companion in.

The Earl swept his daughter into his arms then gently, hurriedly, pushed her away and went to the bed where his wife sat waiting. Over his shoulder he said softly, 'Keep watch outside, Peter.'

His squire hastened to do his bidding and Philippa watched him leave, then anxiously barred the door from within. She stood back a little, her heart beating so fast she thought it would burst from the cage of her ribs as she watched her parents embrace hungrily. She had always known how deeply they loved each other and the sacrifices Cressida had made, cheerfully, in order to remain with her husband in exile. Dully she wondered if she would know such happiness, even if she should only have it for short snatches of time as her parents had.

At last Wroxeter turned to his daughter and, seated upon the bed with one arm tightly clasped round his wife's shoulder, drew her, also, into the embrace. 'My two darlings,' he whispered hoarsely, 'how I have longed to hold you close and comfort you from the moment I arrived and heard the news. I had hoped to speak with Daniel before—' He shook his head angrily as his wife made a conscious effort to stem her tears. He addressed Philippa, glancing towards the door between his wife's and daughter's chamber. 'You have a maid?'

Philippa nodded. 'I am sure she is fast asleep. She is very young and always does so quickly. The door is very stout, as are all the walls, and I doubt she could hear us if we speak softly. Are you safely bestowed?'

'Yes, with Taylor, the blacksmith, he would never betray me, nor, I think, would Daniel's steward or many of the household, but it is as well if the fewer, rather than the many, know of my presence here, for their own sakes.' He grimaced. 'My timing is bad. The house will be full of county nobles by the morrow until after the funeral. I need to get to Ludlow and find quiet lodgings as soon as possible. Young Richard Allard is there; he met me when I landed and has been with me since. He will arrange a safe lodging for me if Peter can reach him there tomorrow. He must find some errand which necessitates him leaving the manor house.'

While he was speaking Philippa was taking in the beloved lineaments of his face; the dark hair, still thick and plentiful, but greying now at the temples, the long face with the thick, black brows and the heavy-lidded eyes that gave their owner a sleepy appearance, which belied the brilliance of the man. How big he was, and strong still; so reassuring to be held close in those muscular arms which had lifted her high and swung her round in play during childhood. Tears came thick and fast as she thought how much she loved him and feared for his peril, yet it was so good to have him here, if only for so short a time as they dared manage together.

Her mother said quietly, 'You know how wonderful it is for us to see you, Martyn, especially at this time of sorrow, when we need your love so badly, but tell us why you are here. Is it for political reasons? If so, when my father says the King is over-anxious concerning security, was it not unwise to venture here?'

'Yes, my heart, and you know well I do not always consider my own safety as paramount, not even when I should spare you your fears. I came for two reasons: first, to test out the reaction of our Yorkist friends to this scurrilous and baseless accusation against the late King which was published following Tyrell's execution. The Duchess Margaret, naturally, is deeply distressed by it and needs to know how it will affect the loyalty of those who profess themselves still true to us.'

Philippa murmured, 'More than likely Sir James was tortured while in the King's hands and forced to sign a confession. You know that Richard Allard was, and could have been, more badly manhandled had not the Queen come to his rescue. If such was the case we have to excuse Sir James, surely.'

'Of course, if that were the case, I would be the first to do so,' her father said, tautly, 'but I think it more likely the confession was never made at all. It would be a simple matter for the King's minions to say what they liked after the man was safely dead and could not refute the accusation. Tyrell was never my favourite person, but he served the late King faithfully and for a time was entrusted with the security of the young Princes. I am here to ensure our friends know, without a semblance of doubt, that both Princes were living until after the fatal summer of 1485 and that I can personally assure them of that.'

Philippa said, 'I believe that Richard Allard was convinced that Perkin Warbeck was the younger Prince. He saw him with young Warwick and said the likeness was uncanny, even though he had doubted earlier when he had served Perkin in the field.'

'Mmm.'

Philippa noted that her father neither refuted nor accepted the comment and she added, 'Richard also said that there was a possibility that another Prince was still living in secrecy in the north. He mentioned it because Jake Garnet and his son-in-law, Josh, from the Golden Cockerel inn, which served as a Yorkist safe base, were headed there when we were forced to leave London after helping Richard escape.'

Her father shot her a frowning glance at this and she flushed doubtfully, fearing that she had touched on some fact he would rather she had not known. He gave a slight shrug. 'Who knows? There were many rumours, as we are all too well aware. I only know that their uncle certainly did not murder them. Indeed, why should he do so when young Warwick, his nephew, who some said had more rightful claim to the throne, was left living to challenge him for it at some later date?' He gave a little irritated moue. 'I wonder that any sensible soul can believe such a tale? Would it have been possible to conceal the bodies when Henry took possession of the Tower so soon after Redmoor and all servants and officials questioned and threatened with torture, as they assuredly must have been? But folk have ever been ready to listen to scurrilous gossip about their betters, especially gossip so ardently fed to them and concerning murder! If Henry is so sure now, having obtained a confession, why has he not had the bodies exhumed? Apparently the tale appears to tell where the murderers put their victims? No, it is my work to seek out the truth of all this and know whether or not the confession was indeed fabricated or obtained, as you say, under duress, as the Warbeck confession undoubtedly was.'

Cressida gave a great start. 'But to go near any of the officials at this time would be putting your own head in the noose, Martyn. Now that my father is dead...'

'I know,' he said gravely. 'Under the circumstances, I must put your safety first and get you and Philippa back to Burgundy the moment the obsequies are over—that is, unless…' he turned to Philippa searchingly '…what Daniel informed me in his letter is true, which was that Rhys Griffith has offered for your hand and that you would be willing to grant it.'

Philippa put a hand to her mouth to cover her sudden cry of distress. 'You came to see for yourself…'

'I did indeed. You are very precious to me, Philippa. I had to know from your own lips what you wished me to reply to this request.'

'You cannot be serious, Father. The man's father fought for King Henry…'

'I know that well enough, Philippa, but Rhys himself was scarcely more than a boy at the time of Redmoor and you not even conceived. What we have to consider is what is best for you now—in the present.'

She said, dully, 'And you consider this best for me, to be wed to the man who inherited your lands, those which were won by his own father's treachery?'

He reached forward and ruffled her bright hair. 'Your grandfather indicated that he believed you had some tender feelings for the man. Can that be true?'

She was about to refute the assertion then found she could not, and be true to herself.

'I believe him to be a good man,' she said falteringly, 'fair to his servants and those under his command and—and he has been good to me, rescued me from several dangerous situations. He has never…' she hesitated '…offered me any discourtesy nor even spoken of his desire—' She broke off, confused.

'And you, what are your feelings? It could be a fair match, Philippa, despite all considerations to the contrary. You would have a secure future and I could wish you to be able to stay here in your native land and live in peace,

but I would not force you to this. If you could live in amity
with this man, of whom I have heard many good reports,
I would be willing to give my consent, though parting with
you will cost me dear.'

'I should not be able to see you and Mother again, be
parted from you for ever,' she murmured brokenly.

'Not necessarily. If you obtained your husband's consent, you could visit us in Burgundy.'

'But there would be a risk. If at any time I should unwittingly betray your confidence to him...'

His expression became grave. 'So, you have considered
that, therefore you have also thought of a possible future
with Rhys Griffith.'

She hung her head. She could never lie to her father nor
yet avoid a direct answer. 'Yes,' she whispered so softly
that he had to bend close to catch her answer. 'Yes, if I
am honest with myself, I have found at times that—that
his nearness excites me and against my own will I am
stirred to tender thoughts of him. Whatever is decided, I
wish him happiness.'

His touch upon her hair was gentle and affectionate. 'I
think, already, I have lost you, child. No loving father is
ever willing to give away his chick, especially if that chick
is his only one and doubly precious, but no loving father
puts his own desires first either but must give way and
decide what is best for his beloved.' He bent and lifted her
chin so that she was gazing up into his eyes. 'This is a
time of deep emotional turmoil, Philippa. You must make
no hasty decisions while your heart sorrows, but your final
yea or nay must be soon. I would have your answer before
I am forced to leave the realm. You understand?'

She nodded and he released her chin and turned to his
wife, who had remained thoughtfully silent throughout the

exchange between father and daughter. 'You have met this man and would approve the match?'

'Yes, Martyn, I would. Rhys Griffith loves Philippa deeply, I am convinced of it and, from what I have observed of his conduct, I am sure he would make her a loving and considerate husband. But,' she added, 'like you, I would not have her over-pressed to accept him against her own strong convictions.'

He took her into his arms and kissed her again. 'I must go, my heart. I will try to see you both again before I leave the country.'

'Take no foolish risks…'

'I swear I will not.' He sighed. 'I would that I could stand beside you openly at this time of sorrow, but I should only endanger you all. Daniel knew well in his heart how I trusted and admired him. He will rest in his grave knowing he kept faith.'

Philippa ran into her father's arms, wetting his rough homespun jerkin with her tears, then she unlatched the door and stood back as it was opened. Peter Fairley appeared and nodded that all was well. The Earl took one quick glance backwards, saying, 'Send me word of your decision soon, Philippa, and the Virgin guide you well in your choice.' Then he was gone and mother and daughter sank back again on the bed clinging tightly to each other for comfort and weeping bitterly.

Both women slept badly and Philippa was in a sorrowful and distressed mood as she went down to breakfast. Her grandmother, naturally, had much upon her mind and appeared distracted. There was still much to be arranged and the moment the hasty meal was over she left them to go to the kitchens to ensure that guests arriving for the funeral on the morrow would be well provided for. The Countess was silent. She sat, nervously pleating the skirts of her black mourning gown. A similar one had been provided for Philippa, but it had had to be altered in haste for it was far too large, having been her grandmother's and a tearful Gwenny had been left to complete the stitching. The girl did not appear to have noted anything unusual during the night and repeatedly said how she had slept heavily, worn out by the stresses of the day before.

'Oh, mistress,' she whispered forlornly, as she dressed Philippa's bright hair, 'who would have thought your visit would have ended so badly? Sir Daniel, he could be strict, but he was a good master for all that, and we all loved him.'

'Thank you, Gwenny, it is good of you to be so consoling. It will be a difficult time for all of us over the next few days and we must try not to distress Lady Gretton by our own show of sorrow any more than we can help. She has much to bear and will need our practical help.'

She went down into the hall and viewed her grandfather's corpse, now decently clad in his best and washed and anointed. Her mother knelt with other members of the household at his side and Philippa bent and kissed the stone-cold features. Her tears came freely again as she felt convinced she had brought about his hasty passing by her own stubbornness.

She whispered in her mother's ear, 'I would like to go into Ludlow with Peter, if I can be spared.'

The Countess rose and moved away from the bier with her. 'There is little you can do here today, but is that wise?'

Philippa avoided her mother's gaze, staring across to the glazed window above the small dais where the family sat at meals.

'I feel so—confused,' she said wretchedly. 'I cannot

come to terms with any of this and—and I feel I cannot meet Sir Rhys again so soon until I—I have made my decision. His presence—disturbs me. He will be here soon to support Grandmother, I am sure of it, and I need to be away—just for a little time.'

Cressida considered and finally nodded. 'Yes, perhaps that is just as well. I know, from experience, how momentous such a decision can be and—and you have much to bear at present. Peter is to see Richard Allard and that may cheer you somewhat. He will be able to tell you news of Anne. I know you miss her companionship sorely.' She hesitated then said quickly, 'You would be enabled to see more of Anne and Richard if—if you agree to remain in England.'

Philippa turned back to her, gazing up into her mother's lovely eyes directly, then she gave a heavy sigh and inclined her chin. 'Our first need is to ensure Father's safety. Do you think he will endanger himself with his need to meet with other Yorkists at this time?'

'I fear so, but I am used to living with this danger.' Her mother's smile was a trifle bitter. 'It is the price of true love, Philippa.'

Philippa recalled, as she made her way to the stables to discover if Peter had yet left the manor, that her dear friend, Anne, had been equally reluctant to give herself to Richard for the same reason and had confessed to Philippa that this constant fear for the safety of the loved one had torn her own mother apart and would do the same for her if she was foolish enough to give way to her heart's wish. Yet she had done so. She had married her Richard and gone into exile with him, parting from all she loved at home, for the first months at least. Could, she, Philippa, commit herself to Rhys Griffith, allow the first stirrings of desire to grow and be fanned in to flames of passion? For today at least she must stay far from him while she carefully worked out what her answer to her father would be.

She found Peter and, though he was reluctant to take her with him, he agreed finally and they rode out together. He seemed preoccupied and she did not press him to talk. Either his thoughts were concerned with arrangements to take his master to a place of safety or he had been told of one of the reasons for the Earl's presence at Gretton and was disturbed by the thought of Philippa's impending decision. Guiltily she remembered that Rhys Griffith believed Peter Fairley entertained tender thoughts towards her and, since she could in no way return them, she was uncomfortable in his presence for the first time since childhood. She was deeply fond of Peter, but always had considered him as friend, almost the brother she had never had, and thoughts of love between them had simply never entered her head.

Ludlow was busy since it was market day and Peter led her to an inn near the castle, the Golden Fleece. A whispered discussion with the burly innkeeper was followed by his return to her side with the information that Master Allard was lodged in the front private chamber and believed to be there. They climbed the stair and were admitted after a knock and an announcement of their identities.

Philippa was overjoyed to see Richard, after an interval of almost four years and he hugged her warmly. He did not appear to be changed, only the little laughter lines around his eyes had deepened and, as usual, his abundant brown hair was unruly and needed a comb.

He seated her upon the bed, for the chamber was small and cramped and boasted little furniture and, after asking after her need of refreshment and discovery that she required nothing, turned his attention to Peter.

'I imagine some crisis has arisen or you would not have sought me out so soon.'

Peter put him in the picture immediately and Richard's normally jovial expression became grave.

'I am so sorry about your grandfather,' he said, turning to Philippa, 'but I can see the urgent need to get your father away from Gretton. There must be many of the guests expected to attend the funeral who know him.'

Peter said brusquely, 'That is all very well, Richard, but you know my lord Earl. He is determined to complete his mission. There are several people in the area he wishes to see and I cannot persuade him to leave for the coast at once which I consider advisable.'

Richard Allard stroked his chin thoughtfully. 'Sir Owen Lewis owns a manor some twenty miles from here. He was my father-in-law Sir Guy Jarvis's squire and, though he later fought for the Tudor at Redmoor, he was sufficiently loyal enough to his old master to help me when I was in trouble at Westminster. It might be possible for me to go and sound him out and discover if he would be willing to accommodate the Earl and I just for the next few days. His house would be the safest place possible. He has served the present King and would be regarded as thoroughly trustworthy, unlikely to receive a company of officials poking their noses into his business.'

'But can he be trusted?' Philippa burst out.

'Sir Owen could very well refuse outright to shelter a man he considers a rebel, but I do not believe he would betray us,' Richard said bluntly. 'I can think of no other safe house for the present. Like Peter here, my advice to your father would be to leave the district at once but I doubt he would heed it.'

Philippa swallowed hard. She was only too well aware that what both said of her father was true. She said awkwardly, 'Peter, could you go below and order dinner for us all here later? I—I would talk privately with Richard for a while.'

Peter cast her a hasty glance, but rose at once to do her bidding.

Richard Allard noted the marks of recent tears upon Philippa's cheeks and her somewhat hunted expression, which puzzled him. Grief he expected, but this strange bewilderment he could not understand. He said gently, 'Are you in some trouble, Philippa, which you would rather Peter is not aware of?'

'I need to talk to someone who—who knows me and would understand,' she said wretchedly. 'Since you and Anne are so very dear to me I thought I might confide in you and feel you would advise me as well as Anne would herself.'

'Then let us walk for a short while in the town. Will Peter object?'

She shook her head. 'I do not think so. He knows—that something is wrong and—and that I cannot unburden myself to him.'

He took her arm and led her below stairs. Peter was engaged in talk with the innkeeper and Richard called to him of their intentions. He turned and acknowledged them but made no objection, as Philippa had hoped.

They walked for a short while in silence then Richard said quietly, 'Is Peter in love with you, Philippa?'

'I do not know, but I fear he is becoming too aware of me as a woman.'

He glanced at her, smiling. 'The Virgin knows that would not be difficult for any man. I recognised your growing maturity when we first met in Westminster Palace four years ago. Anne was decidedly jealous, though she would never confess it.' He chuckled and Philippa smiled also. She was well aware that though Richard Allard would admire her beauty, his heart was given completely to Anne, his wife, and to her alone. He added reflectively, 'Then if it is not Peter's desires which concern you, who is it?'

She gave a little gasp at his perception. 'Sir Rhys Griffith is our neighbour. He has—proved himself a good friend to my grandparents and has been a constant visitor to Gretton since the day we arrived there; indeed, he happened to meet us first at Milford Haven and escorted us home.'

'Does he know who you are?'

'Yes, and he has asked for my hand. My grandfather wrote to my father requesting an answer and that is one of the reasons why he has come to the manor—to see me in person.'

'And what is his opinion of this match?'

'I think—believe—' she floundered '—I think he is in favour of it but—but he leaves the decision to me.'

'And you have some dislike of Griffith, or is that feeling stronger—revulsion, perhaps?'

'No, no, Rhys Griffith is very—personable. He is wealthy and owns my father's lost lands and I—I believe he loves me.'

'And you, what are feelings for him?'

She was silent and he waited patiently for her answer.

'I cannot marry him. He is the King's man,' she whispered at last uncertainly.

'But that is no answer to my question.'

She turned at last and faced him squarely. 'I am not sure,' she murmured miserably, 'but—but he excites me and...'

'Oh, indeed?' Richard's heavy brows rose in amused interrogation and she turned upon him indignantly.

'Do not tease me, Richard, I implore you. Can I trust him? Would I have to part with my parents for ever?'

He gave a faint shrug. 'Who knows, *chérie*? Times change. The King cannot live for ever and, after all, young Henry is Edward IV's grandson. While he will not, I vouch, restore your father's lands, he could well pardon him, as I was pardoned.'

'But all the time you must be circumspect—and my father is never that.'

'Never,' he agreed, a little smile playing about his mobile mouth. 'I take it you would be agreeable to the match if you thought you could trust your groom with your father's safety?'

Again she turned away and he waited, then he said, 'You know Anne was at first reluctant to trust herself to me because she was afraid of my dangerous activities?'

'Yet you have not changed.'

'No, I have not changed, yet she loves me still. Her heart is torn when I am absent from her side, but life with me is preferable to life without me, I imagine. I am a lucky fellow and so is this Griffith, if he has your love.'

Her cheeks were colouring rosily and she was about to answer when she found herself accosted by a familiar voice.

'Lady Philippa, I did not expect to find you in Ludlow this morning.'

To her dismay, Philippa saw Rhys Griffith across the street and striding determinedly towards them.

Philippa panicked. If Rhys Griffith saw her talking to Richard Allard, he might well suspect that she and Peter had come into Ludlow to meet with him and, worse, guess at the reason for that. As if in answer to her silent prayer, a man's voice at her side said gently, 'How good it was of you, Mistress Weston, to come into Ludlow to see how I fared.'

She turned, her eyes widening in surprise, to find the young merchant, Master Maynard, leaning heavily on a cane by her side. He still appeared pale and his leg looked to be tightly strapped to some sort of splinted support, but he was smiling and walking gamely though slowly. Rhys Griffith reached them at the very moment she opened her lips to reply to the merchant's greeting. She saw that he was frowning but, obviously prevented from questioning her, as she feared, by the presence of her two companions.

Master Maynard addressed him. 'I understand, Sir Rhys, that I am under an obligation to you for the care afforded to me. I am most grateful. Unfortunately it will be some time yet before I am able to leave Ludlow but, as I am sure Mistress Weston here is anxious to discover, I am progressing very nicely.'

Rhys Griffith forced a smile. 'So I see,' he observed. He looked pointedly towards Richard Allard who was silently waiting to see how matters progressed, surveying the newcomer with interest. Philippa could hardly avoid introducing Richard to Griffith.

'Master Allard, Sir Rhys Griffith, our neighbour, who has been most kind to us at Gretton, especially during the unfortunate circumstances of my kinsman's death. Master Allard is an acquaintance, his wife my very dearest friend. I was amazed to find that he is here in Ludlow on business. I came, as Master Maynard observed, to see for myself how he is.'

She was surprised to find that her voice had not trembled, though her legs felt like water, and she met Rhys Griffith's challenging stare directly. 'Since Peter and I were the first to discover Master Maynard injured, I felt it incumbent upon me to see how he was.'

Rhys Griffith bowed somewhat frigidly to Richard Allard who responded, smilingly, his grey eyes twinkling. Philippa had observed from experience that Richard could behave with perfect aplomb during difficult and dangerous encounters.

Rhys said tartly, 'You will realise that Mistress Weston is in mourning and will be unable to stay from Gretton long. You say that you were escorted by your squire, Master Fairley? Where is he?' The note was steely and she forced a confident smile. 'He is enquiring in the Golden Fleece for Master Maynard, but I came out to get some air and happened to see him walking and was delighted to note how well he is. Master Allard also happens to be lodged at the inn and we were exchanging news of our families.'

Rhys Griffith nodded. 'I imagine you have business in Ludlow, Master Allard. If I am not mistaken, your father's lands are in Yorkshire.'

Richard inclined his head. 'Yes, and my mother inherited lands in the Cotswolds, near Tewkesbury. I am visiting some acquaintance of hers, who lives in this district.'

So Rhys Griffith was well aware of the circumstances of Richard's father's standing in the Yorkist community and was making it clear to them.

Maynard's wide, guileless blue eyes regarded the group jovially. 'I am sorry to hear of the death of your kinsman, Mistress Weston. It is a kindness indeed that you found that you could spare the time to enquire after my trifling injuries.'

Philippa found herself wondering why the man was so anxious to cover up for her. Had he merely observed her unease when she had seen Sir Rhys approaching and, by quickness of thought, decided to help her? She shot him a relieved glance and found him smiling at her in a friendly but not too familiar manner, though she thought Sir Rhys would probably regard the man's demeanour as insolent. Sir Rhys had been so openly hostile when he had discovered the injured man upon his property that it was no surprise to her that Maynard had guessed at her discomfiture. She herself had been amazed and yet pleased to learn that Sir Rhys had put himself out to attend to the fellow's needs. However, he had warned her against meeting the merchant again and she knew he was displeased if not downright angry to discover her disobeying him and present in Ludlow.

However, he regarded Roger Maynard dispassionately and said, 'You do not appear well enough to be out and about at present. Should you not be back at the inn? Are you not comfortably settled?'

'Certainly, Sir Rhys. Your arrangements for me are excellent. Since it is market day I came to see if the horse coper could provide me with a docile mount for my journey. Alas, he had nothing suitable which I could afford.'

Sir Rhys sniffed. 'What you need is a sturdy little Welsh pony. I will see that the blacksmith in the village finds you one to carry you home. You need not concern yourself about the cost. Since I was forced to dispatch your horse I am prepared to provide a mount for you to travel.'

Philippa was puzzled as to why he should go to so much trouble for a man he apparently still mistrusted, but she could only admit that he was being generous in the extreme. For some reason he was determined to be rid of the man as soon as decently possible.

Sir Rhys said abruptly, 'Perhaps, Master Allard, you would assist Master Maynard to the inn. I am sure he has been on that injured leg for too long as it is.' Pointedly he added, 'I will escort Mistress Weston to the Golden Fleece in a few moments and then, once she is reunited with her squire, back home.'

Philippa's heart sank. Not only was she to be deprived of Richard's company and assurances that he would make arrangements for her father, but she would have to account to Rhys Griffith for her absence from Gretton at a time when she would have been expected to be there, assisting her mother and grandmother with all that needed to be done before the funeral. Richard bowed and his grey eyes met hers deliberately. She read in them the assurance she needed and made a little curtsy in reply.

'Convey to Anne my love and good wishes for the future, Richard, and kiss your little one for me.'

He nodded, smiling, outwardly unaffected by the unwelcome encounter, then he offered an arm to the limping Maynard and turned towards the Golden Fleece.

Before she could move to follow, Rhys Griffith caught at Philippa's arm, his grip hard, and she thought she would see an ugly bruise upon her wrist later.

'What are you doing in Ludlow?' he grated harshly. 'Do you not know that the proprieties require you to remain sequestered on the manor at this time?'

She was seething with fury at his assumed domination of her. 'I came,' she said tartly, 'as I explained, to see Master Maynard. Peter was sent to buy more black cloth, which will be required for the servants attending the funeral, and I took the opportunity to accompany him.' She turned away from his accusing stare. 'You must realise how oppressive it is for me—at—at Gretton at the moment. I needed to get away, if only for an hour or two. There was nothing I could do there.'

He made some slight explosive sound and stood firmly before her, fingers gripped aggressively within his sword belt. 'I warned you not to associate with that merchant.'

'It is not your business to order me, nor yet to issue warnings,' she flashed back. 'You have no responsibility for me, sir.'

'Not yet,' he returned grimly. 'Has your mother not informed you that—?'

'Indeed, she has,' she snapped, 'and let me tell you, sir, the notion does not please me, and less so, having regard to your attitude this morning.'

He relaxed his aggressive stance slightly, reddening, whether with anger or embarrassment she could not tell.

'It is unsafe for you to be associating with known Yorkists,' he said more mildly. 'Master Allard was forced to leave the country, I understand, following the execution of the Earl of Warwick and the imposter, Perkin Warbeck, under suspicion of trying to arrange their escape from the Tower.'

'He was later pardoned,' she said acidly, 'and allowed to return to England. His father, Sir Dominick, was wounded at Redmoor and has never completely recovered. He needed Richard's services to run the manor.'

'Nevertheless, you must realise that he will be under constant surveillance,' he retorted, then more earnestly, 'I have only your safety and that of your mother and grandmother in mind when I remind you of these matters.'

She was somewhat mollified by his change of tone and nodded rather coolly. 'I understand, sir, and I thank you, but say again you have no responsibility to me or mine.'

'But it is the most earnest wish of my heart that I should have, Philippa,' he said quickly and he reached out and drew her close by the shoulders this time, though less cruelly. She felt the frantic beating of his heart through the thick velvet of his doublet and the thin silk of her gown and she was almost unable to draw breath. She could never understand this strange excitement which gripped her when she was close to him. Other men had admired her beauty and remarked upon it, for, like her mother, she had learned to accept, from an early age, that she was an object of men's desires, and, they, too, had tried to hold her, even to steal illicit kisses, but she had always been able to manage them before. She had laughed good-humouredly at their foolishness or flayed them with her tongue for their insolence, but she felt quite helpless now as Rhys Griffith held her close to his heart. She had not even the strength of mind to struggle and was horribly near to tears, though she had no explanation for this sudden, unfamiliar emotional weakness.

She said at last, 'Please release me, sir. I—I—have no answer for you yet. I—I must have time to think. This is no time for hasty decisions.'

He released her obediently, though he kept still a light grasp upon her arm. 'I love you, Philippa, I cannot help myself. I want you,' and more thickly and harshly, 'I will have you, whatever the cost.'

'It could be high indeed, sir, consisting of the loss of royalist friends and, more seriously and dangerously, the loss of the King's good will.'

'Do you not think I have not considered that?'

Knowing him, she was sure he had done so. She said softly, 'But what of the sacrifices I must make?'

'Your father must soon be lost to you. Indeed, every married maiden must part from her family. I know your parents must remain in exile, but if you become my bride I shall allow you to visit them when it is possible and expedient. Your mother will agree to the match, Philippa and I have even sent messages to your father to beg for his consent. Will you not give me your hand in marriage and become mistress of all your father's lost lands?'

She could not reveal to him that her father was only too

willing to give his consent. She could only stare back at him dumbly. Perhaps when she knew her father was safe, then—then she might allow the longing within her heart to overcome the fears, which battered at her brain. She shook her head and turned away. 'Take me to the Golden Fleece. Peter will be anxious and we must return to the manor quickly, as you have reminded me, sir.'

He turned towards the inn and then they saw that Peter Fairley was standing at the door surveying the street, obviously concerned about her.

'Very well, I see I must wait for a while longer and this time of grieving is no time to press you, yet I must assure myself of your safety. You must not come again to Ludlow and meet with those who could bring you into danger. Promise me that you will not do so without me in attendance.'

She looked back at him, puzzled. 'What have you against poor Master Maynard?'

'I have no proof of anything, but strangers are suspect at this time. Heed my warnings. I shall be glad when the man is long gone from this district.'

'You think he may be a King's official spy?'

He shrugged. 'Who knows whom to trust? The King sits still uneasy upon the throne and his eyes and ears are everywhere. You, above all, should be aware of that.'

They reached the inn and she smiled at Peter. There was no sign of either Richard Allard, or of Roger Maynard.

'As you see, Peter, I am safe under Sir Rhys's protection. He has offered to escort us home.'

That Peter was not pleased she could read in his expression, but he could make no objection. Sir Rhys strode off to order their mounts brought round and Peter mouthed, 'Richard will attend to your father's safe lodging. I will bring him to Ludlow under cover of darkness.'

She nodded, relieved, as Sir Rhys returned to them, followed by a groom with their horses.

They mounted and took the road together for Gretton Manor.

Chapter Seven

Philippa knelt in the chancel of the parish church beside the newly laid blue slab of Welsh stone which covered her grandfather's grave. Soon the brass designer would come from Bristol to work on the memorial which would show her grandfather in armour as he had been at Redmoor. She had placed a bouquet of late roses on the stone, of several colours, for she'd not dared to put the white roses she would have wished to place there. In these suspicious times that might well have revealed his past allegiance too clearly. She'd begged leave to come alone for it was but a short step from the manor house and her desire to pray before her grandfather's grave by herself had been very pressing.

Lately the house had been full of visitors attending the funeral and solemn requiem and the feast, which had followed. She'd longed to see her father's face though, just once, and when she had visited the grave with her mother the day following the funeral, she had glimpsed a shadowy figure dressed in homespun hovering near the bell tower. Neither she nor her mother had dared to approach the man but her mother's hand, gently pressing her own as they had knelt there, had told Philippa that the Countess was well aware that her husband had risked himself in coming to see for himself where his father-in-law had been bestowed and had hoped to see his wife and daughter there.

Sir Rhys had been present, of course, throughout the solemn proceedings, close to her grandmother's side, ready to offer help and support whenever it had been required. Though he had treated Philippa courteously, he had not once during these early days of mourning pressed her for her answer to his offer of marriage and she knew that he would respect her need for privacy at this time.

Philippa had needed, desperately, to be alone now. She had still not come to terms with what she believed to be her own culpability for Sir Daniel's death. Certainly he had been ill and it was not unexpected but she could still visualise, vividly, their altercation, her own violent reaction to the proposed marriage he had planned for her. She would always feel guilty, though she was aware that she could have acted in no different a fashion.

She gave a sigh as she rose from her kneeling position. There was little chance now for her to have further words with her father. For his own safety he must remain hidden. She and she alone must make this momentous decision and her awkward meeting with Rhys Griffith in Ludlow had only added to her confusion of mind. She was sure that Richard Allard would do everything in his power to ensure that her father reached Sir Owen Lewis's manor and that Sir Dominick Allard's former squire would be willing to offer Wroxeter a safe haven until he could be smuggled to a port and out of England.

She murmured a final hurried prayer and lit a candle with another prayer to the Virgin, begging for intercession for the safe repose of her grandfather's soul, and prepared to leave the church. She turned hastily from the chancel as she heard the sound of booted feet approaching and knew two men were entering the church, one, or both of them, a knight, by the ring of metal spurs on stone. For moments they were hidden from her view by the bulk of the huge ancient stone bowl which formed the baptismal font.

A familiar voice informed her of Sir Rhys's presence.

'Mistress Weston, I had not expected to see you here and regret if we have interrupted your most private moment of prayer.'

She moved towards him. 'Thank you, Sir Rhys, but I have concluded my prayers and am about to leave.'

Her gaze passed to his companion, a tall handsome man, past his youth but still personable, clearly a knight by his spurs and attire. He bowed to her as Sir Rhys presented her.

'Mistress Weston and her mother are kinsmen of Sir Daniel, Sir Howell. You may well have heard them mentioned during the days when you were well acquainted with Sir Daniel and Lady Gretton.'

'I did not have that pleasure.' The voice was pleasant and the stranger eyed her with frank appraisal and curiosity. He was, perhaps, a little older than Philippa's mother, a tall, well-built man with a square, tanned, open countenance, and strong jaw, whose hair was beginning to grey at his temples.

Sir Rhys said, 'Sir Howell Prosser was formerly a neighbour to Sir Daniel and Lady Gretton. He was from the neighbourhood and, indeed, rarely visits his parents' manor these days since his marriage and so has only recently heard of Sir Daniel's death and has come with me this morning to pay his respects.'

Philippa's heart gave a little jolt of alarm. If this man had known her mother in the old days, and it seemed that he had done, could he fail to note her resemblance to Cres-

sida, Countess of Wroxeter, and was his knighthood a
mark of his past allegiance to King Henry? If so, her
mother must be warned and she herself be wary of what
she said to him.

She curtsied. 'Lady Gretton will be pleased to receive
you at the manor, Sir Howell. She is still in deep mourning, of course, but all friends are welcome. My mother and
I are on a short visit only and have delayed our departure
naturally out of her need for company.'

He bowed his head as his eyes roved towards the chancel and she pointed to the new grave slab. 'There is no
inscription yet, sir, and a brass will be laid there soon.'

His voice was pleasantly low-pitched and expressed regret. 'I am truly sorry to hear of Sir Daniel's passing. I
visited Gretton often in the old days and he was good to
me as a boy. Like his daughter, Cressida, I was an only
child and often lonely.'

She half-smiled in answer. He had ceased to regard her
directly and turned to Sir Rhys. 'I will stay within the
church for a while and pray for Sir Daniel's soul. Thank
you for your escort, Sir Rhys but I know you have business
on your manor and I will not delay you. Mistress,' he
addressed Philippa once more, 'would you please inform
Lady Gretton that I will call on her to offer my condolences formally before I leave the district again.'

She curtsied again and, as Sir Rhys moved towards the
church door, she was forced to accompany him. Outside
the sun was bright but low in the sky and she was reminded that autumn was on the way and that she and her
mother had stayed too long at Gretton and should soon be
on their way into exile once more. The village church, of
solid Welsh stone, and the cluster of thatched cottages
which huddled close beside it was pleasing to her eye as
was the rolling hills beyond and she felt a spasm of regret

that she must return to the flatter, less visibly interesting, countryside of Burgundy.

Sir Rhys was regarding her with a curious intensity and she flushed hotly under the scrutiny.

'Always I have to thank you, sir, for the kindness you have shown to all of us at this sorry time. I hope…' her voice faltered a little '…that you will continue to visit Gretton from time to time after we have left. My grandmother will have need of you, I am sure.'

'And you will not?' he queried.

She lifted tear-brimmed green blue eyes to his dark ones. 'Yes, Sir Rhys, I shall continue to have regard for you and deep—gratitude.'

He said, a trifle harshly, 'I cannot press you at this point, but you know that I hold in my heart far stronger feelings for you than regard, Philippa, and I shall not give up. I shall see you again before you depart and, by that time, I hope you will be in a less distressed state and more ready to accept my suit.'

She shook her head, turning from him.

'I regret that our last meeting was less than cordial,' he continued, 'but I must insist that you take due care. Your presence here, without the protection of my name, could bring you all into real danger. I think you are only too aware of that.'

She nodded again.

'Allard has been pardoned, but he will always be carefully watched. He knows that, as well as I do.'

'Master Maynard will soon be leaving Ludlow,' she said defensively.

'Yes, and I shall not be sorry to see the fellow go.'

He turned from her abruptly. 'I will not press my attendance upon you for you have only a step or two to go before reaching your manor and there are plenty of servants about to watch over you.'

He bowed courteously and moved off towards the fence to which his horse and that of Sir Howell Prosser had been hitched. She watched him go regretfully. Her feelings were so mixed. As he turned once in the saddle to acknowledge her, she forced a smile and began to walk slowly back towards the manor. She hoped she would not see him again. It would be too painful. Her brain was too full of the fear of betrayal while she stayed here and now a new threat had materialised in the person of Sir Howell Prosser.

Her mother and Lady Gretton listened gravely to her tale.

'If he were a constant visitor to the manor he cannot fail to recognise you, ma mère,' she said distractedly. 'He looked so closely at me, so much that I trembled for fear he would see my likeness to the girl he had known. With Father so close…' Her voice tailed off doubtfully.

'Howell Prosser was a dear friend to all of us,' Cressida said thoughtfully. 'Indeed, he may well have been a suitor for my hand had not the King dangled an Earl before my father's bedazzled eyes as a better marriage prospect.'

'Your father had no choice, Cressida. It was the King's wish.'

The countess turned, smiling, towards her mother. 'I have no regrets, you know that, Mother. I love Martyn with all my heart, but during our childhood I was beginning to have tender regards for Howell Prosser. Remember, he was the man who helped me leave England following Redmoor in order to join Martyn in exile. That was not the action of a malicious or vengeful man. He continued to care about me and did his best to ensure my happiness. I doubt that he would deliberately endanger me or mine now.'

Philippa drew a hard breath of relief. It seemed that

much of the time she was finding it hard to breathe these days. So many threats and fears assailed her. She was, however, much less sure than her mother that Sir Howell Prosser would regard the presence of his former successful rival within the country as favourably as did the Countess if he should guess at the truth. She could only pray that neither he nor Sir Rhys had any suspicion that a traitor was within their grasp. They must take no risks.

'I still think it would be safer if you withdrew when Sir Howell comes to Gretton,' she said. 'We are here under assumed names and that would not augur well with the authorities should they come to hear of it. Sir Howell might well gossip, however well meaning he might be.'

Both Lady Gretton and Cressida agreed, Cressida reluctantly, as she would have liked to see her childhood companion after this lapse of time and she questioned Philippa eagerly as to his appearance, pondering over the changes time had wrought in both of them.

Sir Howell did call later that day and, when he was announced, Philippa and her mother took to their chamber and remained there until he had left. If he expressed disappointment in not meeting her kinswomen, Lady Gretton did not mention it to them later.

To Philippa's relief Sir Rhys did not put in an appearance next day and she proposed that the following day they should begin to make arrangements for departure. Peter was summoned and sent into Ludlow to sound out any news of Richard Allard and if he had returned to his lodging at the Golden Fleece. Before they left both women were anxious to hear from him again and be assured that the Earl was safely ensconced in a place of safety.

The terrifying blow when it came struck all of them with utter amazement.

Four days after Sir Daniel's funeral, the women were busied within Lady Gretton's still room when they heard the sound of arrivals from the courtyard. Philippa hastened to the small horn window and pushed the casement wide. There were several horses, she was sure, and caparisoned in military fashion; her ears told her that before she caught her first horrifying sight of them.

Five men-at-arms in leather jacks and salets, mounted on destriers and accompanying a lumbering, covered wagon, drawn by two sturdy percherons, of the type used to convey noble ladies from place to place, were dismounting within the courtyard. Their leader looked up towards the manor house before the steward came hastening from the hall steps to greet the arrivals. Philippa's heart raced upwards into her throat, restricting her breathing, or so it seemed, at sight of him. The man wore the rose and portcullis livery of the King's force.

She informed her companions, then said in a breathless whisper, 'What shall we do?'

Her mother took charge of the situation calmly. 'There is nothing we can do until we know what is required of us. There would be no point in hiding as every one of the servants here knows of our presence.' She removed her apron and folded it. 'We can descend to the hall and wait to see what transpires.' Philippa and Lady Gretton removed their own aprons and smoothed down their skirts. Philippa could see that her grandmother's lips were trembling, as were her own. They had dreaded this; the arrival of the King's men could not be said to be unexpected They glanced quickly at each other, as if seeking support, and then unhurriedly did as the Countess had suggested and descended to the hall to greet their unwelcome visitors.

The steward was clearly alarmed and stood by the door as the sergeant-at-arms advanced to greet the three ladies, his booted feet sounding unusually loud on the stone flagged floor.

He bowed to Lady Gretton. 'My lady, I am informed that you have staying here with you a Mistress Weston and her daughter.'

Lady Gretton acknowledged his courtesy coldly and nodded, tight-lipped. 'My kinswomen are here, as you see, sergeant. They came to be with me during my husband's illness and have remained for his obsequies. I cannot see that their presence should alarm the King's officials. They will be departing soon for their home near Bristol.'

The sergeant's gaze passed briefly and dispassionately over Philippa and her mother who were standing ramrod still beside Lady Gretton.

The Countess said tonelessly, 'I am Mistress Weston, sergeant, and this is my daughter. What business can you possibly have with us?'

'That, mistress, I am unable to disclose at present. I am instructed to take you in charge. You will accompany me without question and I must also command you—' here he turned towards Lady Gretton '—to allow no one in your household to discuss anything concerning our arrival here with any person outside the manor house or demesne…' he paused as if for maximum effect '…on pain of dire punishment. Do I make myself clear? I would suggest that you confine your household servants to the house for the present and send your steward to convey my orders to any of the other servants or labourers working on the demesne.'

His words were so commanding and uttered in so harsh a tone that the steward, standing near the door, gave a great gulp of fear.

Lady Gretton moved a trifle nervously. Her eyes revealed her very real alarm, but her voice was steady enough when she replied, 'Certainly you make yourself very clear, sir. Am I to take it·that my kinswomen are under arrest? If so, I would like to be informed on what charge they stand accused.'

The man's gimlet gaze did not shift from her. 'I did not say anyone was under arrest, my lady, merely that I have instructions to take the ladies into my charge.'

'And convey them where?' Lady Gretton demanded, not to be deterred by his stern demeanour.

'That I am not at liberty to tell you.'

'And can I be assured that they will be returned to Gretton soon?'

He gave a slight shrug. 'Possibly. In any event, you will say nothing of what has occurred to anyone—that is, to no passing caller.'

Cressida said quietly, 'I take it my kinswoman is under no threat of punishment, whatever may happen to my daughter and I?'

'At present, no, mistress. I have no instructions to take any steps regarding Lady Gretton.'

'I see.' The Countess moved towards her mother and held out her hand. 'I am convinced we shall be back shortly,' she said as confidently as she could. 'See to it that our servant, Peter, is not unduly alarmed and tell him to wait here for our return.'

White-lipped, Lady Gretton nodded and the two embraced formally since she dared not take her daughter into her arms as closely as she longed to do. Philippa was similarly embraced and felt the touch of her grandmother's chilled lips upon her forehead. She curtsied and squeezed the gnarled hand reassuringly.

The sergeant addressed the steward. 'The ladies will require cloaks and hoods as it may turn cold later. Summon a servant to bring them. There will be no need for further necessities.'

Philippa gave a premonitory shiver of apprehension. At least they were to be afforded warm garments within any prison to which they might be headed. She waited, woodenly, until a very frightened Gwenny appeared, carrying the requested garments. With stiffened fingers she donned the cloak and put up the hood, more to hide her face from the sergeant than because its warmth was needed as yet.

With the nervous steward in tow, the two accompanied the sergeant through the screen doors and down the steps leading below to the courtyard. The men-at-arms were waiting stolidly for further orders beside the wagonette. The sergeant assisted the Countess to climb aboard and take her seat upon one of the wooden benches, which stretched along each side of the interior. Philippa mounted without assistance, imperiously shrugging aside any proffered help. She seated herself opposite her mother and the sergeant drew to the leather curtains so that they could not be afforded any glimpse of the countryside on the way to their destination, nor could they be seen by any passersby on the road. Silently the two women faced each other and, in the dim light, Philippa could see that her mother's lips were moving in prayer. She averted her gaze, not wishing her mother to see that she was close to tears. She heard the jingle and creak of accountrements and felt the slight movement of the wagonette as one of the men mounted to the driving seat. There was a crisp command from the sergeant and his men could be heard mounting up; soon the heavy, unwieldy vehicle began to lumber towards the courtyard arch. They were denied a last sight of Lady Gretton and the frightened servants standing watching the departure from the manor steps.

They dared not speak least they were overheard by the driver. Each was busy with her own frantic thoughts. Where were they headed? Philippa thought it might be Pembroke Castle, though that was many miles distant, and the sergeant had not insisted that they pack for the journey or require changes of undergarments, which would indicate a prolonged stay. Was their identity known? Common sense told Philippa that must be so, since, otherwise, two unknown kinswomen of Lady Gretton would not have been arrested. It was obvious, too, by the closed curtains, that the sergeant had been given instructions to conceal their presence in the wagonette from prying eyes. Why? Were they to be questioned about her father, the Earl? Cold fear broke over her like a douche of icy water. Her mother's fears looked likely to be fulfilled. They were to be held as hostages for the Earl's voluntary surrender and Philippa knew well that, should Wroxeter hear of their arrest, he would undoubtedly come to their assistance. The vehicle rumbled along what appeared to be a main road, to Ludlow perhaps, on the way to a nearby town where officials of the King had their quarters—and likely some prison where suspected persons might be held and interrogated.

The men rode beside the wagonette without chatter. Obviously they had been warned to remain silent to keep their prisoners unaware of their destination or the reason for their arrest. The silence within the closed vehicle was uncanny. The light was dim and the only sounds that reached them were the creak of harnesses and the sound of the horses' hoofs of their wagonette and of their escort. Philippa reached out and took her mother's hand within her own and squeezed. She could feel the cold smoothness of her mother's betrothal and marriage rings and knew what agonies of fear for her beloved husband the Countess was

suffering. He was so near to them—and yet so far. Philippa
prayed silently that he would have the sense to remain
there. Surely, when it was made clear that neither woman
would speak of his presence in England, they would be
released. Then memories of how Richard Allard had suffered while briefly a prisoner in the Tower of London
flooded back. He had been racked, not badly, but sufficient
so as to render him unable to walk for days. Women, she
knew, were not protected by their sex. If necessary they
could be as ruthlessly questioned as he had been and her
legs trembled on the planked floor of the vehicle as she
wondered if she could withstand such terrible pain.

In order to force her mind from that threat, she wondered who could have possibly betrayed them. Could Sir
Howell Prosser have done so? Her mother doubted that
possibility and he had not been told of their identity, had
not even seen either of them closely, during his visit, only
that brief glimpse of her, Philippa, in the uncertain light
of the village church. Could the young merchant, Master
Maynard, be responsible? But he, too, had not known their
true identities—yet Sir Rhys had distrusted his alleged reason for being in the district. Rhys Griffith! Always her
tortured mind returned to the possibility that he might betray them. Bile rushed into her mouth at the thought. Had
he so resented her apparent rejection of his advances that
he had stooped to this?

Now she could hear sounds of the town, the hustle and
bustle of people and the rumble of iron cart wheels upon
the road, the cries of apprentices. Could they now be in
Ludlow? It was the nearest town and it would have taken
longer to reach another. The noises grew louder and their
passage was halted momentarily by some obstruction on
the road ahead. Philippa heard the sergeant shout a brusque
command and, after a short pause, their vehicle began to

move slowly forward again and she heard some members of her escort move in more closely. Now it was imperative that the prisoners should not be seen on the crowded thoroughfare.

She could not gauge her mother's expression. The Countess moved restlessly on her seat and Philippa leaned forward to reach out to her and offer silent comfort.

The wagonette came to another sudden halt and, again, the sergeant called out an order, instantly obeyed, for, after a short pause, they lumbered on once more. The side of the vehicle had pressed against something, Philippa was sure. So they had passed through a gate!

Now the sounds of the town were hushed, but she could hear other, familiar noises, the mewling of hawks from the mews, the rustling of wings and the gentle voice of the falconer reassuring his charges, the heavy repetitive beat of the blacksmith's hammer as he plied his trade, the restless movement of horses in a nearby stable. They had arrived. She caught her breath hard. They could only be in Ludlow and, if so, then this must be the castle courtyard.

The sergeant called a halt and then an order to dismount. Already the wagonette had stopped and the driver was climbing down heavily from his seat. The leather curtains were hastily drawn back and Philippa blinked in the sudden entrance of sunlight and saw the sergeant waiting to hand down her mother. She gazed round and realised that her surmise was correct. They had drawn up within the inner bailey of Ludlow Castle. She took the sergeant's hand and found herself stiff as she stepped down the portable wooden steps brought for the purpose. She had been sitting too tensed upon the hard wooden bench.

They were given little opportunity to look round. Philippa had only a moment to recognise the castle chapel nearby before they were hustled up the keep steps and into the most guarded and fortified part of the building. Immediately they were in gloom again and bewildered by their hasty arrival and their fears for the outcome.

Two of their former escorts accompanied the sergeant and his prisoners as he led them down several gloomy corridors and into a larger room, which received direct sunlight from several glazed windows. A man rose to his feet from a high-backed chair and faced them. Obviously he had been waiting for their arrival. Philippa gave a sharp cry of disappointment and fury, but she had no time to speak one word to Rhys Griffith before two guards, armed with crossed halberds, standing before a heavy oaken door, lowered their weapons at the sergeant's low tone of command as he knocked. The door opened and a youthful page, clad in the silken livery of the court, bearing the device of the Tudor rose and portcullis, appeared in the opening and ushered them into the inner chamber.

Philippa turned just once and directed a glance of pure hatred towards Rhys Griffith. He moved forward slightly, and held out one hand, as if in entreaty, but the page was waiting impatiently for her to follow her mother, and the sergeant and his two men-at-arms stood impassively beside the door, obviously on guard until the judgement given inside the chamber should be concluded, and their services required to direct the prisoners to their place of confinement. She was forced to follow the boy.

She had only a moment to take in the appointments of the chamber, which was furnished richly, with a central oaken table, several high-backed chairs and stools and a court cupboard on which silver and pewter dishes were displayed. Philippa felt the thickness of carpet beneath her feet and noted the bright colours of the tapestries upon the lime-washed walls in the full sunlight, which flowed in through the glazed oriel window opposite.

A woman rose from the padded window seat within the embrasure and came slightly towards them, handing her embroidery tambour to another, younger, lady who had been seated with her. With one dismissive wave of her hand she dismissed the girl, who curtsied deeply, then moved to the door and exited.

Cressida gave a swift exclamation as the woman held wide her arms and she ran into them, murmuring brokenly her joy and relief at sight of their hostess.

'Oh, your Grace, this is such an honour and delight. I had not expected ever—to see you again.'

Philippa's lips curved into a smile of joy as she recognised Queen Elizabeth, her former mistress, and she brushed back emotional tears as her mother stepped back slightly and she, too, was drawn into the Queen's embrace.

'Come, sit with me. I have ordered the fire lighted as the evenings are beginning to grow chill and I find myself feeling the cold more and more lately.'

The Queen sank into a padded armchair before the hearth and gestured for Cressida to sit beside her on a high-backed chair nearby. Philippa sank on to a joint stool close to the Queen's chair. Elizabeth was smiling at Cressida and holding her hand tightly and Philippa remembered that she and her mother had formed a close friendship long ago when Cressida had been briefly attendant upon Queen Anne, the wife of the late King, until her death in the spring of 1485.

The two said nothing for moments, overcome by the pleasure of their renewed acquaintance and Philippa was able to assess the changes in the Queen's appearance since their last meeting four years ago.

Now Elizabeth was mourning the death of her first-born, Arthur, Prince of Wales, and was clad in the deepest of black mourning velvet, as were her two visitors. Only a golden pendant from which depended a crucifix and the small seed pearls embedded in the gilt-braided cloth of the Queen's gable headdress relieved the sombreness of her garments.

There were lines of suffering upon the formerly serene and smooth features and the pale gilt hair she had inherited from her famed mother, Elizabeth Woodville, showing one smooth band upon her forehead, had faded and was touched with silver.

Philippa's mother frowned and Philippa knew that she, too, had recognised the signs of deep unhappiness in the Queen's demeanour.

She said quietly, 'I feel for you deeply, your Grace, in the loss of your first-born and heir.'

The Queen's answer was very low. 'It has been a terrible blow to both of us and unexpected as...' she hesitated, turning away '...the loss of my uncle Richard's child must have been to him.'

It was a strange comparison and both women were a little nonplussed by the Queen's thinking.

After a moment Elizabeth continued. 'Henry has been very good to me. He came to me when—when we heard the news—to be with me and console me.' She turned back to her two companions, her eyes brimming with tears. 'You know, Cressida, Henry is not usually demonstrative.'

Philippa, who had witnessed some of the King's visits to his wife in her apartments at Westminster, was well aware of that. She recalled the occasions he had complained bitterly and querulously about the expenses of the Queen's court and she compressed her lips in silent anger.

The Queen was speaking tonelessly, 'I have come to Ludlow to be near to Arthur, since this where he spent most of his life. I saw little of him, you see. It is a Queen's lot to be parted from her children too early.'

That was a reference to the custom of placing royal princes in households of their own while extremely young and the necessity of making marriage alliances with foreign princes for the young Princesses of the court. The Princess Margaret was already given in marriage to the King of Scotland and the young Princess Mary Rose would soon be leaving her mother's side.

Philippa put in eagerly, 'Your Grace, how fares Prince Henry and Princess Mary? It is long since I saw them and that time when I accompanied the hunt with the King and Prince Henry, the little Princess was ailing.'

The Queen smiled brightly. 'Henry grows daily more personable and confident. You know he took a very active part in arranging the celebrations for his brother's wedding to the Infanta of Spain, the Princess Catherine. Despite his youth he made an excellent job of it,' she said proudly. 'Henry has a fine mind and is strong of physique. He will make a good ruler when the time comes.' She added wistfully, 'He reminds me much of the King, my father. How fortunate it was that young Richard Allard was present at the hunt that day and managed to save Henry from that charging boar. Henry was always too adventurous for his own good. Mary grows yet more beautiful—and wilful, I fear. She and Henry are much of a kind and have deep affection for each other.'

Philippa guessed at what was not said, that the Queen's children were drawing more and more away from her and she was feeling isolated.

Abruptly the Queen leaned towards her former friend. 'How is Wroxeter, Cressida? I must offer my condolences for the loss of your father. It seems we are all suffering loss at this time. It makes it more difficult for you that Martyn cannot be with you at this sad time.'

The Countess nodded. 'And even more difficult, your

Grace, because I cannot remain here to comfort my mother. She knew, of course, that the possibility of losing my father was near. He had already had one bad seizure which was what brought Philippa and me to England, knowing that time might be short for him, but we hoped we could be together for a little longer, but it was not to be…' Her voice tailed off sadly.

The Queen turned to Philippa. 'I believe you had not seen your grandfather until these last weeks. If I remember correctly, he and your grandmother were about to come to Court when you were forced to leave.' She closed her eyes momentarily, recalling the urgency of that leave-taking and her sadness at losing her two youthful ladies-in-waiting, Anne and Philippa. She smiled slightly. 'I am glad Richard and Anne have been allowed to return to England in safety and I hear that she is a mother. I suppose you have seen nothing of them. You will regret that.' She was looking searchingly at Philippa and the girl was forced to lower her gaze so that the Queen would not read in her eyes the knowledge that she had, indeed, seen Richard recently and in this very town. It might be dangerous for the Queen to be aware of his presence here and so close to the hiding place of her father.

'No, I have seen nothing of them,' she said softly. 'I miss my friends, but Anne has been able to write and send messages to me from time to time.'

The Queen sighed. 'Perhaps, one day, all these troubles will be over and meetings between friends from the old days will be possible.'

There was a moment of silence then the Queen said, in a little rush, 'You have not spoken of Wroxeter. Is he well?'

'He suffers the ill effects still of the wounds taken at Redmoor, but he is much improved recently.' Cressida paused, then added, 'He keeps busy on the Duchess Margaret's business.'

The Queen exchanged a knowing glance with both of them. 'This—alleged confession of Tyrell's will have given him much pain,' she murmured. 'You must know, Cressida, that it distresses me, too, greatly.'

The Countess gazed around hurriedly as if she might detect the presence nearby of someone eavesdropping upon their private talk, then she said very softly, 'Your Grace does not believe—'

'Of course not…' the Queen's blue eyes became steely '…and, if the truth is known, neither does his Majesty the King. We do not discuss the fate of my young brothers— ever—and it is my belief that he is as bewildered by those events so long in the past as we all are but—' she drew a hard breath '—it is necessary at this juncture to again reassure the King and Queen of Spain that no obstacles would lie in the path of young Henry's accession to the throne and, also, that he obtain a dispensation from the Pope and their consent to Henry's betrothal to the Infanta.'

'And it is the Prince's wish?' Philippa said wonderingly. Her remembrances of the madcap young Prince did not lead her to believe that he would be over-willing at this stage to be betrothed to any one, least of all to his brother's reputedly staid young widow. And there would, of course, be some considerable opposition to young Henry's marriage with his late brother's wife since such a union was forbidden by Holy Church, despite the fact that the marriage would be desirable for the welfare of both countries. She had heard it rumoured that the Princess Catherine had sworn upon Holy books and reliquaries that the marriage with Prince Arthur had never been consummated, and that physicians had examined her and confirmed the truth of her oath. If that were so, there were no obstacles for the marriage to take place, as the King wished, but Philippa doubted whether most people would believe it. She could not resist a small inner grin as she remembered grimly what terrible steps King Henry had taken to ensure the alliance with Spain in the first place. Both the young Earl of Warwick and the hapless Perkin Warbeck had gone to the scaffold in order to convince King Ferdinand and Queen Isabella that their daughter would, in time, become Queen of England and that no shadowy heir lived to counter the Tudor's undoubted right to that throne. Certainly the death of his heir, Prince Arthur, had been a terrible and untimely blow to King Henry.

She came from her reverie to find that the Queen was regarding Cressida, her mother, very intently.

'When I discovered that you were here in England, Cressida, I was concerned that Martyn might have followed you. I know he is prone to rash acts—valorous they might be, but extremely dangerous to him and to your family. Henry will brook no opposition to his will at this difficult moment and would deal ruthlessly with anyone who sought to frustrate his plans. You must see that Martyn does nothing foolish.'

Philippa said hurriedly, 'What makes your Grace fear there is any possibility of that? Could we be informed as to who betrayed us?'

The Queen's slightly myopic blue eyes fixed themselves in a puzzled expression upon her former young lady-in-waiting.

'You use a strong word, Philippa. No one betrayed you. Sir Rhys Griffith—'

'I thought as much,' Philippa said through clenched teeth, her eyes stormy. 'Who, on our manor, would betray us? And no one else knows of our presence here. What has he been promised in payment?'

The Queen gave a little sharp gasp. 'You mistake the situation, Philippa. I have known Sir Rhys Griffith for some time. He came to Court two years ago following the death of his father and gradually showed himself to be in sympathy with my situation....'

'Your Grace should take care that he does not betray you as well,' Philippa cut in.

The Queen reached out and took Philippa's hand within her own. 'Child, what makes you so hot against this man? I came to Ludlow to be near to Arthur. He spent so much time here that I feel curiously close to my son here. Sir Rhys is aware of that and of my despair. He believed that a meeting between myself and two very dear friends and attendants would comfort me, as indeed it has. He revealed to me, in utmost secrecy, your presence nearby and arranged for you both to be conveyed here, again in utmost secrecy. I understand that no one was allowed to see either of you upon the journey. My captain is fiercely loyal to me and his men-at-arms were chosen for their loyalty to him. You will be returned to Gretton in the same fashion. Only my most intimate companions will ever be aware that you came here.' She turned back to gaze into Cressida's hurt and bewildered eyes. 'You cannot believe that I would ever seek to do either of you harm or place you in any real danger.'

'Of course not, your Grace.'

The Queen's facial muscles relaxed and she smiled and squeezed Philippa's hand. 'I had thought to see you happily wed by now, like Anne and Richard, but, knowing what I know now, perhaps that it is as well that you are not contracted in marriage as yet to one of your father's impoverished companions in Burgundy.' She said brightly, 'If you will ring the little silver hand bell on the window seat in the oriel embrasure, Cressida, Lady Harding will come to attend me. I think you will remember her and you two will be happy to meet again, if only for a short time.'

Cressida rose at once to obey and moved away from the Queen and Philippa, who was aware that the Queen had deliberately arranged matters so that they might talk in private together.

Her guess was proven correct as the Queen drew her a little closer to her chair and bent to speak softly.

'It appears to me that you have some aversion to Sir Rhys Griffith that you judge him so harshly. Believe that he has only your welfare at heart. He has confessed to me that he loves you well and has begged for your hand in marriage.' She bent even closer and said, a trifle laughingly, 'I see that you blush at the thought, child. Is Rhys Griffith so abhorrent to you that you would dismiss him out of hand? It would be a fair match.'

It was the first time the Queen had ever truly revealed herself to Philippa and the girl could not hold back a sudden gasp.

She said falteringly, 'I saw Sir Rhys in the anteroom as we entered and I think I showed him in just one revealing look that I thought the worst of him. He must think ill of me.'

'Do you love him, Philippa?'

There was only the slightest of hesitations before the answer came. 'Yes, your Grace, I believe that I do.'

'Then, child, go immediately and tell him so. At the very least, inform him that you are now aware that your conclusion was hasty and misjudged. Your mother will be occupied here with Lady Harding and myself for some moments. It will give you the opportunity to put things right.' She reached down and gently impelled Philippa to her feet, then gave her a quick little push towards the door.

She turned and afforded the Queen a deep curtsy and

exited backwards. She had half-hoped that she would find the anteroom deserted or, at least, that Sir Rhys would have left by now, but he was standing gazing out of the window at some activity below in the courtyard. Philippa stood for a moment with her back to the door and then came forward in a little rush. The susurration of her gown brushing the rushes upon the floor alerted him to her presence and he swung round at once to face her, a frown forming between his brows on recognition.

She said humbly, 'Sir Rhys, the Queen has informed me of your kind intent in having us conveyed here. It seems we are for ever in your debt.'

He stepped a little closer and she observed that his chest was rising and falling as if in a state of agitation.

He said thickly, 'But you, as usual, thought the worst of me.'

She attempted to move back a trifle, for the first time in their acquaintanceship aware of a feeling of fear in his presence, but he frustrated her intention by seizing her wrist and held it tightly. 'What is this, Lady Philippa, that everything I attempt to accomplish for your happiness ends in disaster? I could see by your glance of pure vitriolic hatred as you entered just now that you believed I had betrayed you both and, it seems, for the very worst of motives: gain. Then know, my lady, that I am very well aware of your father's presence in England. I knew from almost the first moment he stepped upon English soil and that Richard Allard was there to meet him and conduct him here, also that Allard has taken him to Sir Owen Lewis's house where he is at present. Do you not think I would have accomplished far more in the way of favour with the King by betraying him rather than his wife and daughter?'

She gave a great cry of horror and covered her face with her free hand.

'Yes,' he continued ruthlessly, 'the safety of you all has been in my hands from the beginning. I have my own informants, you see, and my reasons for keeping myself informed. I love you, Lady Philippa, have done from the first moment I clapped eyes upon you and your so-obvious aversion to me has not changed my attitude towards you. I have wanted to take you to myself, to hold you safe. Can you imagine I would cause you unhappiness by bringing harm to those you love?'

She made a little helpless choking sound.

'But I am fast losing patience, my lady. I cannot hope that you will ever return my love and will always regard my actions with suspicion. We cannot live together like that, my lady, however I would wish it otherwise. You must go your own way and I pray the Virgin will find happiness in the arms of another more patient and less exacting lover. I cannot hope to find such happiness, but that is no concern of yours. You will be conveyed safely back to Gretton and I assure you I will not impose myself upon your presence there again. You can inform Lady Gretton that I will be at her service the moment you and your lady mother have left for Burgundy. Your father is in no danger from me. I can only hope, for your sake, that he will bring no disaster upon his own head by taking an unnecessary risk. I will bid you goodbye, my lady. Perhaps one day, in the distant future, you will be able to look back on these last days and recall that you met a man who deeply loved you and will continue to do so till the end of his days.'

Before she could utter a word in her own defence he had torn himself free and marched to the outer door, opened it and, turning once to give her a stiff bow of leave-taking, he strode out, slamming it to after him.

'No,' she gave a little moan of protest, 'no, no, please come back. It is not as you believe. I do…'

It was useless and she knew it. He had gone and she was left with nothing but empty regret.

She slipped down to the rush-strewn floor, crying helplessly. She had rejected him this one time too many. She could see now that on each occasion when their wills had clashed it had been because he had needed to save her from some foolish impulsive action, which could bring her into danger. Even his antipathy towards Peter Fairley had been brought about by his desperate love for her. She knew now, with a terrible bleak sense of loss, that she loved him, and her very antagonistic reaction towards his nearness was because she feared for her own need to surrender. All her life she had lived with this constant fear for her family's safety and her own blind awareness that she must trust no one she was not completely sure of. Yet her father was sufficiently convinced of Rhys Griffith's worthiness that he was prepared to give the man his most precious daughter's hand in marriage. She had fought against the match because she could not trust herself.

The Queen had spoken of her own deep loneliness and urged her to confront the innermost feelings of her own heart. And he had given her no opportunity to reveal to him her longing to be truly his. This final betrayal of trust had wounded him to the heart and he had accepted his rejection at last and gone from her. Was he here in the castle still? She must find him, tell him in simple words of her love, convince him of her sincerity. He could not have left yet, not without a formal leave-taking and dismissal from the Queen. She stood up determinedly and dabbed at her streaming eyes, hoped her lids had not been reddened and that the guards she would surely find keeping watch in the corridor would not notice and be curious. She brushed that thought aside impatiently. That was of no importance. She needed to find Rhys quickly before her courage deserted her and she would return miserably to the manor house and leave England without ever being entirely sure whether she could have found the total happiness she sought in his arms.

She moved resolutely to the door and opened it hesitantly. Immediately the two guards saluted and lowered their halberds.

'Sir Rhys,' she ventured hesitantly, 'the knight who was here in the anteroom recently—where is he, have you any idea where he went when he left the Queen's apartments?'

The men eyed her cautiously and the taller of the two cleared his throat in an embarrassed fashion.

'Sir Rhys Griffith announced his intention of walking in the town for a while.' The guard's scrutiny did not waver and Philippa was aware that the men had noted the temper which had consumed the knight and his need to put a space between himself and those beings who had caused it. The man continued. 'He informed us he would return later to take his leave of her Grace after your departure, my lady.'

So he intended to deliberately avoid her. Philippa bit down upon her lower lip.

'I see,' she said in a small voice. 'There is some urgent matter on which I need to consult him. Perhaps I could find him. Would you inform my lady mother that I will return shortly? She knows that I am acquainted with the town and the Queen is aware of my intentions and gave me leave. Will one of you escort me to the gate and afford me means of leaving the castle?'

They exchanged embarrassed glances, unwilling to leave their posts, yet if the Queen had given leave the matter must indeed be one of some urgency. The taller man bowed and nodded to his companion. He stalked beside her in dignified silence as they left the keep, crossed the inner and outer baileys, and reached the main gate where she was passed through with the proviso that she would return shortly and require admittance once more.

Chapter Eight

Philippa found herself standing uncertainly outside the main gate house of the castle, the focus of several pairs of curious eyes. The day was already drawing to a close for those engaged in marketing and passers-by were moving towards the town gates. She was grateful for the fact that the sergeant had instructed her to wear a cloak, for, already, the evenings were beginning to become chillier once the sun had set. She drew her hood up and her cloak more tightly round her as it would serve to keep her from being observed too closely by onlookers.

She had become reasonably familiar with the pattern of streets in Ludlow and turned at once in the direction of the inn where Peter had taken her to meet Richard Allard, the Golden Fleece. Since it lay in the vicinity of the castle she judged that Sir Rhys Griffith would chose to drink there before returning to the castle, as he had promised, to take formal leave of her Grace the Queen.

She was aware that a noble woman walking without escort would attract undue notice, but she was dressed simply and her cloak was of dark brown fustian; she believed she would be taken for a merchant's wife going about her business. She hesitated for a moment at the door of the inn. It was unlikely that Rhys Griffith would greet her warmly and she had no wish to cause a scene. Perhaps it might be better if she enquired after Richard Allard. If he had returned to Ludlow he might be persuaded to enquire after the whereabouts of Rhys Griffith for her.

The tap room was crowded, as many of the market folk were drinking and taking refreshment there before commencing their homeward journeys. She glanced round quickly but could discern no sight of Rhys Griffith. More than likely he had bespoken the use of a private room since he had been in no mood to counter the jovial banter of the other customers.

One of the serving wenches came towards her, noting her hesitation.

'Can I be of service, mistress?'

'I was wondering if either Sir Rhys Griffith or Master Allard were here.'

The girl shook her head. 'I do know Sir Rhys well, mistress, he often gives us his custom, but he ain't been 'ere today. As for Master Allard, he left us some days ago and we don't be expecting 'im back.'

Philippa thanked the girl and declined her offer of ale or food and hurriedly left the inn. Neither her mother nor Sir Rhys would thank her for drawing undue notice to herself and it was clear that she must seek Sir Rhys elsewhere. Outside she stood perplexed. Where would he have gone? Obviously there were several respectable inns and taverns in the town, but she doubted the wisdom of visiting each to enquire after him. It was possible he had acquaintances in the town whom he might have decided to visit and she had no knowledge of any of them.

She was very close to tears. She had been so sure she would find him at the Golden Fleece and that it would be easy to talk to him there or to request him to accompany her outside. She needed desperately to explain herself to him before she left Ludlow. Since he had declared his intention of remaining clear of Gretton until after she and her mother had left there was scant opportunity of seeing him again unless she could find him now. She could not, in all honour, seek him out at his own manor. That would be too humiliating. He could refuse outright to receive her and what could she tell her mother?

There was nothing for it but to return to the castle. Soon her mother would be looking anxiously for her when she had been dismissed from the Queen's presence. She must not be kept waiting.

She gave a little helpless shrug and turned reluctantly towards the castle gate. Almost immediately she was hailed by a familiar voice.

'Mistress Weston, is it not? I had not expected to see you again so soon in Ludlow, that is, after the funeral.' The pleasant tones of Roger Maynard halted her in her walk and she turned at once, pleased to see a friendly face.

His expression was a trifle more grave as he added, 'Are you alone?' He glanced round uncertainly and she thought he believed that she might well have been escorted by Sir Rhys Griffith; she knew well the two men had no liking for each other. He said gently, 'You should not really be walking alone in the streets, Mistress Weston. You are a stranger here and do not know the dangers. This has been market day and markets attract pickpockets as honey attracts bees. While they can often be only a nuisance and inconvenience, occasionally they can attack vulnerable people. Will you allow me to escort you wherever you might be going? Isn't your servant with you today?'

She gave a little nervous laugh. 'Why, no, Master Maynard, Peter is not with me.' She hesitated, then plunged on somewhat inaccurately, 'Sir Rhys Griffith was coming into town on business and I requested that he escort me. My mother and I will be leaving Gretton shortly and there are one or two items I wished to purchase. Unfortunately we became separated. I am sure I shall find him shortly.'

She was convinced that mention of the man he had most reason to dislike might well put Master Maynard off remaining with her. She could not allow him to know she was on her way to the castle. The visit of her mother and her on the Queen had been arranged in the utmost secrecy and must remain so. If, indeed, he had happened to see Sir Rhys, he might well be able to point her in the right direction.

He looked much better today. He was still limping slightly and leaning upon a cane, but it was clear that his broken leg was healing nicely and that soon he would be fit enough to ride. Rhys Griffith would be relieved to see the back of him.

'I am pleased to see that you are recovering well, Master Maynard. Does the leg pain you still?' she enquired politely.

He gave her his little respectful bow. 'Only when I put too much weight upon it, but I am, as you see, fortunate, Mistress Weston, that there was no infection and the bone appears to be knitting well. I have you and your servant to thank for the prompt treatment I received.'

'And Sir Rhys Griffith,' she reminded him.

He nodded. 'Indeed. Despite his wish for privacy and disinclination to allow trespass on his land, he has been very generous towards me. I have much to thank him for.' He paused and smiled down at her. 'Actually I am now in a position to do him a service for which I am sure he will thank me profusely. He must be half out of his mind with concern about you, mistress, and I am able to reunite you. I happened to see him entering a house on the other side of town. Perhaps you know of it, that he has friends living there?'

She shook her head and said eagerly, 'No, I know nothing of his acquaintances. It is possible that he went there to request assistance in finding me. Can you direct me to the house, Master Maynard? I will be very grateful.'

His smile broadened. 'Why, certainly. I am charmed that I can be of service to both of you. Please, take my arm, mistress. The house is not far away and Sir Rhys will be delighted that he need not call out a hue and cry.' The last words were spoken teasingly and she responded shyly.

Timidly she took his arm as he requested and gave one hurried glance, back towards the castle gate. She must not be too long in her search for Rhys Griffith but, surely, he, too, would not delay since the Queen would wish to conclude any business that she might wish to entrust to him.

She noticed that Roger Maynard was still walking somewhat slowly and wondered if, in fact, his leg was paining him more than he liked to admit. He talked to her easily, pointing out one or two of the more interesting places of the town as they passed.

'You will be pleased to get back to London,' she said. 'I imagine your business has been inconveniently delayed.'

He shrugged. 'I have one or two people on whom I need to call before returning to the capital, but that can wait.' He smiled down at her. 'My master is an understanding man and will be prepared to give me all the time I need.'

'That must be a relief to you.'

'It is well to know one is trusted.'

'Certainly.'

They had passed through the centre of the small market town, which was familiar to Philippa by now, and the streets were less frequented. She noted that the houses here were more down at heel and clustered together, many in a dilapidated condition. She paused for a moment and glanced round uncertainly. It seemed most unlikely that Sir Rhys would be acquainted with the denizens of these types of properties, yet he was a strange man and she wondered if, like many noblemen of her father's company, he employed private spies to keep ears and eyes out for any possible danger which might lurk for those unwitting victims. In these uncertain times men feared their neighbours. The King's new Court of the Star Chamber had been invented to track down any men who entertained ideas or beliefs not acceptable to the new monarch and she knew men could be punished by swingeing fines and even greater penalties if they were summoned there and found guilty of any hint of disloyalty. She doubted that Rhys Griffith could ever come under such suspicion, but he was in somewhat dangerous correspondence with the Queen— she had seen that for herself—and he had always been suspicious of strangers on his demesne. It was, quite likely, that he might engage underlings to spy out any whiff of intrigue in the area.

Roger Maynard paused before a house, set back somewhat and apart from its neighbours. It appeared to be in better condition than others in the area and Philippa felt somewhat reassured. Her escort unlatched the gate in the rough-hewn fence and beckoned Philippa courteously to precede him up the overgrown path. She could glimpse no sign of occupation although it was already becoming dusk and she thought the inhabitants would soon need to light their candles and prickets.

Roger Maynard knocked peremptorily and after a few moments of delay the door was opened and a man appeared, holding a lighted candle. He glanced at Philippa uncertainly and she could see, even in the waning light, that he was dressed in homespun like a servant and yet there was a touch of military bearing about him, which suggested that he had been a soldier.

Roger Maynard spoke politely. 'This lady wishes to see the master. She is in search of a friend she believes is visiting here.'

The man gave a faint grunt in answer and stepped back so that the two of them might enter. Philippa was surprised to see that Roger Maynard should choose to go with her and had expected that, once having delivered her to the right house, he would take his leave or possibly wait outside, since his previous encounters with Rhys Griffith had been less than pleasant. Instead he followed her closely into the small gloomy hall and the heavy door closed with a sudden bang behind them.

The man, who had admitted them, led the way through into a backroom, probably the solar of the house, though, at the moment, it was impossible for Philippa to recognise it as such, since the shutters were already closed over the casement and the room had not yet been illuminated with either candles or oil lamps. It was so dark that she stumbled against something near the doorway and hurt her shin, so giving a little cry of pain. She was now beginning to get alarmed. Why should the servant show her into an unlit room, an action discourteous in the extreme? Before she could utter a word of doubt she was unceremoniously shoved further into the room, the man with the candlestick advanced and Roger Maynard came up close behind her and seized her arm. His grip was so fierce she let out a second cry, then stifled it hurriedly as the door to this room also was banged shut behind them.

She made no attempt to free herself, knowing, instinctively, that it would be useless.

Drawing herself to her full height she turned and faced Maynard. 'I do not understand, sir. Where is Sir Rhys Griffith?' Her eyes roved the chamber hastily, finding it to be almost unfurnished. There was a truckle bed, set against the far wall, on which she discerned a straw-filled pallet partially covered with a homespun rough blanket. Beside it was a wooden bucket and near the door she discovered the object over which she had stumbled on entry into the chamber, a simple oaken joint stool. Apart from these utilitarian and poorly fashioned articles the room was empty. The wall had been lime-washed at some time in the past but that had clearly been pealing for years and there were damp patches near the shuttered window.

Roger Maynard stood leaning easily, his back against the door, for he had now released her so quickly that she stumbled again and almost fell. He made no attempt to prevent her from hurting herself.

'Well, Lady Philippa Telford,' he addressed her sneeringly, 'did you really expect to find Sir Rhys Griffith in such a hovel?'

She stared at the sound of her true name and her heart began to beat even faster than when she had felt the first twinges of alarm at sight of this room.

She had recovered herself now and faced him as haughtily as if she had been in the Queen's audience chamber.

'I do not know what this is all about, Master Maynard—'

'My name is Hilyard, in fact, a slight deception but, since your true identity was kept from me, I think it can be allowed.' He smiled a trifle mockingly and folded his arms. 'Ah, I see the name is familiar to you, as much so as yours is to me. John Hilyard was my cousin and, like me, in the service of his majesty.' He paused then added, very deliberately, 'He was killed in that service and his body thrown ignominiously behind a hedge. I think you were present on that occasion, Lady Philippa.' He emphasised her title mockingly and she drew back a trifle, though still holding her dignified stance. She would not allow her fear of him to be shown.

Since she made no reply to his challenge, he regarded her thoughtfully. 'I wonder that you were so very anxious to find Sir Rhys Griffith. In the past you have never displayed any liking for the man, the opposite, in fact.'

Stung, she replied, 'That is no business of yours, Master May—Hilyard,' she corrected herself, 'since it appears that he is not here.'

He shrugged. 'I have not the faintest notion of where he might be, but your need of him served my purpose well, since I have been waiting patiently to find one of you ladies unescorted and able to be made my prisoner.'

Philippa knew that despite her resolve she had betrayed herself with a slight shiver of apprehension at his final word. She was aware that the man who had admitted them to the house was standing stolidly behind her, on guard, though she did not turn her head to look directly at him. So he was a man-at-arms.

'I am unable to discover any possible reason you might have to imprison me, Master Hilyard,' she said curtly. 'Neither my mother nor I are proscribed under any act made by King or council, though I now understand you to be not a merchant but a spy of King Henry.'

'*You* may not be, Lady Philippa,' he said suavely, 'but your father, the Earl of Wroxeter, most certainly is and will, undoubtedly, surrender himself to me once he receives my message that you are my prisoner.'

She shook her head vehemently. 'My father is in Burgundy, well away from any harm you might do him.'

Slowly he shook his own head, smiling. 'Now, Lady Philippa, you know that to be untrue. The Earl is in England and has indeed, visited you and his lady wife at

Gretton only days ago. I saw him myself in Ludlow with
another gentleman of your acquaintance, Master Allard. I
am not entirely certain of his present whereabouts, but am
convinced that my men will be able to ascertain that within
a very short time. Indeed, you might well be prepared to
supply me with that information and thereby shorten your
own period of detention which…' he gazed round deliberately '…will not be entirely comfortable, as you can see
for yourself. I have four men within this house whose duties will be to guard you continuously, never to let you out
of sight. In fact, one will be with you inside this room at
all times. They are veteran soldiers and they have instructions not to offer you insult or harm. That is, of course—'
he grinned meaningfully '—unless you should give them
cause to do so, in which case they have carte blanche from
me to take whatever steps necessary to ensure that you
remain my honoured guest; then, I think, you will find their
presence discomforting.'

The very thought of such close confinement and the in-
dignity it suggested to her personal privacy caused her to
go dry mouthed with dread but she made no answer.

He grinned again, and she thought how his appearance
had become so changed by her discovery of his perfidy
and wondered that she could have ever considered him
pleasant and affable. Her lip trembled as she recalled that
Sir Rhys had ever been aware of a deep aversion towards
the man and had warned her against placing any trust in
him. Had he known that the fellow was a creature of the
King, a paid spy? Probably he had not been certain, but
had been cautious in his dealings with the fellow and revealed a desire to get him from the district without delay.
She looked down at Hilyard's injured leg. Had he deliberately thrown himself from his horse that day, knowing
she was riding close by? If so he had taken a grave risk,

since that fractured bone could have lost him his life. It was more likely that he had expected to suffer a sprained ankle or some less serious injury. At all events he had thought the reward he might gain for her father's capture well worth the pain and trouble he had been caused.

And he was anxious for vengeance! She thought back wearily to that encounter on the road to the coast four years ago when John Hilyard had attempted to arrest her and return her to the King's custody—and paid for it with his life. Then, as his cousin's was now, his intention had been to obtain her father's surrender to the King. The Queen had feared that and been determined to send her into exile for that very reason even though she'd been reluctant to part with Philippa's company. So Roger Maynard, or whatever he chose to call himself, had a double reason for imprisoning her and capturing her father: a rich reward of preferment from the King and vengeance for his cousin's death. She bit down savagely upon her lower lip. He would have so tight a hold over these men who served him that the likelihood of any one of them relaxing his guard over her would be nigh on impossible.

She was trapped here. She had seen for herself that the house was set apart from others, had been well chosen for a prison, so no cries or pleas of hers would be heard by passers-by. Sir Rhys had abandoned all interest in her. Whatever desperate measures her mother and grandmother took to discover her whereabouts would be entirely frustrated and Sir Rhys had declared his intention of absenting himself from Gretton until she had departed the country, so they could expect no help from him in their search. She had foolishly placed herself in Hilyard's hands and could think of no way of obtaining a release from this terrible predicament. The one thing she had feared, from the moment they had stepped ashore in England, had come to pass. Her father must not be lured to his death. She would prefer her own demise to that, but she knew, instinctively, that he would come to her rescue—and she could do nothing to prevent him.

She turned away from her tormentor, her shoulders shaking in utter revulsion.

Hilyard said abruptly, 'I just wish to impress upon you one fact, Lady Philippa. Each one of my men is aware that if he touches you, apart from the necessity to keep you safe, he will hang for it. The King would offer me no reward should the daughter of any one of England's nobility be violated. You will be kept close, but your virginity is safe.'

She did not so much as turn her head at his attempt to reassure her. Her despair was too great. After some moments she heard the door open and then close again and knew that she was alone with her guard. Her legs were trembling so much now that she thought she might fall and she groped her way to the truckle bed and sank down upon it, her face hidden in her hands. She was determined that she would not burst into tears before her grim-faced jailer, who stood watching her dispassionately with his back against the door.

It was about an hour after Philippa had left Ludlow Castle that Sir Rhys Griffith returned to present himself and take formal leave of her Majesty the Queen. When he was ushered into her presence, he was startled to discover the Countess of Wroxeter still with her and both women appeared to be in a state of considerable alarm. Lady Hartley had admitted him and then taken her stance some distance from the Queen and her visitors.

The Queen addressed him without preamble. 'You have seen Lady Philippa, Sir Rhys, since she left our presence?'

He hesitated and glanced awkwardly at the Countess. 'I had a brief conversation with Lady Philippa before I left the castle, your Grace.'

'The two of you quarrelled?' The Queen's question was blunt.

Again he hesitated. 'No, your Grace, I would not say that we quarrelled, merely that matters came to a head between us and I made it clear to Lady Philippa that I no longer considered myself her ardent suitor and that I would withdraw from her company, as she appeared to desire that I should.'

The Countess gave a little gasp of alarm and the Queen reached out and touched her arm lightly.

'Sir Rhys, we are closeted in private here. Nothing of what was said will be repeated. Will you tell us what took place between you two?'

Griffith was beginning to feel distinctly uncomfortable. In fact, he was becoming aware that something was gravely wrong. One glance at the Countess's distraught features made that clear to him.

'Before I answer that, your Grace, I must know, where is Lady Philippa? I would hate to reveal what went on between us without obtaining her permission to do so.'

The Queen gave a heavy sigh and the Countess let out a distinct sob.

'That, Sir Rhys, is exactly what we hoped you would be able to tell us. Apparently Lady Philippa left the castle over an hour ago and has not returned. We have been waiting for her appearance so that she and her mother can be returned in secret to Gretton—but there is no sign of her. We are afraid that some harm might have come to her—unescorted—' The Queen broke off and appealed to Sir Rhys mutely with her eyes. 'We had hoped that she might be with you, sir. Now we realise that is not so.'

Startled, Rhys Griffith almost forgot protocol in his angry expostulation. 'But, why, in the Virgin's name, was she not prevented from leaving?'

Mildly the Queen reminded him, 'Lady Philippa is not a prisoner, Sir Rhys. The guards at the gate had no orders to detain her.'

Cressida said tearfully, 'What we cannot understand is why she should wish to leave the castle. When the guard was summoned he informed us that she left in search of you. That is, she enquired if you had left and so we presume she went to find you, but,' she added anxiously, 'why should she do that?'

He shook his head angrily, 'I cannot—I do not know.'

'When you informed her that your pursuit of her was at an end, did she appear to be relieved or sorry?' the Queen pressed him.

He gave a little muffled sound of suppressed fury and shook his head again helplessly. 'I confess that I left her little or no time to answer me at all. I simply thought it was what she wished—to be left in peace.'

The Queen said, very softly, 'When she left me, Sir Rhys, I was under the impression she wished to inform you that she had misjudged your motives. She believed...' she hesitated '...that you have informed on her and her mother and wanted preferment as the price of that betrayal.'

'I was aware of that, I saw it in her expression when she arrived here. I told her that it was untrue and that if she thought so hardly of me I would remove herself permanently from her company—and then—I left—to drown my sorrow in some tavern,' he added bitterly.

The Queen said gently, 'This was all such a waste. I think—Philippa had a completely different solution in mind. She must have been deeply distressed and tried to find you to explain.'

'Then, dear God in Heaven, *why* has she not returned?' he stormed wrathfully.

The women gazed at one another in utter bewilderment and he drew his dark brows together in a scowl.

'It is likely that she sought me at the Golden Fleece where she had previously gone with Fairley, but I chose another tavern.' He paused and half-turned from them, his lower lip jutting out in thought. 'Yet I cannot imagine why she has not returned. She knows Ludlow well enough and, at this time of day, there would be many unescorted women abroad, stall-holders, merchants' wives. She should have been safe enough. Pickpockets abound, of course, but they would not prevent her—' He broke off and rubbed his chin. 'She might, of course, have met with…' He hesitated, glancing meaningfully at the Countess, then thought the urgency of the moment could displace natural caution. 'We saw Richard Allard the last time we met in Ludlow and she might have gone with him, but I doubt she would have delayed returning, knowing that to keep you waiting would be discourteous in the extreme, your Grace.'

The Queen sighed. 'Then it is as we feared. Some harm has come to her and we should send out men to search.'

Rhys Griffith nodded. 'It would be best if you send with me the men who escorted the Countess and Lady Philippa here. They can be trusted to keep close mouths. In the meantime, could the Countess continue to remain here in privacy?'

The Queen glanced towards Lady Hartley, who nodded. 'That can be arranged and I will send a messenger to Gretton to inform Lady Gretton of what has occurred here and that her daughter, at least, is safe here with me.'

The Queen gestured to Lady Hartley, who went immediately to the door to summon the sergeant at-arms, as the Queen required. The man presented himself almost at once and the Queen nodded towards Sir Rhys, who put the man in the picture hurriedly.

'I need you and two of your most trusted men to accompany me into Ludlow to search for Lady Philippa. I want no word of this to leak out and the guards on the gate who allowed her out must be made to realise what the penalty would be should they gossip.'

The sergeant saluted and bowed to the Queen. 'May I take my leave, your Grace?'

'At once, sergeant, and report to me immediately you have news.'

The sergeant exited, having informed Sir Rhys that he would meet him at the castle gate-house.

Sir Rhys went to the Countess and took both her hands within his own. 'My lady, you know I would gladly die to save Philippa. Everything that can be done will be done. You have my word.'

She brushed away a tear and forced a smile. 'I know that, Sir Rhys. It is just that I cannot dispel from my mind the thought of Philippa lying injured or dead in a town alley.'

He shook his head and said gruffly, 'Unfortunately that thought is not far from my mind either, but it is also my dread that she might have been abducted with a more deadly purpose.'

The Queen gave a little strangled sound and he looked towards her apologetically. 'Your Grace entertains the same fear?'

'Four years ago I feared she might be used as a pawn to entrap her father and for that reason sent her away from me. I should not have sent for you both, Cressida. There is the dread within me that I might well have caused this.'

'Your Grace would never willingly endanger my child,' Cressida said, horrified.

'Never, knowingly, but unwittingly…' The Queen left the rest of the sentence unsaid but her eyes appealed to Rhys Griffith.

He was frowning again in thought. 'There is a man in Ludlow whom I have distrusted since I set eyes upon him. He represents himself as a wool merchant's apprentice, yet it is not the time for such men to be doing business and unlikely for one to be upon my demesne.'

'You think he is a King's spy?'

'It may be so, your Grace. As you know, since the proclamation of Sir James Tyrell's confession there has been some disquiet amongst some of the former Yorkist gentlemen in the district.'

'Men who are angered by the undoubted falsehood of its claims,' she murmured bitterly.

'Aye, your Grace, and I suspected the man was sent to sound out the depth of feeling in this area and where *he* is—' he paused significantly '—there will be others, his trusted minions. I will send to enquire if he is still at the inn where I lodged him after he suffered a broken leg, and, if not…' he gave a gusty sigh '…well, then I shall believe the worst.'

The Queen nodded sagely. 'And it is well known how deeply the Earl of Wroxeter would be anxious to refute that confession and that he could well be in England to try to convince others that its claims are false.'

There was a short silence, then Sir Rhys bent his knee before the Queen and she offered him her hand.

'Go with our blessing and our prayers for your success in your mission to find our beloved Philippa, Sir Rhys.'

He gave a comforting glance in the Countess's direction and bowed himself out of the presence chamber.

* * *

An hour later he was back in the castle and admitted at once into the Queen's presence. He found both the Countess of Wroxeter and Lady Hartley closeted with the Queen.

He came immediately to the point. 'So far we have not found Lady Philippa, your Grace, but it is as I suspected, the man, Maynard, has left his lodging, apparently departed for London, so I am informed…' He paused, then added deliberately, 'accompanied by two companions.'

'That may well be the truth,' the Queen said doubtfully.

'Indeed, your Grace, but I beg to suggest that we should pray that what I feared earlier could be closer to the mark.'

'But if he has abducted her,' Cressida put in fearfully, 'surely that is more to be feared.'

'No, my lady, if Maynard has abducted Lady Philippa he will see to it that she comes to no harm, at least until she has served her purpose.' He gave a brief uneasy shrug. 'Otherwise we have cause to fear that she might have been attacked by some other who had no requirement to keep her alive.'

Cressida went white around the lips at his grim assessment and the Queen reached out and took her cold hand.

'Philippa is a resourceful young woman, as she was when a child,' she said consolingly. 'As Sir Rhys says, we must pray that she is held safe a prisoner somewhere.' She looked coolly up at Sir Rhys. 'What, sir, is your proposal now?'

'I have already instituted a thorough search of the town, which will continue through the night, if necessary, your Grace.' He bit his nether lip and added harshly, 'Meanwhile, I have my own sources of information. I intend to find this fellow Maynard. If he is on the road to London, as he gave out, then all my suspicions pertaining to his character can be set aside and we must continue to make the usual enquiries for Lady Philippa. I suggest that I escort Lady Wroxeter to Gretton personally, then set out to my own manor to commence my own enquiries.'

Cressida rose to her feet, clearly agitated. 'Should I not remain in Ludlow until we hear some news…?'

'No, my lady, your presence here could only compound our problem. If you should be recognised, then you would add a further dimension to the dangers which threaten the Earl. Your part must be to wait patiently at Gretton. Do not think that I underestimate your agonies while you are doing so.'

Her lip trembled and she rose and turned to the Queen, bending her knee in a deep court curtsy. 'Then if you will excuse me, your Grace.'

The Queen rose and embraced her former friend. 'My anxieties are as great as yours until I hear—' She broke off hurriedly. 'The Virgin guard and aid you, Sir Rhys, in this mission.'

He took the Countess's arm and, together, they bowed themselves out of the chamber.

Rhys rode beside the wagonette with the Queen's sergeant-at-arms bringing up the rear of the small company. Once at Gretton, Lady Wroxeter clung to his hand as he assisted her down. Already he saw that Lady Gretton was standing anxiously on the hall steps, with Peter Fairley beside her, and her steward hovering worriedly in the rear.

Rhys said quietly, 'Send your man Fairley to me first thing in the morning. Try not to worry too much, though I know how almost impossible that is. I am convinced that Lady Philippa lives.' He touched his breast briefly. 'If she did not, I would feel it here.'

Cressida gave a wan smile. 'You love her.'

'With every particle of my being. We will find her. The only thing which concerns me is the length of time that will take. I would not have her afraid for one second of time longer than necessary. I know you are afraid for your husband too. If God is good, he can be kept safe out of this.'

'If he should learn…' she faltered.

'He would surrender himself immediately. I know it. If Philippa is discovered as quickly as I hope, he may never need to be informed.'

She was slightly turned away from him when she said very softly, 'Sir Rhys, if she has been harmed—' Her lip trembled and he was aware of her meaning.

'Trust me, Lady Wroxeter. I was prepared to let Philippa go because I believed she wanted that. Now, whatever may have occurred, if she lives she will be mine. I will allow nothing to come between us, not even her own desire.'

Cressida gave a little shaky laugh. 'She does not know how fortunate she is, sir.'

'I assure you I shall make her aware of it and very quickly.'

Again she gave a little half-strangled laugh and he reached out and tilted up her chin. 'I believe Philippa is like her mother in more ways than one. She inherited your beauty, my lady, and your fortitude and spirit in adversity. I can only guess at what sufferings of mind and, not to say, the privations you have endured over the years since Redmoor and I sense your great and enduring love for your husband. I pray Philippa will come to love me as deeply as you do the Earl.'

Her smile now was very wondrous. 'I will pray fervently that it will come to pass, sir.'

He bent and kissed her palms and straightened up as Peter Fairley strode towards them. He sensed the man's innate hostility and frowned.

'Lady Wroxeter will inform you of what has occurred,'

he said a trifle harshly. 'I shall need your services tomorrow morning and hope that you will put aside all suspicion and work with me to bring Lady Philippa home soon.'

Fairley bowed, but he did not relax his rigid stance as he took his lady's hand.

'I will present myself tomorrow early, sir,' he replied curtly.

Rhys waited to see them safely within the manor house, then led the way to his own demesne.

After supper he was informed by one of the Queen's men who had been left to continue the search in Ludlow that no information regarding Philippa had come to light. The only comforting thought was that there had been no reported findings of any injured girl or of a body either.

Rhys went to bed at last seething with conflicting emotions. Though he was trained as a soldier to induce sleep when necessary, tonight he found it well nigh impossible. Despite his reassurances to the Queen and to Lady Wroxeter, he could be by no means sure that Philippa had not been set upon by some thief or outlaw, murdered and her body conveyed out of town and weighted down in some nearby stream. He tossed and turned upon his bed, picturing her frightened and threatened, hurt—and he almost choked upon his own fury. Who dared lay one finger upon the body of his love? Whoever had done so would pay with his life.

He had managed to fall into an uneasy doze just after dawn and was awakened by his cousin and squire, David, who was shaking him urgently.

'Sir, the man you sent to scour the London road has returned and is anxious to report to you.'

'Send him in while I dress and order bread and meat to

be brought here to me at once. I will not delay to break fast in the hall.'

As the boy reached the door to obey him he called, peremptorily, 'After you have eaten I want you to ride over to Sir Owen Lewis's manor and request speech with Master Richard Allard, whom, I am sure, is staying there. Tell him I wish to confer with him urgently here and, David, try not to alert Sir Owen's other guest to the knowledge that we have some crisis here. You understand me?'

'Yes, Rhys.'

'Then off you go. Lose no time. Every second is urgent.'

The Queen's man-at-arms looked dusty and wearied. Obviously he had ridden through the night without pause.

'There was no sighting of the man, Maynard, upon the London road, Sir Rhys. I made enquiries at every tavern upon the way, giving a description of the man before turning back, knowing how quickly you would want my news.'

'You are convinced, then, that he did not set off for the capital as he had told the innkeeper of the Golden Fleece?'

'If he had done so, sir, surely someone would have noted him upon the road. He still carried a distinctive limp, or so I was informed.'

'He did,' Rhys said grimly. 'Then it seems I was right. The fellow is still skulking somewhere in the town. Why? It seems more than likely that he encountered Lady Philippa soon after she left the castle and conveyed her to some safe house for his own purposes. No one else in the town would have had reason to detain her apart from common robbery and we appear to have ruled out that from our other enquiries.'

'But—' The man was clearly reluctant to put into words the notion he might have entertained himself and Sir Rhys glanced at him sharply.

'You think she might have been seized upon by some brothel keeper?'

The man hesitated, then blurted out, 'She is so very beautiful, sir.'

'Aye, she is, but the town sheriff has been alerted to my need to discover her whereabouts and, since he knows all the houses of ill repute in the area, and has the authority to make searches, I doubt that that has been her fate. If it has, we shall know very shortly.' He waved the man away. 'Get yourself to the kitchen and take some refreshment, then get what rest you can, you'll need it. I may summon you soon. One of my servants will find you a pallet.'

The man saluted and made to leave, almost colliding with a young servant girl who came into the chamber bearing Sir Rhys's breakfast upon a tray.

He ate hastily and without tasting anything. He had only just finished when a tousle-haired boy thrust his head round the chamber door and informed him that Master Fairley had arrived from Gretton Manor and had asked to speak with him.

Rhys descended immediately to the hall and beckoned Peter Fairley into the room he used as a study. He wasted no time in empty preamble.

'Lady Wroxeter has informed you of the situation?'

Fairley nodded, his eyes wary and, testily, Rhys waved him to a chair.

'Sir down, man, and let us call a truce in hostilities for Lady Philippa's sake. We have much to do and little time at our disposal. I understand that you are the Earl of Wroxeter's squire and fought with him on Redmoor field, therefore you are an experienced warrior. I take it I can rely on your services and expertise?'

'Of course.'

'Do you agree with my surmise that she may well be

held somewhere as hostage? I am aware that the Earl is being sheltered at Sir Owen Lewis's manor.'

Peter Fairley's eyebrows rose in shock. 'You are, indeed, very well informed, Sir Rhys.'

'I make it my business to know my neighbours and their loyalties. In this day and age it is as well to do so. It also seems likely that I am not alone in knowing the Earl's whereabouts. I warned you several times to be wary in your dealings with the man, Maynard, but you chose to disregard my hints and allowed Lady Philippa to continue to interest herself in his welfare. This behaviour was incautious in the extreme and likely to endanger her father.'

Fairley jolted to an upright stance upon the stool and leaned toward his host, his eyes stormy.

'You knew the man was a King's spy?'

Rhys shrugged. 'I was simply not sure, but all strangers in the district are suspect, as I would have thought you would understand.'

'I thought the man was a merchant…'

'Aye, well, the harm is done and naught to be done on that score. He did not set out for London as he gave out and it is my opinion that he is the one man Lady Philippa would have trusted and the one man in Ludlow to lead her into a trap.'

Fairley scowled and moved his feet restively. 'But we do not know where he is.'

'No, and that is our main problem. Under the circumstances we cannot knock on every door in Ludlow and demand to search. We have no warrant and such behaviour would bring us under official scrutiny and further endanger Lady Wroxeter and the Earl.'

Peter Fairley gave a snarl of anger. 'If he harms one hair of her head—'

'You love her. I suspected as much.'

'Aye, I love her, have done since the moment of her birth, but I am almost twice her age and have no resources to keep her, even were her father to accept my suit. She regards me as a trusted elder brother. There it stands between us and will ever do so. I will give my life willingly to save hers and there you have it.' He turned abruptly and faced Griffith. 'I have my own understanding that she loves you—therefore, for her sake, I will do everything in my power to find her, rescue her and give her safely into your keeping.'

Rhys Griffith gave a long sigh and reached forward across the table to take the other's hand.

'Then we shall be truly comrades-in-arms in this and sworn to her service.'

Fairley sank down upon his chair again and gave a long, lugubrious sigh. 'I pray to God we shall be able to do so, but at present we seem helpless to move.' He looked up suddenly. 'Richard Allard is in the district still and would help us, but I imagine you know that as you seem to be well informed of all our movements.'

'I have sent for him. No—' he held up one hand to silence Peter as he was about to spring to his feet in alarm '—I have warned my cousin, David, whom I sent to summon him, that he was not to alert either Sir Owen or his guest to the fact that we have a serious problem here. I am only too aware that should the Earl discover that his daughter is missing he will come to her aid immediately.'

'He will not thank us for keeping the truth from him.'

'Let that be. I consider it necessary and what Philippa would wish and I'm happy to suffer the consequences in good time.' Rhys grimaced. 'And, as I am anxious to remain in the Earl's good opinion, I have much to lose.'

They were interrupted by Sir Rhys's steward, who ushered in Richard Allard and, at a sign from his master, withdrew and left the three men together to confer.

Richard Allard listened gravely to Fairley's explanation and his face whitened. 'Sweet Virgin, it is what we all most feared, yet we cannot be sure.'

'Since this man, Maynard, did not take the road to London, though he informed all and sundry that that was his intention, we imagine he must have had some other plan in mind. That, and the fact that we've had no other news of Lady Philippa, despite numerous searches.'

Richard nodded, stroking his chin. 'Yet, if we are unaware of his hiding place, we can do nothing.'

'I think gentlemen—' a quiet voice came from the doorway '—I can help you with the required information.'

They had all three been so intent on the matter in hand that they had not heard the door open and they spun round instantly to face the speaker. Rhys Griffith rose from his chair and scrutinised the newcomer curiously.

He was tall, though just a trifle stooped now, despite the arrogance of his bearing; a lean man, of soldierly bearing, still handsome, with a long face and deep-set eyes beneath half-closed lids, giving the false expression of lazy indifference. There were but faint touches of grey to the temples and Rhys judged him to be about fifty years of age. He could be in no doubt of his identity. Despite all their efforts to keep him in ignorance, Martyn Telford, Earl of Wroxeter, had come to his daughter's assistance.

Chapter Nine

Philippa had spent a sleepless night, lying still and tense upon her pallet in case she moved and alerted her guard. He was seated on a joint stool near the door. She had managed to rig up a blanket diagonally across one corner of the small foetid chamber to shield the bucket left for her toilet from view, assisted by the oldest of the guards, who had produced a hammer and two nails, genuinely affected by her modest distress at the lack of privacy afforded her. He had, he told her, two young daughters of his own and their mother would castigate him for his treatment of his prisoner if she were to hear of it. He had left, leaving his junior on guard, but warning the man sternly to leave the improvised curtain in place and to do nothing to embarrass the prisoner. Philippa could not help entertaining the fear that, should he discover the simple act of kindness, Hilyard would order the curtain to be torn down. In that one brief moment before he had left her, she had seen the vindictiveness of his true nature and her fears had begun to mount and she had thrust a hand hard against her mouth to prevent herself from dissolving into desperate tears, which would be heard by her guard.

Through the dark hours she had lain watchful, her only

comfort were her prayers. There seemed no way out of her terrible predicament. Either her father would surrender himself into the hands of his enemies or she, herself, would eventually be taken to London and become the King's prisoner, more than likely accommodated within the dark recess of the Tower. Yet she knew that would not happen. It was not her greatest fear. Her father would come for her, she knew that, and he would lose his life. Though King Henry had pardoned most of the remaining Yorkist gentlemen who had survived the field at Redmoor near Bosworth, he would never forgive her father, who had been one of the late King's principal advisers. She had refused to reveal his whereabouts and would keep staunchly to her resolve. Hilyard would not dare to harm her; the Queen would protect her, Philippa was convinced of that, but in the worst moments of her dread she realised that the Queen would not know of her imprisonment. Even if she were conveyed to London and the Tower, it was likely that the Queen would not be informed, neither would her mother or grandmother. She shivered with cold beneath the thin covering, yet knew it was not really a cold night. Her fear was freezing her to the marrow.

She continued to pray soundlessly. Though her situation appeared desperate, surely the Virgin would aid her. Then, suddenly, she knew that her prayer for courage was answered. She knew, without a shadow of doubt, that Rhys Griffith would come and find her. Her doubts yesterday that he would abandon her, after his conviction that he could never win her trust, were groundless. Rhys Griffith loved her. He might say that he would let her go but, once informed that she was missing, he would come to her aid. Relief washed over her as a cleansing tide. She had but to wait for him. Somehow he would find her and come and now her one prayer was that he would do so in time to prevent her father from endangering himself. How he would manage to accomplish her rescue, she had no idea. Her faith in him was complete. He would do it.

She pictured him vividly as she remembered him so many times when he had come to her assistance, tall, unyielding, strong, yet compassionate beneath that air of domination she had told herself that she despised. She saw how he had stood up to the mob when Nan Freeman had been threatened, one man, alone, but with the innate authority to subdue the infuriated villagers. Her heart pounded as she recalled the moment when she had first realised his underlying compassion, the moment he had held her close in silent comfort after the death of her beloved grandfather. She had turned to him blindly then, knowing instinctively that he was the one being in the world who would understand her torment.

When Roger Hilyard came unceremoniously into her prison early the next morning she was suddenly aware of her disordered appearance. She had slept in her gown, afraid to undress with her guard ever watchful. It was crumpled and dusty at the hem from her walk through the streets with Hilyard yesterday and she had no comb. Her hair had come free from its pins during the night and she had caught it up, smoothed it with her fingers as best she could and braided it beneath her linen cap which she had hastily pinned into place after rising. She had no idea if the cap was straight, but she smoothed down the folds of her mourning gown and faced her jailer with as much defiant courage as she could summon up.

He made her a mocking bow after dismissing the guard with instructions to bring up my lady's breakfast in a half an hour or so after he had left.

'You see, Lady Philippa, I have your welfare in mind. We shall not let you starve.'

'And if I choose to do so of my own free will?' she snapped.

He smiled affably. 'I shall not allow you to do that either,' he said mildly. 'You realise how important you are for my purpose. If necessary I will have you fed by force, but that is unlikely to become necessary since your father will have given himself into my hands before then.'

Deliberately she lowered her gaze that he might not see the flash of stark fear revealed in her eyes. 'I do not see how that can be possible, Master Maynard—or is it Hilyard? I confess I cannot remember, since you are such an insignificant creature in my eyes. You do not know where my father is.'

'No?' he questioned, his grey eyes dancing. 'You think that I do not without your divulging it? Ah, Lady Philippa, you must think me a fool and without resources. I understand your father employed an efficient spy network in the service of the late murderer who called himself Richard of England. Well, my network is smaller, but just as hard working and efficient. I know of one man in the district who might agree to shelter an enemy of the king. Sir Owen Lewis was once squire to Sir Guy Jarvis, I am told. Is not your very good friend, Mistress Anne Allard, the daughter of Sir Guy? Now I know Master Allard was very recently here in Ludlow. Did I not see him in talk with you and Master Fairley, your father's former squire? Oh, yes, I know that too. Fairley fought beside your father at Redmoor. Now why, I asked myself, should Master Richard Allard come to Ludlow? His father's manor and that of his wife's father lie far from here. He came for a purpose, I am quite sure. Now, could it have been to meet and help to protect the Earl of Wroxeter? Since Wroxeter's wife and daughter are here at Gretton it would seem likely that he would venture himself to be near them, especially at a time of deep sorrow for Lady Wroxeter.'

He knew instantly that his arrow had struck home for Philippa's eyes had widened, first in doubt, then in horrified discovery that he was right. She bit hard down upon her bottom lip to prevent it from trembling.

'You are guessing wildly, Master Hilyard,' she said tonelessly.

'I am sufficiently confident that Lewis still harbours Yorkist loyalties,' he said lightly. 'So much so that I have dispatched a messenger to his manor to alert his honoured guest to the knowledge that his daughter is a prisoner in my hands and issued instructions as to the wherewithal to find this house. I am reasonably sure that he will heed my summons. After all, I am sure he has sufficient affection for his only child to come to her aid when she is in peril.'

Philippa managed to keep control over her emotions, though she was very close to tears. She would not allow this creature to see her desperation.

She lifted her head and stared back at him defiantly. 'Sir Owen Lewis fought for the present King both at Redmoor and at Stoke. He is the King's man. My father would never seek his aid.'

He gave a little snort of amusement. 'We shall see, my lady. If I am, indeed, wrong in my assumptions, we can always try the homes of other gentlemen in the area whose loyalties have ever been suspect, but I do not believe that I am wrong. I expect my lord Earl to present himself here before the day's end or at the very latest in the morning.'

He made her another mocking bow and left, ordering the guard to keep a still tighter watch over his prisoner.

She sat upon the pallet bed, her heart racing. It seemed that Master Hilyard knew more about the loyalties of the gentlemen of the district than she could ever have suspected. And if he did, the King, more than likely, was aware of them also. Not only was her father in peril, but many other good men with him. She shivered again, and turned so that the guard would not glimpse her growing panic. During the night she had been so sure that Rhys Griffith would come, but would he now be in time? Another terrible thought struck her forcibly. If he did so, would he place himself in peril? Had his love for her put him in mortal danger?

Later, when another of the men-at-arms entered with a tray of food, consisting of a dish of gruel, coarse rye bread moistened with a smear of honey and a cup of watered sour wine, she forced herself to eat. She would need all her strength and courage to endure the long hours of waiting.

Rhys Griffith rose to greet his noble visitor and courteously offered him his chair.

'I am glad to welcome you to my home, my lord, but wish it were under happier circumstances.'

The Earl waved to his host to seat himself again and hooked a joint stool forward, nearer to the table and between his two companions, and sank down.

'I only hope that I have not put you under suspicion,' he said, fumbling inside his doublet to find a folded piece of parchment, which he laid open upon the table. 'I am afraid I have upset your steward by my unexpected arrival and insistence upon being brought to you immediately, but I thought you should see this at once.' He glanced round at the small, assembled company and grimaced. 'I take it this is a council of war.'

Rhys looked up irritably as his steward apologetically poked his head around the door.

'Sir, this man forced his way in and—'

'Yes, I know, man. All is well. When the sergeant returns send him up if we are still in conference. In the meantime, see that no one else is admitted and, Crawley, make sure none of the household servants gossip about what is happening here. Keep them well occupied within the manor house.'

'Yes, Sir Rhys.'

The head disappeared and the Earl gave a brief snort of a laugh. 'It seems that you impose discretion upon your household, Sir Rhys, which is just as well.' He tapped the parchment with his forefinger. 'I received this message this morning soon after Richard, here, left, I imagine. He went without informing me of his destination, but Owen and I drew our own conclusions. I decided that, dangerous or not, for Philippa's sake you would need to see this.'

With a muttered word to excuse himself, Rhys snatched up the parchment and scanned the contents.

'We were right, then,' he informed the others, who were leaning forward eagerly. 'The man, Maynard, is holding Lady Philippa hostage. He demands that the Earl surrender himself immediately or face the consequences. He does not state what they might be,' he added grimly then, peering closer at the parchment, he murmured, 'I see that he signs himself Hilyard, not Maynard, which is interesting.'

Richard Allard uttered a soldier's oath. And the others glanced at him blankly.

'You know the man, Richard?' the Earl queried.

'No, I think not, but John Hilyard was King Henry's esquire of the body. He showed a particular interest in my wife, Anne, while she served the Queen at Westminster. It was Hilyard who followed us when we were escaping to the coast, escorting your daughter, my lord. In the skirmish Hilyard was killed.'

'Ah.' The Earl leaned back slightly upon his stool. 'Then this fellow is most likely kin of his and is anxious for revenge as well as preferment.' He was watching Rhys Griffith closely as he traced his finger across the crude map scrawled upon the parchment. 'You know this house, Sir Rhys?'

'I know the district. It lies somewhat clear of the town and appears to be apart from other properties.'

Richard Allard said curtly, 'Then it lies open to attack without the likelihood of being observed by townsfolk.'

'It is also likely to be well guarded from within,' the Earl drawled, his heavy lids narrowed. 'This is a King's man. He will have men at his beck and call, fighting men.'

There was a brief silence, then Peter Fairley said heavily, 'And Lady Philippa is at their mercy and could be killed while we are about it.'

'Exactly,' the Earl agreed.

Rhys made a little explosive sound and the Earl turned to him. 'I know you have a deep regard for my daughter, sir, but you have much to lose if you venture yourself with us.'

Rhys gave a harsh laugh and dismissive movement of his hand. 'I will fight for her with the last breath in my body. Do you doubt that, my lord?'

'No, I merely point out the disadvantages of allying yourself with us.'

'That is of no account. Now that we know where she is, our plan of action is clear. We must free her.'

There were nods of agreement from the others. Peter said quietly, 'How many men would you estimate are within the house, my lord?'

The Earl shook his head and turned to Rhys. 'You would know the size of the property, sir.'

'It is quite small but, because that is so, easy to defend.

I would imagine Hilyard has, perhaps, five or six men, to have more at his command would have excited notice amongst the townsfolk. It seems obvious that he instructed his men to remain apart from him for the most part while he was engaged in spying out the situation. Had a troop of men arrived in the town we should have learned of it.'

Peter asked, 'Can we rely on the services of the Queen's men who have been searching the town, Sir Rhys?'

'I would be reluctant to do that, Master Fairley, as that could embarrass the Queen.'

'That is not to be countenanced,' the Earl said quietly. 'No action of ours must place her Grace in danger.'

'Agreed,' Sir Rhys said. 'I take it, gentlemen, that all of us here are prepared to risk ourselves in order to save Lady Philippa.'

There was a murmur of assent.

'What we *can* do is allow some of the men the Queen placed at my disposal to spy out the house and its environs and report to me,' Rhys proposed. 'I think a night attack will be advantageous.'

'Any attack will be dangerous for Philippa,' the Earl said firmly. 'I propose, gentlemen, to do just what this message instructs me to do. I intend to present myself at the door and allow Master Hilyard the pleasure of arresting me.'

Rhys sprang to his feet in horror. 'I cannot allow you to do that, my lord.'

'And how, pray, would you prevent me?'

'By force if necessary. Philippa would never forgive any of us if anything were to happen to you.'

'Philippa is truly my daughter. She knows when to obey me and when to bow to the inevitable. Always she is conscious of that fact that I might be killed in the service of the Duchess Margaret. She fears it but, like my wife, Cressida, she has learned to live with it and face it bravely, but I am by no means sure that anything will happen to me.'

'But, my lord, you propose to walk into the trap unarmed.'

The Earl shrugged. 'It would seem to me that it is the only plan possible to allow us any chance of success.'

'How so?' Richard Allard demanded harshly.

'While Hilyard's men are occupied in securing me, you would have a better opportunity of taking the other men by surprise and, once in, I shall be in a better position to reassure Philippa.' The Earl gave a little crooked smile. 'Assuredly, at my request, Hilyard will allow me to see my daughter. It will give him an added sense of satisfaction to witness her distress, a fillip to his revenge for the death of his kinsman.'

'But he could dispatch you at once with the intention of taking your head to the King at Westminster,' Rhys grated, while Peter Fairley moved restlessly on his stool, his eyes dark with alarm.

'He will not do that. I tell you, Henry will wish to speak with me.' The words were spoken lightly but Richard Allard winced at the thought behind them. The Earl would be subjected to interrogation in the dark dungeon within the Tower where he, himself, had suffered.

'Don't do this, Lord Martyn,' he pleaded. 'Philippa would not wish it and many things could go wrong. I am the first to admit that we could be badly outnumbered and you taken and held, despite our best endeavours.'

'Then what would you suggest?' The Earl queried blandly, opening both palms facing upwards upon the table top. 'Philippa lies in their hands and cannot be left to Hilyard's mercy, not even to his continued insults.'

Rhys's brows drew together in a black scowl of fury.

'The Earl is right,' he grated. 'His surrender does offer

us the best chance of success. We are like to be outnumbered and surprise is the only tactic which is open to us at this stage in the game.'

He paused as there came a tap upon the door and he called an imperative instruction to enter. The Queen's sergeant-at-arms stood on the threshold and saluted.

'I regret, Sir Rhys, that I have to report no success in our search. It appears to me that we have exhausted every possible place of concealment, except within one of the houses, of course, and we have no jurisdiction to demand entrance to any of those as yet.'

'We have discovered where Lady Philippa is held and for what purpose. Our difficulty now is the best way of effecting her release,' Rhys said.

'Then what can we do to help you, sir? Each one of us would gladly die in the service of her Grace the Queen, and Lady Philippa is her favourite.'

'As each one of us would,' Sir Rhys assured him gravely. He prodded the parchment with one finger. 'I can give you instructions about where to find this house. I suggest that each of your men, who is willing, remove all livery and go with you to the street and discover as much as you can about the place's defences. We shall join you later, just before nightfall, I think.' He turned to receive the affirmation of the others. 'We shall then enter the house and try to free the Lady Philippa. I think it best if you surround the property for us and try to ensure that none of the men of Hilyard's company escape to carry tales. I do not want any of us embroiled in any skirmish in the town. Information of that sort reaching the King would not only endanger you all but also injure the reputation of the Queen.'

The sergeant considered for a moment, then gave a brief

nod of acknowledgement. 'But you four could easily be outnumbered and the lady hurt or killed in the attempt.'

'We are only too aware of that,' Sir Rhys conceded.

The sergeant said huskily, 'I am willing to risk myself…'

'No, for the Queen's sake, better not.'

'But just four of you and hindered by the need to protect the lady…'

'There will be five of us, if you will grant me permission, Rhys,' a youthful voice spoke from the doorway.

Rhys turned and smiled a little grimly as his young cousin and squire entered the chamber. The boy was attired in martial clothing, a boiled leather jack and heavy riding boots, and was armed with sword and dagger.

Rhys nodded. 'I think you are ready to see action, boy,' he said quietly, 'but remember to obey my instructions implicitly.'

'You have my word.' The boy gave a broad smile. 'After all, it is likely that Lady Philippa will become the chatelaine of this house and my mistress and very soon, so I should have the honour of taking part in her rescue.'

'If God wills it,' Rhys said heavily, and he looked towards the Earl for confirmation of his claim to Philippa's hand.

After the sergeant had taken his leave to instruct his men in their duties and the other three had set about their own preparations Rhys sat alone in his study with the Earl. He had already sent young David to Gretton with a letter informing the Countess that he intended to take steps very shortly to restore her daughter to her.

While he was penning it the Earl queried sharply, 'You have not mentioned my intended part in this rescue?'

'No, my lord.'

'Good. Let that remain a secret between us.' The Earl

paused, then said quietly, 'I know I do not have to ask you to care for Philippa if the worst should happen to me but…' and he hesitated momentarily '…but I do need to ask you…'

'To ensure the welfare of the Countess Wroxeter and Lady Gretton,' Rhys finished and the other gave a little shrug of acknowledgement. Rhys continued. 'You know that I will do so, you have my word and, indeed, if later, after the Duchess of Burgundy can no longer offer her protection, I would wish Lady Wroxeter and Fairley to come to me here.'

The Earl gave a little contented sigh, then leaned forward towards his host, 'You realise all this could cause you trouble—if not place you in very real danger?'

'Yes, my lord, I am fully aware of that.' Rhys then sealed the letter with his signet ring and handed it to David. 'See that you give it into the hand of no one but the Countess or, failing that, into the hand of Lady Gretton.'

The boy nodded and took his leave. The two men sat on in silence for a moment, then Rhys said softly, 'What hope do you have of success in this?'

Again the Earl gave a faint Gallic shrug. 'I think, like you, we have a fair chance. Our comrades are brave and true which I doubt can be said about Hilyard's men. They serve him for gain and their hearts will not be set on a fight, but we cannot escape the knowledge that they will be experienced warriors.'

'Yes.'

Again the two seemed lost in thought, then Rhys said abruptly, 'You said the King will be most anxious to question you personally. Information concerning the whereabouts and movements of other Yorkist gentlemen could be obtained by others, by lesser officials. You imply that

Henry has his own reasons for ensuring he has you in his hands. Is it that he wishes to know the fate of the Princes?'

A slight smile curled the Earl's long lips. 'Ah, you, too, are not sure that Tryell's confession is genuine.'

'I never for one moment believed that it was.'

'Then you would wish to know about the Princes for yourself?'

'On the contrary, the fewer who are entrusted with that deadly secret the better. It is just that it is one more reason why you should not surrender yourself. Can we even the balance of risk by arming you with a poniard, at least, well hidden on your person? It would give you some means of defence.'

Regretfully the Earl shook his head. 'I shall be immediately searched. If I am found to be armed and you and your companions fail to enter the house, Philippa could be further endangered. That risk I must take. My late master would understand my need. At all events it would be difficult for the King to take action against his most dreaded enemies now. It is merely that, if possible, I would wish him to remain in ignorance of the true situation.' He gave a little bitter laugh. 'It grants me a measure of satisfaction, that is all and,' he added thoughtfully, 'it is better for the Queen's peace of mind that the truth should not be made public.'

As evening approached the five comrades-in-arms, clad in dark, serviceable garments over brigandines and well armed, but for the Earl, mounted and rode from the manor. In Ludlow Rhys arranged for them to stable their mounts at an inn and they then proceeded on foot to the rendezvous agreed with the Queen's sergeant-at-arms.

A dark shadow emerged from the bushes that bordered

the neglected garden of one of the properties and revealed itself to be the sergeant.

'Two men entered the house about an hour ago. They appeared to be carrying food supplies and an ample supply of wine bottles. I could not estimate the number inside, but two, beside Master Hilyard, would be guarding the prisoner, I imagine. There might be more. The two we saw were ruffianly in appearance, but undoubtedly fighting men still in early middle age, both of them, and capable of putting up a fair fight and an unfair one too if pressed.'

Sir Rhys nodded. 'What of windows and doors?'

'There seems to be one main door at the front, made of stout oak, not easy to broach but an axe should suffice.' He produced one from beneath his cloak and handed it to Richard Allard. 'It will take some time, but if the men are engaged in another part of the house it might be managed.' He glanced back towards the house in question, from which they could see a glimmer of candle light from between closed shutters. 'There is one window, heavily shuttered at the back and I would guess that that is the room where Lady Philippa is confined. There is a very small upstairs casement, also shuttered, but it would not be easy to climb to that, or, indeed, for a big man to enter it, especially as he would have to deal with the shutters, while suspended in an ungainly and difficult position and without adequate foothold. There are no sturdy creepers in evidence nor, I regret to say, a suitable tree near with overhanging branches. I have managed to deal with the bottom casement shutter with the point of my dagger. It had to be done very quietly. While there I detected no sound of voices within the chamber but there is a pricket burning and I believe it to be occupied.'

Rhys nodded grimly.

'It would seem that we have no alternative but to do as

my lord Earl proposes, allow him to surrender himself while the rest of us hold ourselves in readiness to make an assault upon the front door and rear window.' He addressed the sergeant-at-arms. 'You have done well, man, and have my gratitude. Now I think your men should retire to the cover of those bushes and watch for what happens, particularly to deal with any one of Hilyard's men who runs out to seek help.' He glanced around. 'The houses nearby are sufficiently away from this property to avoid undue notice, which, I imagine, is the reason why Hilyard chose it. That should prove an advantage to us, too. Well...' he turned to the waiting, silent, little company '...I take it that we are all ready?'

There was a mutter of assent and the Earl put a hand upon Rhys's shoulder. 'God guard us all and especially you whom I trust to help Philippa whatever the consequences to the rest of us.'

Rhys nodded and answered gruffly, 'You can trust each one of us to do his part, my lord, and I pray the Virgin to bring you safely out of this.'

The Earl turned and briefly embraced his squire, Peter, who had been his trusted and loyal companion over many years. 'I know I can trust you with the safekeeping of your mistress, should you come out of this unscathed.'

Peter's voice was husky with emotional tears. 'Come, my lord, we have come through worst scrapes. Did I not believe you dead on Redmoor field and yet you survived? Our cause is righteous. We'll bring the Lady Philippa safe home to Gretton, never fear.'

The Earl gripped his arm tightly, acknowledged the rest with a nod and then strode off towards the house. The sergeant saluted and withdrew to join his men and Rhys signalled silently for the others to draw closer to the house, ready for action after the Earl had entered and they had given sufficient time for the occupants to be busy with his capture.

He glanced briefly at the others. 'Master Allard, you are too big a man to go easily and silently through that window and I would prefer that young David here remain close to me during the attack. I think, Master Fairley you will be the best man to broach the casement and, if you can, to get to Lady Philippa that way. The rest of you come with me to make an assault on that door.'

Peter made no objection, simply moved off to take up his position.

Rhys looked briefly up at the sky. It was a dark night, with only a fraction of the new moon peeping through the cloud. It was calm but cold and he could discern no sound of people moving in the vicinity. He hoped, if it were possible, to manage this rescue without causing any trouble within the town which could involve the Earl and bring him eventually to the notice of the authorities. He bared his teeth. By all the saints, he would save Philippa and dispatch Hilyard whatever the consequences to himself or any other man. He gave the signal to advance and felt David's heavy breathing at his back.

Philippa stirred uneasily on her pallet when she heard the sound of raised voices outside the door of her prison. Her guard, seated on his stool as usual, lifted his head and had turned to listen intently, too, but turned his watchful gaze to her again and made no move to stand or unlock the door. The noise continued, the scraping of booted feet upon the flagstones of the hallway, the mutter of voices, then the voices were muted. She bit down hard upon her bottom lip to prevent it trembling. She was aware that the two men Hilyard had sent out earlier for supplies had returned some time ago. All his men were within the house, yet she was sure that the outer door had been opened. She sat back against her pillow, her ears straining. Who had been admitted? She dared not even think that her worst fear might be realised.

Then, abruptly, there came a harsh command in Hilyard's voice, and the guard rose, moved his stool and un-latched the door. Philippa found her heart racing as it seemed an age before it finally opened and she saw Roger Hilyard standing on the threshold with his arm raised high, brandishing a lighted candle in its holder. She saw clearly in that instant of time that he was deliberately illuminating the face of the man who stood by his side. She gave a sharp cry of anguish and Hilyard smiled.

'You see, my lady, I was right. Honour determined my lord Earl's decision. He could not allow his only daughter to remain a hostage. He has come to surrender himself into my hands, his only request that he might see you and speak with you. Naturally,' he mocked, 'I could not be cruel enough to refuse that request, but for moments only.' He addressed her guard. 'Leave them together, man. He has been well searched and was found to be completely un-armed as I ordered.'

Philippa sprang from the pallet and rushed to her father as he stepped into the chamber. He drew her close to his heart as Hilyard gave a final mocking laugh and he and the guard exited. Close to her ear the Earl murmured softly, 'Give your heart peace, child, you are not aban-doned. Rhys is outside with three good men. No, do not cry out again. Just be ready and do what I or Rhys com-mand. Stand clear and allow us to do what must be done.'

He felt her tremble against him and steadied her gently. 'I need you to be very strong, my daughter. Do not faint on me, now.' As she gave a little sob, muffled against his heart, he said aloud, 'Do not upbraid me, Philippa. I could not leave you a prisoner, you know that.'

She stifled her weeping and said hoarsely and loudly enough, she hoped, for Hilyard to hear through the cracks of the ill-made door, 'You should not have come. You have walked into a trap. He will not release me. You must be aware of that.'

He said, 'I do not believe the man to be completely without honour. He gave his word…'

He held her tightly by one shoulder, as there came the sound of splintering wood and the hoarse cries of men taken by surprise. Almost immediately her guard unlatched the door and, with an oath, sprang at the pair in the centre of the room. He swung the Earl aside, tearing him apart from his daughter, and Philippa felt the bite of cold steel against her throat as the man's dagger grazed her skin. She knew her father would do nothing at this moment to endanger her and so would not make his move against her assailant. Her breath was coming in hard, dry pants but her eyes peered round desperately.

As if in answer to her unspoken prayer, a soft voice sounded from behind her as Peter wrenched aside the shutter and crashed through the horn window.

'Harm her and you are a dead man, my friend.'

For moments there was stalemate. The Earl glared at her attacker and Philippa felt, rather than heard, Peter come close up to her captor's back. She dared not struggle, as she could feel the harsh beat of the guard's ragged breaths and smell the rank body stink of his raw fear. Outside the room she could hear the noise of conflict, shouts, trampling of feet, thuds, as if an axe was being wielded, and the scrape of steel on steel. Nobody moved in the little prison chamber.

It seemed an eternity as the noise of battle went on, yells

of pain as a weapon found its mark and soldiers' oaths flowed freely. Caught tight against her jailor, she could do nothing but pray. Sweet Virgin, Rhys was out there and probably Richard. Let them come through this safely. Through her own heedlessness she had brought them all into this peril and, if Hilyard's men were triumphant, in moments they would all be killed or carried off as prisoners.

Her father's eyes were fixed relentlessly upon her captor and Peter did not move. They were helpless to join the combat, since their one aim was to ensure her safety. She longed to call out to them to leave her to her fate and go to the help of the intruders, but her father's implacable gaze warned her to remain silent. Her captor was turning his head desperately as he could hear the battle, but not see one sign of how it was progressing. His breath was becoming even more ragged and Philippa felt a thin trickle of blood run down her throat and on to her breast as his dagger bit yet closer, though she felt no real pain.

Suddenly her captor's attention was drawn from her as a man's body fell against the door of the chamber and Roger Hilyard stumbled backwards through, then righted itself, his sword held protectively forward. Abruptly, taken by utter surprise, her captor released his hold and she fell forward, almost into her father's arms. At the same moment Peter gave a cry of triumph and thrust his dagger into her erstwhile captor's back, so that he gave one terrible scream and fell forwards almost at her father's feet. Held against the Earl, she watched with mounting horror as the wounded man's feet drummed against the floor in his death agony and his breath rasped in his throat, then he fell silent and his sprawled body stilled. Peter knelt and retrieved his and the man's weapon.

Philippa's father urged her gently backwards as he made

a clear way for the two men who were fighting their way into the chamber while Peter also moved. He was watching the combatants carefully, alert for any sign that he might aid Rhys without hindering him. Roger Hilyard had recovered his balance and appeared now to be unhindered by his injured leg. He was expertly defending himself against the sword thrusts of his opponent and Rhys Griffith pushed him ever more relentlessly further into the chamber.

Horrified, Philippa watched as the two fought doggedly on. The other men in the room were silent and that emphasised the clang of weapons and the ragged breathing of the two fighting men. Philippa had thought that Roger Hilyard would be inexperienced in the use of sword and dagger, but that was not so. Evidently he had been well trained in the King's service and he parried and attacked with considerable skill. Also he was as light on his feet as a dancer. She had no idea if he had kept clear of the fighting until now and, if so, he would be much fresher for the fray than Rhys was. Had he deliberately feigned lameness when he had brought her here last night?

She saw that her father was watching the conflict with frowning interest and since he had come unarmed into the house he could not intervene. Peter evidently considered that as matters stood he would only make matters worse for Rhys by plunging into the fight and he, too, stood aside, lips pursed, his sword at the ready to jump in if necessary. Philippa could only stand still helplessly, in desperate fascination. Her lips moved in silent prayer.

Once or twice one or other of the combatants let out a cry and she stifled her own answering one with the back of her hand across her mouth in case her distress should draw Rhys's attention to her and so bring about his downfall.

Rhys was the bigger man, less agile, but stronger and

tireless in the use of the heavy broad sword. Steadily he pushed his opponent back further into the room. Someone outside in the corridor groaned and, for a second, Roger Hilyard hesitated and Rhys thrust home at his sword arm calling forth a sharp cry of pain, but immediately Hilyard riposted, infuriated by the cut, and appeared unconcerned by the heavy flow of blood dyeing his doublet sleeve. Surely one or other of the two must tire and make a fatal mistake now, Philippa thought, and as if in answer to that thought, Rhys suddenly stumbled and fell to one knee. He appeared to have taken a cut across his right wrist and his weapon faltered momentarily and almost fell from his hand. Despite her determination not to hinder him by her fear, Philippa let out a scream of terror as Roger Hilyard came on eagerly and leaned forward for the kill. In that same moment Rhys, magically, it seemed, retrieved his weapon and his sword leaped forward as if by its own volition and Philippa glimpsed the lightning flash of the rushlight on the tempered steel. As an echo of her own cry, Roger Hilyard let out one shrill scream of agony and fell backwards across the shattered window casement. There was a strange, tinny sound of splintering horn, as his body was bent across the broken wood of the sill and, for a moment, Philippa thought it would topple further backwards into the darkened garden beyond, but it convulsed, as her former attacker's had done, and then lay horribly still. This time she detected no death rattle and she caught at her father's hand as Peter Fairley strode forward and bent over the stricken man.

He straightened and turned back to Rhys who was struggling to his feet, nursing the deep cut in his wrist from which crimson blood flowed onto his hand so that he cursed and let fall his blade.

'You got him squarely in the throat with that final thrust.

A daring move and a desperate one, if I may say so. Are you badly hurt, Sir Rhys?'

Rhys was attempting to stem the blood welling up in his wrist with his free hand and the fingers of both his hands were stained and slippery. Now, at last, as if released from some malign spell, Philippa rushed into his arms, unmindful of the bloodied fingers, which reached up to stroke tenderly her disordered hair.

'There, there, my heart,' Rhys murmured, bending to nuzzle the bright gold waves, 'it is not so bad and you and your father are safe finally.'

She pulled herself free, as he was unable to hold her, hampered by the wound as he was, and she bent and impatiently tore strips from the hem of her cambric petticoat to tie around the wound, pulling the bandage tight to staunch the heavy blood flow.

'Do not dare,' she murmured through gritted teeth, 'tell me that you have had to rescue me from yet another foolish scrape.'

He gave a shaky laugh and pulled her protesting into his arms again. 'I was not about to. Frankly I am too wearied to argue with you, only thankful to have you alive, that is enough for me.' He leaned forward and peered intently into her eyes. 'Did one of those devils so much as touch you? You are unharmed?'

She shook her head vehemently. 'No, I have been frightened and humiliated but Hilyard threatened them with hanging if they so much as insulted me.'

'As for me, Sir Rhys,' the Earl said quietly, as he came to their side, 'you have my eternal gratitude.'

'What I want is your permission to wed this shrew of a daughter of yours,' Rhys grinned, 'and I hope and pray she will learn gentler ways with the sick and dying. Ouch,' he said sharply as she pulled even tighter the improvised bandage.

'You are a very long way from dying, sir,' she said tartly, then burst into sudden tears of relief from the unbearable tension, 'though every moment I feared that you were, and when he had you on one knee like that—I thought—dear God—I thought it would be the end.'

He cupped her chin in his two, still bloodied hands, but she gave no heed to the unsightly smears upon her skin. 'My heart, I was beginning to glimpse the gates of Heaven or Hell myself,' he chuckled darkly. 'Thank the saints I was not to discover which, at this time, at least.'

Richard Allard and Peter were counting up the dead. Young David had sustained a chest wound and was clearly pale and shaky, though the gash had been padded by one of the victorious men and he was protesting loudly that he was not feeling faint. Peter, Philippa now noticed, was disfigured by several gashes on face, throat, hands and arms, where he had burst through the broken horn casement.

Rhys said sharply, 'Sit down, David, and keep still. We need to get you to a surgeon and soon, after we have cleaned up here.'

The Earl was looking round at the carnage. Richard could be heard mounting to the upper room to make sure there were no further opponents in hiding and awaiting an opportunity to make yet a further assault. Though still somewhat trembly from shock, Philippa went and knelt by Roger Hilyard's sprawled body. His face, she was relieved to see, was not contorted and his wide blue eyes were open and gazing blankly upwards. His expression now appeared as she had first seen it, bereft of guile, like the simple youthful merchant's journeyman he had purported to be and, she sighed heavily at her loss of trust in humanity in general. Very gently she closed his eyes and Rhys joined her, looking down dispassionately at his fallen enemy.

'Do not pity him too much, my heart,' he said soberly, 'his only intention was to snare your father and many other good men of dubious loyalty within this county and his motive was gain. I doubt very much if he would have released you, even after he had given his sworn word to your father. You would have been too great a prize and you might well have ended up within the gloomy dungeons of the Tower, accused of treason for the simple act of trying to protect your own father.'

She rose to her feet with a little sob and he enclosed her in his arms again, turning her so that she might cry into his shoulder, as she had done on that dreadful day when her beloved *grandpère* had died and he had comforted her.

There came a thundering noise from the stairs, which made them all turn and stare. Richard Allard erupted into the chamber, pushing before him a man he held roughly by one shoulder.

'I found this fellow hiding behind a chest upstairs.'

The man was whimpering a plea for his life, promising complete surrender.

Rhys regarded him sternly. 'You are one of Master Hilyard's men?'

'I was, my lord, but I was taking no part in the fighting. I...'

Rhys turned a contemptuous gaze upon the man, older by some years than his companions who had engaged in the fight.

'Take him outside and kill him,' he ordered Richard Allard 'and, for God's sake, do it quietly. We need to keep this business from the attention of prying neighbours.'

The man fell to his knees, holding out two hands before him in supplication.

Philippa went slightly towards him and gave a little start of recognition.

'Please, Rhys,' she begged, 'spare him. He was the only member of this household who treated me with the slightest consideration. He did try to spare me humiliation. He told me he has children of his own, young girls and...'

Rhys shook his head angrily. 'That may be so, Philippa, but he can do us irreparable harm. None of Hilyard's men must leave this place and talk of what has occurred here. Your father's life depends on this and possibly the lives of the rest of us, too, to say nothing of the lives of other good men he may harbour secret information about. I understand your pity but this is war, and we cannot afford to be merciful.'

She appealed to her father. 'If he swears that he will go far from here and say nothing...'

'It is a risk,' he said quietly. 'We have the right to play with our lives but not those of our friends.'

The man had fallen forward on to his knees and was whimpering or praying softly, Philippa could not tell which.

She turned away, shocked. 'I do not think I can bear this,' she whispered, looking down at Hilyard's sprawled body and that of the other man who had held her by the throat, 'so much bloodletting and all because I was incautious in placing my trust.'

The Earl lifted both shoulders and let them fall. 'I ask you to let the fellow go, Rhys,' he said. 'Philippa is right. There has been killing enough and this dispatching in cold blood sickens me.'

Rhys looked from one to the other of his companions

and they each hesitated for a moment and then nodded, averting their eyes from the proposed victim.

Rhys said harshly, 'Very well, then. On our own heads be the consequences.'

Richard had released his grip on the prisoner who had not moved from the spot but had lifted his head now to turn in mute appeal to Philippa. Rhys moved near to him and stirred him with his foot.

'All right, you heard my Lady Philippa. You can thank her for your life for what is left of it. You can go, but I ask your word that you will leave this district at once and delay any report to your masters in London for at least two weeks.'

The man still did not climb to his feet, but gazed uneasily around the chamber at the impassive faces of his captors as if he could not even now believe his good fortune.

'I was simply engaged by Master Hilyard there to keep guard on his prisoner and do common tasks about the house while we were waiting for him to capture her. I'd no notion who'm it was to be, not even that it was to be a woman. I knows no one of importance in London, and I swear to you, my lords, that I'll be off back to my family the moment you let me and never stir.'

Rhys frowned slightly as if he were uncertain as to the truth of the fellow's tale, but he turned away at last, signalling to the man to stand up.

'Then take yourself off and remember that one word from you to anyone about what has happened here could threaten the life of your benefactress.' He turned back abruptly and bared his teeth in a grimace. 'Do that, fellow, and you will have all of us to answer to and, make no mistake about it, one or other of us will hound you down and end it once and for all.'

The man was backing towards the chamber door. Not one of his captors moved a muscle, but he felt the steel-like gaze of them all. He knuckled his brow as a salute to Philippa, then turned and dashed out. They could hear his stumbling steps on the flagstones of the corridor.

Philippa said a trifle huskily, 'Thank you, all of you. I know I have been perhaps a little—unwise in asking this of you but—' Tears sparked her eyelashes and she gave a little choking sound. 'I could not have borne to have him summarily taken and killed. If he had died in the conflict I could have accepted it—but—but—'

The Earl took her briefly into his arms and patted her shoulder as her body heaved with tearful distress.

'Sir Rhys, is there somewhere I could take Philippa, out of here?' He looked round distastefully at the signs of carnage.

Rhys looked questioningly at Richard Allard who said, 'The kitchen would seem to be a more appropriate place, for the moment. There was less—disturbance in there.'

Following Richard's instructions, the Earl led his daughter into the back part of the house and was relieved to see that there was an overturned joint stool beside the neglected fireplace. He righted it and gently set her down upon it, sensing by the violent shivering of her body that she was very close to complete collapse.

Richard stood in the doorway, his expression sober. 'What do you think we should do about cleaning up, my lord?' He gestured with a backward glance towards the bodies sprawled in the sleeping chamber.

Rhys had come up behind them and was looking with concern at Philippa.

The Earl said reassuringly, 'She is very shocked, has been through much. She is strong in body and will. She will recover. Give her time.' In answer to Richard's question he addressed Rhys. 'You should make the decisions, sir. You live in the district and will have to face up to any consequences after the rest of us have gone.'

Rhys inclined his chin. 'I think we should leave them all where they lie. To attempt to bury them would take too long and shallow graves would soon be discovered.' He gave a grim smile, 'Stray dogs could root around—I do not think I need elaborate.' Again he glanced towards Philippa who gave a great shudder and turned away.

He continued. 'The sergeant-at-arms said the men had returned with wine bottles and supplies. I suggest we leave food and overturned wine bottles about. The investigating constable will assume the men have quarrelled over dice or some wanton and a fight broke out. He will not know how many men were here or how many others have fled.' He gave a little dismissive shrug. 'I imagine he will see they have paupers' burials and make few enquiries. Naturally we must search the house and the bodies before we leave and make quite sure none of them, especially Hilyard, carried any official papers or warrants. If you will remain with your daughter, my lord, we will see to that. With your permission I will send Master Fairley to the inn for our horses and dismiss the Queen's men. The sooner they are dispersed the better and the sergeant will be able to reassure her that Lady Philippa and you, my lord, are safe and will be soon in hiding again.' He frowned, considering. 'I would rather not have had the horses brought to the house, but I need to get young David to a surgeon in the town and neither he nor Lady Philippa are in any condition to walk. It is safe enough, I think. Most of the respectable townsfolk are tucked up in their beds and—' he gave a little dismissive shrug again '—we must risk them being noticed and remarked upon later.' He dropped upon one knee before Philippa. 'Can you hold on here for just a little longer? I would spare you this but—'

She reached out and took his hand. 'Do what you must, sir, to protect all of us and I pray Master David will soon be well again. Is his wound grievous?'

'I think not, but it requires more attention that I can give. It is a chest wound, but I do not believe vital organs have been affected. There is no lung damage or he would be coughing frothy blood by now. We must get it stitched and cleansed against future infection.'

He gripped her hand tightly and rose. 'I will be back very shortly. David is resting quietly on a pallet we managed to find, for the present. His wound is well padded and there is not too great a blood loss. Give your gentle heart ease on his account.'

She watched him leave to give instructions to the others and turned to her father with frightened eyes. 'I pray no one will pay with his life for this night's work.'

The Earl sank down beside her on the rush-strewn floor. 'Philippa, I may not have another opportunity to speak with you again. When we leave here I must go into deep hiding. You understand?' She nodded, her bottom lip trembling.

'Tell your mother I love her deeply and will, God willing, see her again soon at Malines, if not before.'

'She knows how you love us. She will be anxious to join you. Papa.' Philippa's voice was very soft. 'Take no more risks, for her sake and mine.'

His hand squeezed hers. 'Trust me.' He looked at her intently. 'I have given Rhys Griffith permission to wed you, but, the decision is up to you. I am convinced he will make you a good husband and I know he loves you with all his heart, but the choice must be yours. Can you love him in return?'

'Oh yes, Papa, I love him with all my heart, only...'

'Only?'

'I fear if he weds me I will endanger him. The King will be informed and will withdraw his favour. Rhys should not marry a traitor's daughter.'

The Earl was silent for a moment, gazing down at the rushes. 'That choice is his, Philippa. He wants you and it is for you to accept him or no. I will not press you in this, but...' He hesitated, then said, clearing his throat a trifle as if to stifle emotion, 'To have you near Gretton would be a great relief to me. You will be able to comfort your grandmother and...' he paused and she leaned forward to stare into his face, striving to read his expression '...if—if anything should happen to me—I believe your mother would be able to come to you here, and I would trust Griffith with her care.'

She said slowly, 'I will consider very carefully what is best for Rhys. I love him too greatly to bring him to harm.'

She looked up as Rhys entered again. 'The horses are outside and we are ready to leave, my lord. Will you take up Philippa before you? I must carry David.'

Philippa rose with her father and joined the others who were gathered in the corridor, Richard supporting the injured young squire.

It was almost pitch black outside and very cold as it often is just before dawn. Philippa turned once to stare behind her at the house which had held such terror for her and from which she had not expected either her father or herself to emerge free. The men were mounting up. Richard was assisting David to mount behind his cousin and Peter lifted Philippa up behind her father. There was no sign of any of the Queen's men. A dog barked somewhere, otherwise, except for the jingle of their horses' harness, the silence was profound and eerie. They set off for the town centre.

Peter waited with the Earl and Philippa in a little copse just outside the town while Richard Allard and Rhys conveyed David to a surgeon whom, Philippa was informed, lived near the Golden Fleece inn. David had made no sound during the short ride, but Philippa had glimpsed his pain-contorted young face just as they had left the house and she was very concerned for his recovery.

She was relieved to hear the clatter of hoofs approaching and Peter rode forward slightly to assure himself that the newcomers were, indeed, Sir Rhys and Richard.

Rhys rode up to the Earl and Philippa gave a little cry as she saw he was riding alone.

'Where is David? Is he—?'

'He needs special care. He will stay with the man for a day or two. I am assured he will recover.' He smiled a little grimly. 'This man is known to me. I have ridden beside him in combat on the Marches. He is skilled in the treatment of combat wounds and also extremely discreet. I can trust him rather than the town physician, who is a notable gossip.' He turned to the Earl, his horse sidling a little as he drew level.

'I think you and Allard should leave us now, my lord, and I would advise you both not to return to Sir Owen Lewis's manor.'

The Earl grinned mirthlessly. 'We have already come to that conclusion, my friend. If Hilyard was able to discover my whereabouts, it is obviously unsafe for Owen to be burdened with my company any longer. Give your heart peace. We have other bolt-holds.'

'If Master Allard can be at the Golden Fleece round about noon in two days' time, I can send a messenger there to let you know how young David progresses and how the ladies at Gretton fare.' Rhys leaned forward a little in the saddle. 'And now, my lord, if you will allow me, I will take your most precious burden from you and return her to Gretton. Master Fairley will accompany us.'

The Earl dismounted and lifted Philippa down. She clung to him tearfully as he kissed her, then he lifted her up before Rhys who drew her tightly close against his body. She strove once to glance behind her at the two men, still lingering in the copse to see them go, and then she nestled close to Rhys's heart, moving a little fretfully as she rubbed against the protective metal pieces of his brigandine, and settling close again, nestling her head against the soft leather, as he rode slowly from the copse and took the road to Gretton.

Chapter Ten

Philippa sat in the herb garden, which appeared as bleak
as her spirits. The earth was brown and barren, though one
or two of the more hardy herbs were still struggling to
throw out new leaves. An autumnal chill was in the air
and she clutched her black frieze cloak yet closer and
pulled up her hood against the biting wind. Her mother
and grandmother were busied in the house with the brass
image maker who had come from Bristol to discuss the
design and wording of the memorial which was to cover
her grandfather's tomb. Gwenny had accompanied her into
the garden, but had sat shivering uncomfortably and was
clearly so miserable that Philippa had dismissed her, giving
her duties within the house, and, for the first time since
she had arrived back at the manor, held close to Rhys's
body, she had been left alone. She glanced at the gar-
dener's boy, some distance away clearing remaining dead
leaves and sweeping up the paths. Gwenny had considered
the boy sufficient chaperon for her mistress, but he was far
enough from her for Philippa to feel free of his watchful
presence.

This was the third day since she had returned to Gretton
and Rhys had not called. In spite of all his protestations

of love, had he decided to abandon her, and give way to his doubts about allying himself with the daughter of the King's enemy after all?

When he had lifted her down into a waiting groom's arms after arriving at Gretton Manor, she had been reluctant, even then, to part from him. Shocked and frightened though she had been by the night's events, and relieved to be once more restored to her family, she had watched his departure with mounting despair. His arms had been so strong, so dependable around her, that she had wanted never to be parted from him again. Peter had supported her trembling form while Rhys had spoken briefly with her mother and then he had ridden away and she had been led inside and handed into Gwenny's care. Her grandmother had called for a bathtub to be carried up to her chamber and filled with pails of steaming hot water, despite the lateness of the hour, knowing Philippa's need to ritually cleanse her body and mind, for she had felt soiled by the sights she had witnessed, and sickened by the betrayal of the man she had believed to be sincere. She had trusted and helped Roger Hilyard, defended him against the suspicions Rhys had entertained towards him, and it hurt her now to know that he had so deliberately sought to use her. She had sat shivering in the hot, rose-scented water and her mother had come in and helped Gwenny to rub the soft homemade soap into her skin and then had wrapped her snuggly in the heavy white tufted towels which had been imported from the East. Gwenny had combed out the wet tangles of her hair, but even after they had dried her, and clothed her in her own bedgown and seated her by the hearth fire, hastily kindled within the chamber, she had still felt deadly cold.

Finally, the Countess had insisted that her daughter sleep with her in her own bed for what remained of the night and had gently and firmly dismissed Gwenny to her own truckle and, at last, Philippa had given way to a storm of weeping which had, in some part, relieved her of the terrible numbness which had taken her prisoner following the death of Roger Hilyard and his followers.

Her grandmother had come in, anxious to be told more fully the details of her abduction and the subsequent happenings in that house in Ludlow, but Philippa had found it impossible to describe the rescue and its horrible consequences. She had not been present before at the violent deaths of men after combat and it had been later, next day, before she had felt herself able to relate the full story and give tongue to her continued fears for her father and Richard Allard.

Her mother had tried to reassure her. 'Your father has spent so much of his life in avoiding dangers such as this, that I am convinced that, by now, he has found a safe hiding place and will soon be off back to Burgundy where I shall join him as soon as possible, that is...' and she had hesitated, smoothing back Philippa's bright hair and looking deeply into her daughter's eyes, '...once I have assured myself that your welfare is in safe hands here or—' and again she had paused deliberately '—you are well enough and prepared to accompany me.'

Philippa had given a little sob and shaken her head. 'I know that Rhys Griffith cares for me, but he will sacrifice so much if he marries me.'

'He knows that well enough.'

'But suppose that he is entertaining second thoughts and who could blame him?'

She had said that then and the same thoughts were running round in her head as she sat in desolate mood, kicking idly at a flint edging stone near her seat.

She knew that he was there without even turning her

head. She sat quite still for moments then did turn slowly, imploring him with her eyes to come close.

He was standing tall in the entrance arch, one hand holding lightly to the wooden trellis which, in summer, supported a climbing rose. He was dressed, as she last remembered him, in serviceable dark velvet doublet, his warm cloak thrown back from his shoulders, and he was smiling, yet she sensed a question which lurked behind that smile which made him hesitate before advancing towards her.

She stood up and held out one hand. Huskily she murmured, 'I thought that you had deserted me.'

Immediately he came to her and gathered her into his arms. She nestled against the muscular strength of him, smelling the familiar male, clean scents of soap and horseflesh, the faint tang of oil he used for protecting the metal of his weapons. He drew back for a second, gazing deep into her eyes, 'You have recovered? I was impatient, but thought it best to give you time. I know how the sight of those horrors in Ludlow distressed you. And, my darling, I thank the Virgin they did. Those reactions conveyed to me the knowledge of a sensitive, compassionate heart.

She nodded, suddenly shy in his presence without knowing quite why as he drew her down beside him on the wooden bench.

Head bent, her fingers toying with a fold of her black mourning kirtle, she asked, 'How is David? I thought, when you did not come to us, that his condition might have worsened and you felt the necessity of staying by him.'

'No, no. David is progressing well. Tomorrow he will ride home. The wound was deep and he lost a deal of blood but, fortunately, the sword did not penetrate his lung. My surgeon tells me he no longer fears infection so all should be well. I confess to feeling guilty for allowing him to accompany us, but there—' he lifted his shoulders in a slight shrug '—all boys must face a first taste of combat and a possible blooding. He is feeling remarkably pleased with himself for the part he played in the activities, as well he might.'

She gave a little shaky laugh as he captured her hands, then held both in one of his and with the other, tilted her chin so that she was forced to look full at him.

'I wanted to give you time to consider my proposal though, I tell you now, I have already bespoken the priest and made my arrangements for our nuptials which must be soon since your mother will leave soon for Malines.'

She tried to look away, but he continued to hold her chin fast. 'Well?'

'I love you,' she confessed, 'I was seeking you to tell you that in Ludlow when—when it happened. I know you were angry with me for my lack of faith—'

'Philippa, my heart's love, that anger was soon spent. That accusing look at me cut me to the heart and yet I knew how it must be with you and that all your life you have suspected treachery and sensed hidden dangers directed at those you love. I came straight back to the castle to claim you, to compel you to trust me and—' he drew a hard breath '—when I discovered you had not returned I feared that I had lost you for ever.'

'I want to be your wife, Rhys, yet I fear for you. The King—'

'Tush, sweetheart, Henry cares little about what I do. I am no courtier to fawn upon him at Westminster. If strike at me he does, and I doubt he would even stoop to do so, so unimportant he considers me, then we must fly together to Burgundy as your mother did when your father was forced into exile.'

'Then you would lose everything.'

'Nothing I value as much as my possession of you.'

She lifted shining eyes to him and he swept her possessively close, again raining passionate kisses upon her forehead, nose, lips and throat. She had never before tasted such ecstasy and she became dizzy and swayed in his arms so that he lifted her lightly off her feet and she clung yet closer to him, heart to heart, thigh to thigh, revelling in total surrender.

Triumphantly he murmured close to her ear. 'Tomorrow, then? David should be well enough to attend and he demands to be present and we must not delay, for your mother's sake.'

She nodded, as he drew back, holding her at arm's length, devouring her loveliness with his eyes. 'I dare not hold you so a moment longer, my heart, or I will not be able to wait,' he murmured huskily. Then he said gently. 'Give me your hand.'

Wonderingly, she obeyed him and he placed his betrothal ring upon her finger. It was a simple signet ring bearing an unknown crest and she looked up at him questioningly.

He explained. 'I would not have you wear my mother's ring, as is sometimes customary. It brought her nothing but unhappiness. This ring was given to me by the man I most admired, the man who trained me to arms. I have had a special one fashioned for you for your marital ring and with that will go all my love and pledges that you shall never live neglected nor shamed as my mother did. Will you trust me, my heart?'

'Oh, Rhys, my dear love, I do now and will ever do so.'

He bent and kissed her more gently this time upon the brow, then drew her back to the bench and seated her.

'I think it best if we hold the ceremony in the hall at

my manor. It is fitting that it should be private since your family is still in mourning, but we cannot afford to wait in order to summon the county gentry to our nuptials. Will you mind that, my love?'

She shook her head vehemently. 'You know I would have the ceremony quiet and in private for many reasons.'

'Aye.' He gave a faint sigh. 'I wish your father could be present to place your hand in mine, but that cannot be and we must accept that. I will send a wagonette for your party early tomorrow and arrange for the priest to attend at noon.'

She bowed her head in acceptance of the arrangements, knowing how secretive and hurried they must be.

He stood up and adjusted his cloak. 'My man met with Richard Allard at the Golden Fleece yesterday and learned that all is well with your father and I also ascertained that Sir Owen Lewis has not been bothered by over-officious King's men and he will be able to attend our wedding.'

Her lips curved into a smile. At least some of her father's friends would be present at this, the most momentous day of her life. Rhys bent and kissed her palm then bowed and took his leave. Afterwards she sat on for moments, her heart pounding wildly.

An hour before noon next day she stood within the master bedchamber of Rhys's manor house attended by her mother, grandmother, Gwenny and Rhys's trusted housekeeper. She had already taken the ritual bath and knew that her skin glowed with scented oils and that her hair fell, unrestrained by pins, combed lovingly by her grandmother. The servants and lesser women were dismissed at last as she stood with her mother and grandmother, looking anxiously down at her bridal gown. Both her loved ones had assured her that for this special day she must lay aside her mourning and the gown was simple and yet splendid, of white silk with an undergown of brocaded white and cloth of gold. Her mother touched that tenderly. 'This cloth was given to me by King Richard's Queen Anne. The bolt was a Christmas gift from the King and she wore a gown fashioned from it at the last Twelfth Night feast of her life.' She put a trembling hand to her mouth, as she re-called that the present queen, then the Princess Elizabeth, had worn a similar gown, of the same material, a choice which had been ill judged and caused a scandal within court circles. 'Anne had a small piece over and made a present of it to me and I have kept it until now and sewed it only days ago into this undergown for you, knowing how proud your father would have been to see you wear it.'

Tears sparked momentarily in Philippa's eyes as she longed for his presence, but she brushed them impatiently aside. This was no time for such recriminations. Her hair she would wear uncovered as a virgin bride and Rhys had sent up a page with four white rosebuds, apologising for the fact that they were all that were left of the past sum-mer's blooms in the pleasance. Gwenny had formed them into a simple wreath with strands of rosemary and her mother crowned her bright hair with it and stood back to admire her handiwork. She nodded, satisfied. 'The silk gown was one of mine left behind when I travelled to Westminster to see your father for the first time and it fits you well and is becoming, if a little outmoded.' She held up a small Italian glass mirror for Philippa to view herself and smiled as she saw a rosy blush suffuse her daughter's cheeks and knew she was well pleased with their efforts.

'Rhys cannot be anything but proud and delighted, as your grandfather would have been,' her grandmother said.

They could hear the noise below of final touches being completed in the hall for the ceremony. Lady Gretton raised her eyebrow to enquire if Philippa was ready and, on receiving an answering nod, went to the door to inform the page outside that they were ready when summoned. Philippa placed a trembling hand in that of her mother and forced a smile. They had talked together well into the night and, though she was prepared, she could not but be a little afraid of what was facing her now, a fact, her mother assured her, that was natural to every virgin bride.

'I am convinced by what I have seen of him throughout this visit that you have nothing to fear,' she had assured her daughter. 'Rhys will be a considerate bridegroom, but a loving and lusty one.'

Philippa turned sharply as her grandmother made a sudden exclamation. She was standing by the door with one hand pressed to her heart. Philippa hastened towards her and then went pale herself. A man was standing on the landing, waiting for the bride to emerge from the chamber. Dressed though he was in a servant's livery, Philippa could be in no doubt of his identity. She suppressed a little cry of joy.

He said softly, 'My lady, Sir Rhys has sent me to escort you into his presence,' and he held out one hand.

Philippa turned to direct one warning glance towards her mother and then she stepped outside and accepted the strong clasp of her father's hand. She dared not make any comment, as there were men at the stair foot looking upwards expectantly for the arrival of the bride. She stepped beside the Earl, her mother and grandmother close behind and, heart beating wildly with delight and anxious anticipation, went down to greet her groom who was waiting in the great hall before the priest who was standing, breviary in hand, beside the makeshift altar.

Though, later, she was to gaze round and marvel at the efficiency of Rhys's servants who had transformed the hall into a beautiful place for the ceremony—green garlands adorned the walls and the altar was covered with a fine white silk cloth and the brass candlesticks and Pyx shone brightly in the light from the fine thick wax candles—she was in such a daze of hopefulness and joy that the ceremony passed over her completely. As if from a distance she heard Rhys's strong, melodious voice with its faint Welsh lilt making his vows, and her own timid replies. The ring he placed upon her finger was heavy and cold and she remembered that he had had it specially fashioned for her so that no sad memories of the past should mar their union. She was aware that her father was standing within the crowd farther back in the hall and that her friends Richard Allard and Sir Owen Lewis came quickly afterwards to offer their congratulations and that her mother and grandmother both embraced her warmly, their glad smiles mingled with emotional tears.

She sat beside Rhys afterwards at the lord's table upon the dais, realising for the first time that she was now lady and mistress of her father's former lands and demesnes. Rhys's hand was clasping hers beneath the napery-covered trestle and his dark eyes were shining with his love for her. She peered hopefully for a glimpse of her father's tall form amongst the lesser folk who sat feasting at the boards below the dais, but could not see him. She knew he must take his leave quickly, for he had risked all to see her wed and she hoped he would have had time and opportunity to speak privately but briefly with her mother.

This was not a great feast, for the bride's family were acknowledged to be still in mourning and it had been hurriedly prepared, but the dishes and delicacies were of excellent quality and well served and she found herself partaking of the food with more appetite and pleasure than she had expected, for she had thought that she would be too excited and anxious to do so. Rhys pledged her in the traditional loving cup and she drank after him, placing her lips where his had been and smiling up at him in gratitude for all he had arranged for her to make this day a happy one.

She went with her mother to the master bedchamber later and, once the door was closed on the clamouring well wishers outside, they had embraced avidly.

'You saw him?' Philippa breathed excitedly. 'He looked well and happy. Rhys must have arranged it. Oh, Mother, will he be safe, do you think?'

'Dressed so, I am sure he could not be recognised, except by eyes so loving as ours,' her mother assured her. 'I managed to speak with him briefly and I shall join him aboard ship at Milford on the fourth day from now. I regret I must leave you so soon, but I am sure I do so with confidence that Rhys Griffith will love and cherish you to the end of your days together.'

They were alone and no mention of the time to come was mentioned as her mother helped her to undress and then slipped a silken white shift over her daughter's head. There was no need. Philippa knew the duty she owed to her new lord and was ready to pay it in full. After her mother had kissed her fondly and left her, Philippa sat on a joint stool watching the firelight play upon the furniture of the room. Her mouth was strangely dry and her heart raced with expectation, but there was no fear in her. She longed for the moment when Rhys would escape the bawdy badinage directed at him below and come to her.

When at last she heard his familiar step upon the stair and the latch of the door was lifted, she turned to welcome him.

He stood upon the threshold, regarding her. She had

risen and the light of the candles and the firelight played upon her lovely form. The thin silk of the night shift hid nothing of her youthful splendour and his eyes went to the mass of reddish-gold hair which cascaded in soft waves down her back well beyond her waist. His heart raced at the sight of her and the ache in his groin to possess her which had troubled him throughout the day worsened. His throat thickened so that he could find no words with which to greet her and he felt like a callow boy again. She was his at last. He had wanted her from the moment he had first met her at the Milford inn and now he could not believe that his ardent prayer had been granted, that he had managed to overcome her reluctance to wed the man she believed had stolen her father's lands from him. He swallowed awkwardly and turned to close and latch the heavy door behind him, which would shut out the world outside.

She did not move but stood and watched him as he steadily advanced towards her, then she gave a little shaky laugh. 'I see you managed to escape. I thought—feared—that those friends of yours would insist on entering our chamber and assisting you to undress.'

He made a dismissive gesture and gave a throaty chuckle. 'My heart, even had I been forced to fight them off with sword and dagger, I would not have allowed that.'

'I am relieved.' She lifted a tentative hand to touch his shaven chin, then traced the lineaments of his nose and mouth as if anxious to re-acquaint herself with those loved features.

He bent to take her in his arms but, abruptly she pulled away a little and turned from him. Perplexed, he made to advance on her again, then thought better of it. He must not be too impatient now. She was his, at last, heart and soul, he was sure of it, but he must not frighten her with too great an ardour. She must be wooed gently.

He said quietly, 'I made a vow to myself that I would make you my wife, if only to keep you safe, and then I would wait until you were ready, but I find I am quite unable to keep that vow.'

Head turned from him, she murmured, 'I would neither expect nor want you to.'

Still she was hiding her face from him and he turned awkwardly to the bed and began to hastily divest himself of his fine clothing. His doublet of mulberry velvet with its expensive silver buttons was thrown on to the bed, his shirt of finest cambric followed and then his hose. He could hear nothing from her and his breathing quickened as he reached for a brocaded bedgown laid ready to hand, but he could not stem his impatience and swung round blindly to face her.

His lip parted in startled amazement for she had slipped the white silk shift from her shoulders and it lay at her feet, a shimmering mass, then she stepped clear and stood gazing at him proudly as the firelight flickered upon the ivory beauty of her form, the breasts firm and high but already ripening to the roundness of womanhood, the slender hips, the high white throat and the head held as high as any queen. With a little nervous movement she shook back her hair and lifted one hand as if to receive him, then dropped it back to her side as if she were unsure of her welcome. This was no faery child but a woman, full grown and ready for his love. He made an inarticulate sound deep in his throat and drew her into his arms so that she was crushed against the hard maleness of him, held tight against his shoulder while she gave a little sigh. He bent and lifted her chin with one finger and she held her head high again and smiled into his dark eyes.

'You are not afraid?'

She shook her head and he saw the movement in her

slender throat as she swallowed and knew that though she faced him bravely, as any maiden would, she was pleading with him silently to be gentle with her.

He was, indeed, lifting her high and carrying her to the bed, pausing to gaze at her again and let his eyes take in the wondrous beauty of her before he lowered himself into the bed beside her.

She was shivering with fearful anticipation, but he would not let her fear him for that would spoil their union, which he would not allow. He kissed her gently, teasingly upon the forehead, lips, throat and then his questing lips moved lower and lower until her body arched in an agony of impatience too and she made little throaty sounds to match his own. Then, and only then, he knew that she was ready and lowered himself fully upon her to take what was his.

His patience was rewarded for he felt her respond at once and he was able to carry her to the heights of ecstasy so that she almost swooned in the wonder of their final coming together. The pain had been momentary and almost a delight in itself and he laid her back until he felt her eager body ready for his again and they made love passionately, uncaring of any sound from beyond the chamber and the wide bed which held their two responsive bodies.

He cradled her at last, when both were spent, her head against his heart, one hand of his cupping her breast. Her lovely hair spilt, sweat dampened, across his body and his breath stirred the silken strands smelling sweetly of rosemary and lavender.

'I have waited for this hour all my life,' he said hoarsely, 'and now my one question, sweetheart: are you content?'

'Have I not proved it to you?' She started up, her expression anxious as if she feared she had failed him in some way she could not comprehend.

His lips claimed hers again demandingly. 'Hush, do not ask such a thing. You are all I ever needed or craved for and ever will be. Can you forgive me now, for possessing that which should have been your inheritance?'

She gave a little half-strangled laugh. 'It will be our child's inheritance. How could I fault that?'

And he kissed her again.

Later she murmured sleepily, 'I have to thank you for the finest marriage gift, my father's presence.'

'He wanted it so. I felt it was a risk, but only a slight one, when I had thought it through. We had few members of the county gentry here who would recognise him in any guise and those who might do so would wish him no harm.'

She frowned slightly. 'Yet he should not linger in England. Have you heard any news from Ludlow about—about the house and what the constable must have found there?'

'Aye, I received a report from him yesterday and it is as I thought. He surmised that friends had fallen out in drink, with tragic results. Have no fears, my darling, I arranged for a respectful burial of all those who died and the parish officials will rest content and ask no more difficult questions.'

'But, eventually, Roger Hilyard's masters at court will miss him.'

'True, they will suspect foul play but will be unable to prove anything against us. But you are right, it is necessary for your father and mother to leave England hastily now and arrangements are well on the way to see them safely to Milford.'

He kissed her brow as he felt, rather than saw, her give a sigh of regret.

'I will take you to Burgundy when I feel it safe to do so,' he reassured her.

She slept at last, safe in his arms, and woke to find him gone from her. Alarmed, she sat up and then rose and ran to the door. He had been so loving to her throughout the night that she could not believe he would have deserted her so soon.

Young David Griffith looked up from the foot of the stair, pale and still leaning upon a cane for support. She saw that he was glancing worriedly at his new mistress as she stood, in her bedgown, hair cascading below her waist.

'Sir Rhys?' she demanded.

'He is at breakfast and will soon prepare for a journey, my lady.'

He was leaving her so soon. She said softly, 'Ask him to come to me before he leaves and send Gwenny to me.'

He made her a little bow and she turned back into the chamber and stood, uncertainly, looking around for suitable clothing.

Rhys came running up the stair and the moment he entered the chamber she threw herself tearfully into his arms.

'What have I done or failed to do that you should abandon me so soon?'

He bent to kiss the top of her head. 'My heart's darling, I go only to escort your mother and to see her and your father safely to Milford and aboard ship. She wrote me a message to say that she thinks it necessary that she leave immediately. She has heard that King's officials will arrive in Ludlow to escort the Queen to Westminster and is anxious to be gone from here before they arrive.'

'Can I not go with you?'

He hesitated, then nodded. 'Yes, I think it would be acceptable for you to be escorting your mother on her journey. Her true identity is not known, but you are her daughter and now my wife. It should be safe enough, but it is a longish journey. After your recent troubles, do you think you can keep up the pace?'

'Of course I can.'

'Very well. Dress quickly. Gwenny can accompany us to see to your needs. Do not be alarmed. Your father will join us two days from now and travel in a servant's guise. All should be well.' He rumpled her hair with a gentle hand. 'I confess I cannot bear to be parted from you so soon and will be heartened and delighted by your presence.'

And so it was that Philippa re-trod the journey she had taken when she had first met Rhys. Her joy at her reunion with her father made every problem along the way worth while. Though he could not ride by her side, Philippa was constantly aware of his loving presence and, when in groom's guise, he did approach to hold her leading rein or to lift her from the saddle, she felt her heart throb with mingled distress that they must part so soon and relief that he and her mother would soon be safe in Burgundy once more and together.

The nights she spent clasped in her husband's arms and gloried in his lovemaking. Though she was often weary and saddle sore for, as Rhys had warned, they were forced to keep a steady pace, lest they miss the sailing of the ship he had arranged for the Earl and Countess to board for the port of Damme, she never once complained or regretted her decision to accompany him.

The journey was accomplished without incident and when Philippa was tearfully embraced by her parents in parting, she knew that, in spite of her loss of their company, she had made the right decision. In exile in Burgundy she would have been a greater burden to them, since they had heard from the Burgundian shipmaster that the Dowager Duchess of Burgundy's health had worsened and Philippa was aware that her parents must eventually find themselves in a state of penury, should the Duchess's favour be lost to them. She also knew that they were heartened by their knowledge that their daughter was madly in love with her husband and that he would devote his life to ensuring her happiness. She took a regretful farewell of Peter, hoping he would find some woman he could soon find happiness with, as she had found hers.

The journey home they were able to make more leisurely and comfortably and it was with a sense of deep happiness and homecoming, even after so short a time of residence there, that she rode into the courtyard of her husband's manor.

Before she could be lifted down from her mount or Rhys dismount, she was struck by the same terrifying fear which had possessed her at Gretton when she had seen the King's officials arrive at her grandmother's house. The courtyard was alive with bustle and confusion and she recognised immediately the King's personal badge of the Tudor rose and portcullis upon the livery of the recent arrivals. Rhys rode alongside and reached across to take her gloved hand within his own.

'Can they know of my father's escape?' she breathed and he looked at her steadily.

'That can hardly be possible. Keep a good heart and behave naturally.'

He dismounted as his head groom rushed breathlessly to his side. Clearly the man was greatly agitated.

'What is it?' Rhys enquired casually enough and the man gulped hard as he said, 'Sir Rhys, you have a royal visitor. We do not know what to do. Mistress Cheswick is entertaining him within the hall and…'

Rhys lifted Philippa down and felt her body shake with terror against his own. Though the day was warmer today he could tell she was icy cold with dread.

'Come, my lady,' he said encouragingly, 'as chatelaine of my manor you must greet our distinguished visitor.' He half-supported her up the steps and into the screen's passage.

Philippa forced herself to stand upright and proceed without her husband's assistance. This sudden arrival of King's men could only herald disaster and she must meet it with a display of courage. Could her husband's part in her father's escape be known? If so, was an imminent arrest possible or had Rhys come under the King's extreme disfavour for his alliance with the Earl of Wroxeter's daughter? He was still holding her hand and, together, they entered the hall which, like the courtyard, seemed unaccountably crowded with strangers, some elegantly dressed, obviously courtiers, and others more soberly, clearly members of their distinguished visitor's household.

For a moment her eyes were too blurred to see the man who was seated near the hearth fire being waited upon by her husband's steward while Mistress Cheswick hovered nearby, anxiously harrying their pages and serving women about their duties.

A youthful clear voice greeted her jovially as their noble visitor rose courteously to greet his hostess. 'I regret that we appear to have come at an inconvenient time, Sir Rhys and my lady, but I am delighted to see you returned, as I was charged by my royal father and by my lady mother, to offer my congratulations to you both on your recent marriage in person and, of course, to wish you happiness.'

Philippa was momentarily too confused to curtsy deeply as she was in duty bound to do as she stared into the wide-spaced blue eyes of young Prince Henry. She had seen him often at the Queen's court at Westminster, but he had been scarcely more than eight years old then, and now he must be almost thirteen and a man grown. He was tall and would soon, she thought, be massively built and truly handsome like his famed grandsire, King Edward IV, who had been termed the Rose of Rouen because of his extreme beauty of form and face. He was dressed, as she herself was, in mourning black for the death of his elder brother, but jewels gleamed dully in his velvet cap and in the gold and enamelled chain around his neck. As he held out his hand for the now kneeling Sir Rhys to kiss, she saw the richness of rubies and emeralds in his heavy rings there too. His red-gold hair curled into the elegant collar of his velvet doublet.

He was laughing merrily. 'I see you find it hard to recognise me, Lady Griffith, but it is full four years since we last met and I have grown and filled out considerably since then. Please, do be seated. Do not stand on ceremony in my presence. I am sure you must be wearied after your long journey.' He led her to a chair opposite, with the manners of an accomplished courtier, his bright blue eyes raking over her in admiration and she recalled how, even when he had been but a child, she had noticed what a practised eye he had then for the younger ladies of his mother's household. Now she felt uncomfortable in presenting herself before him in her travel-stained garments. He was now Prince of Wales, she remembered, and heir to his father's throne.

He was addressing Rhys. 'I have come to Ludlow Castle

to escort my mother back to Westminster and, as she is
slightly indisposed, she charged me with the task of wishing you both well, as I explained. My father also, once he
received the news of your betrothal, was glad to hear of
your approaching nuptials and hope you will both prosper
and be granted an heir.'

Watching him in jovial talk with her husband, Philippa
could not think that there might have been something more
sinister in the last remark, but the prince turned to her, his
face beaming.

'I have never forgotten, Lady Philippa, that you were
present at the hunt at Sheen that day when I almost lost
my life under a boar's tusks. Master Richard Allard came
to my assistance then, although…' and he grinned in remembrance of his childhood impetuosity which had almost
proved fatal '…we knew him by another name then. Since
you were Mistress Anne Allard's friend, I am sure you
have kept in touch and know that he is once more settled
in England, pardoned after his part in meeting with the
unfortunate Earl of Warwick.'

Philippa murmured an almost incoherent reply. She felt
she was living in a dream, or was this a nightmare? Could
this courteous and elegant young man, who was the son
of her father's greatest enemy, be really offering them congratulations upon their marriage and could he be truly sincere?

As if aware of her doubt, he turned to her and said
charmingly, 'I am sure that it is time for old enmities to
be laid aside, Lady Griffith. It pleases us well that you
have come into possession of your father's lands.' He
paused, then added, 'It may also be possible, in time, for
him to be able to return from exile. I am sure his presence
here would present no threat to me or mine.'

He rose and picked up his riding gloves. 'I must return

to Ludlow. My mother will be delighted that I have seen you both. I trust, Sir Rhys, that once you have had time to settle into matrimony—' and here his teeth gleamed in a smile again '—you will bring your lady wife to court. We shall all be delighted to receive you both.' He bowed over Philippa's hand. 'And, Lady Philippa, I can assure you, all the court will worship at the feet of your beauty.'

She stood awkwardly, still numbed and confused by the suddenness of the encounter as he swept out with his retinue, Rhys at his side, to escort him, as a host should, to the courtyard and to oversee the efficiency of his household in the arrangements for the royal departure. The hall emptied abruptly and Philippa could hear the sounds of bustle from the courtyard again and she forced her limbs to move and go to the hall steps to see the company ride off. Henry turned in the saddle and doffed his hat to her and she leaned against the door post for support as, eventually, Rhys returned to her.

'Well, it seems that the King has decided to accept our marriage and all your fears for my future can be laid to rest.'

She looked deep into his eyes. 'Do you believe that my father could ever be given a pardon by the King and that we could be welcomed at Court?'

He thought for a moment, then bent and kissed her. 'I believe that what young Henry was suggesting was that that will be possible after his accession.'

She stared at him in amazement. 'He is still scarcely more than a child.'

Rhys chuckled. 'But a very precocious one. I think England will see great changes when once the reins of government are in his hands, and, my darling, I will see to it that he will see you infrequently at court. He was right in his assumption that I intend to keep you to myself for a long time yet, and later, I shall be very cautious at bringing you too much into that young man's company. I saw his expression when he gazed at you.'

'But, Rhys, I am all in my dirt and…'

He laughed heartily. 'My treasure, you are the most beautiful woman in the kingdom and all mine. Later, just later, I may be prepared to share your loveliness with others but—not yet.'

He lifted her into his arms and carried her into the hall again and then up to their chamber, slamming the heavy door to with a bang as he laid her upon the bed.

'Our return to our own chamber has been too abruptly interrupted,' he said, as his lips closed on hers, and she gave a little sigh of relief and satisfaction. No one would dare to come up to the chamber and later—much later— they would summon refreshment. For the moment they were too engrossed in each other to even feel hungry.

* * * * *